FOLLOW THE DYING LIGHT

DAVID DONALDSON

We Follow the Dying Light

Copyright © 2017 by David Donaldson

All rights reserved. No part of this publication may be reproduced, distributed, or transmitted in any form or by any means, including photocopying, recording, or other electronic or mechanical methods, without the prior written permission of the author, except in the case of brief quotations embodied in critical reviews and certain other non-commercial uses permitted by copyright law.

This is a work of fiction. Names, characters, businesses, places, events and incidents are either the products of the author's imagination or used in a fictitious manner. Any resemblance to actual persons, living or dead, or actual events is purely coincidental.

Tellwell Talent
www.tellwell.ca

ISBN
978-1-77370-184-4 (Hardcover)
978-1-77370-183-7 (Paperback)
978-1-77370-185-1 (eBook)

For Sunny and your unfailing support
For Bentley and the smile you put on my face everyday

ACKNOWLEDGMENTS

Three years and countless drafts later, this book was a journey that wouldn't have reached a conclusion without the help of many great people. I can't thank my wife enough for putting up with my constant nattering about the story. She remained supportive throughout and was always a great source of advice.

When it comes to big ideas, my brother Ben was instrumental in sorting out plot and developing the exciting technology Dr. Chambers relies upon to do her work. One particularly long car ride was spent talking out changes to the final draft.

I'd like to thank Carolanne Duncan for doing one final read of the book to ensure the novel didn't accidentally break on the editing room floor.

A shout out is necessary for Rob Britton and Sarah Wishart who provided feedback on the hot mess I called a second draft. Their commentary helped me release my grip on an ending that wasn't working.

The Tellwell team were an excellent and professional resource throughout the process and there's no way I could have finished without their help.

Finally I'd like to acknowledge everyone out there struggling with their mental health. This book started as a writing therapy project while I struggled with anxiety. As the words spilled out of my head on to the page and the anxiety subsided, somehow a thriller was born. But the struggle was real and I hope that in my small way these pages shed light on the challenges of mental illness.

WE FOLLOW THE DYING LIGHT

Happy Reading Bailey's Bay!
Your resident author at PV4

David

CHAPTER ONE

The eyes that stared back at me in the mirror concealed the shards of horrific memories that clung to an afterlife in my head. Pill popping my own concoction was the only thing that kept these recollections from consuming my life. Day in, day out, I laid bare the worst traumas of those most desperate for relief. PTER allowed me to experience what they begged to forget. But the technology was taking its toll.

My trembling hands gripped the wet washroom counter. The walls closed in. Tunnel vision consumed me. I was about to receive a long-awaited answer. One that would determine if I could continue healing the minds of the city's most broken. The fact that I was called to a meeting at a rehab center should have made me optimistic about my proposal's prospects for approval. So why did I feel like curling up into a ball in the corner?

"You're straight dope sick," said a woman's voice to my left. My eyes darted in her direction.

"Excuse me?" I said.

"Worst gas panic I've seen all week. It's a good thing you're here to help with your withdrawal." She wore black denim jeans and a crimson blouse. Her makeup was dark and heavy on her pale face. She rubbed my back and shoulder blades.

"Oh, no I'm not looking for a fix, not, you know, jonesing. Just nervous," I said. The dark halo that surrounded my vision subsided. I towelled off my hands and smoothed out my blazer. At nearly five ten I stood a good five inches over the woman.

"You're not the first suit I've seen in here," she said.

"Honestly, I'm actually here for a meeting."

"They always are."

She's quick. "I'm serious."

"Oh, so you're with the city then?"

"You could say that. I'm Dr. Catarina Chambers," I held out my hand.

The woman screwed up her face. "Don't normally make a point of shaking people's hands in bathrooms."

"Right…" I put my hand away as we laughed off the moment.

"My name's Maggie," she said.

"Nice to meet you. Listen, I just need a minute to compose myself."

"See you, Doc." She swung open the bathroom door.

I looked back at the mirror. Sweat beaded my hairline and the back of my neck. I took a minute to clean up. As I left the bathroom and turned the corner, my face collided with the shoulder of an older man. The hairs of his graying beard scraped against my forehead. He towered over me. I craned my neck up to apologize, but the words caught in my throat. He looked down. His vacant pale-blue eyes pierced through me.

I stepped automatically out of his path. Without a word, he carried on his course, as if I was never there. Long, tangled hair rained over his shoulders. He flexed the fingers of his right hand, and then balled them into a fist. A chill ran up my spine.

With my bag clutched close to my chest, I scurried down the hall until I found the rehab center's meeting room. Lydia Qiao, the city's Director of Social Services, sat on the other side of the desk behind a mountain of paperwork. Her head was down, and her jet-black hair gleamed in the light.

I recognized the documentation I had sent to her and her colleagues three months prior, back when I originally pitched the idea to use Post Traumatic Exploratory Restitution to tackle Vancouver's fentanyl epidemic. It looked like she had printed out the entire bibliography to my research. Red ink was scattered across the majority of the pages. The topmost had the acronym PTER written in that red ink under Post Traumatic Exploratory Restitution.

"Ms. Qiao?" I said.

"Mrs.," she replied without lifting her head. She slid her left hand to the top page and let her large diamond ring glitter under the fluorescent light.

So it's going to be like that then.

"Mrs. Qiao, it's Dr. Chambers, I'm here for our meeting," I said.

"Obviously." After another couple scribbles of red ink, she lifted her head from the paper. She had the tanned and weathered skin of an avid runner. Her makeup was subtle and tidy. She wore a gray blazer over a cream-colored blouse. A diamond pendant crested the notch of her neck. I extended my hand across the table.

"You're late," she said, her hands clasped across her papers.

I retracted my hand, wiped off my sweaty palm and sat down. From the grilling I took from Lydia three months ago, I knew that to survive this meeting I would have to pull myself together.

"Why don't we discuss why you called me down here Mrs. Qiao. I see you've printed off what looks like every shred of documentation available on PTER."

"Catarina, I have the power to approve your project and make you a well-off woman. You'll never have to chase after patients who don't pay ever again." She paused, smug.

How did she know my clinic was struggling financially? Did I reek that badly of desperation?

She continued, "But I have more questions than answers and, frankly, I'm not comfortable moving forward."

"So you'd like me to answer your—"

"—The other people who were at your presentation, like the chief of police, were impressed by PTER's potential and *encouraged* me to make you a proposal. If it were up to me we wouldn't be having this conversation."

My heart thundered in my chest. What was she saying? Was it approved or not? The past decade of my life was a blur of patients. Using technology-enhanced exposure therapy, I helped rid them of the traumatic stress that haunted them daily. PTER let me walk in their memories. There was the Syrian refugee who watched his family die in a bombing, the veteran returning from a tour of duty, the first responder to a fatal drunk-driving accident, and hundreds of stories like them. I brought peace to every one of them. But when they came through my door, they were often poor and destitute. Roughly half actually paid, but I didn't have the heart to turn them away. If the city approved the program, it would validate ten years of toil. PTER would no longer be considered some sideshow, some quack psychotherapy technique. It would give me an opportunity to focus on patients like-

"—*Doctor* Chambers," Lydia sneered. "Welcome back. Don't start mentally spending the money before you get it."

She was wrong. It wasn't about the money; it never was. My husband's job was enough to keep us comfortable. But I couldn't help others, or myself, if lack of money shut my clinic down.

"Catarina, what I don't understand is why you're the only person using PTER to witness memories. Why didn't its inventor, Dr. Dietrich, capitalize on his work?"

This was the same question I had been asking myself for years. Dr. Dietrich had written numerous academic papers in the mid-nineties about a device that could be used to render a visual depiction of an individual's memories and repair damage to the memory caused by the corrosion of time. A device that can close the gaps the imagination fills and uncover the truth that lies beneath. When I first read about the concept, I was instantly inspired. I latched onto the idea, and I haven't let go since.

"I've wondered the same. His writing on the subject stopped suddenly. All I know is that he built a prototype. During my PhD, my speculation was that Dr. Dietrich never figured out how to keep a patient's memories from invading his own. After four years of research I discovered the answer."

"Extirpation," said Lydia.

"That's right."

"You see, it's your little chemistry experiments that make me nervous. They were why I objected to this project. What's to keep you from doping-up the patients who already suffer from drug addiction?"

She tossed two papers onto my side of the table. On the left was the compound formula for the sedative SLUMB-Rx that I used to calm the minds of those about to relive their most traumatic moment. On the right was a technical paper about extirpation tablets, the pills that helped me forget my patient's worst nightmares.

"From what I've read about extirpation, I'm inclined to believe you have a substance abuse problem yourself," said Lydia.

Who does this woman think she is?! I wanted to scream. "Believe what you want," I said, fighting to maintain my composure. "But I can assure you that if you explored my past you'd never think that."

Lydia stuffed her papers back into her briefcase. She withdrew a manila envelope from her bag and slid it across the table. "These are the city's terms."

Below the table my hands were shaking. *Pull it together, Cat, this is it!* I took a slow breath and withdrew two sheets of paper from the file.

Lydia said, "The city reserves the right to select each patient entering the program and will use its discretion to choose the best candidates. The project will begin with a probationary period where I will audit every aspect of the procedure as you work on the first patient. If anything happens that I don't like, I pull the plug. In return, you will receive an annual contract valued at one million dollars, spread out over twelve, monthly instalments. Any questions?"

My mouth turned dry as paste. "When do we start?"

"Next week."

"NEXT WEEK!" There was no time to get ready. PTER was hanging together by threads. The cost and scope of the repairs to get the machine in good enough condition to withstand a Lydia Qiao audit would be monumental.

"Spending allocations for the next budget year must go in by the end of the quarter," Lydia said. "For final approval, the probationary period needs to be complete and an assessment prepared. We go now or not at all. Is that a problem?"

It was a huge problem. "No, no, not at all. I'm excited," I assured her.

"Good." Lydia stood up from the desk. "Follow me." She exited the conference room.

"Where are we going?" I said, chasing after her. She marched down the hall.

"To meet your first patient."

CHAPTER TWO

Everything was moving so fast. As Lydia strode away from me the floor seemed to melt away into darkness. Chains wrapped themselves around my chest. My breath came short.

Lydia stopped in front of a door. "He's in here," she said. There was a water fountain between Lydia and myself. I took a long sip. The anxiety attack subsided; my body became my own again. I walked behind Lydia into the therapy room.

It was him! The man I bumped into coming out of the bathroom. His frame darkened the back wall. He swayed from one foot to another. His eyes didn't register our presence as we entered. The room contained a television, couch, computer and private bathroom.

Leaning against the couch next to the older man was a bulldozer of a woman dressed in nursing smocks. She was almost my height but had the shoulders of a football player. Her name badge said 'Suzy.'

"Dr. Chambers, I'm a nurse with the center. Nice to meet you," she said.

"Likewise," I replied. I walked across the room to the man on the other side. I clasped my hands in front of me to appear as diminutive as possible.

"Hello again," I said.

"I wouldn't bother," said Suzy.

"Excuse me?"

"He's mute. I've worked with him for months and he's never said a word to me."

That would be a problem. Fundamental to PTER's success was the discussion of the traumatic memory with the patient after a session.

"What do you know about him?"

"Very little. Not even his name."

Another woman's voice interrupted us. It was Maggie from the washroom. "We're helping him with his substance abuse issues by providing a regimented prescription of opioids an-"

"—The details aren't important," interrupted Lydia. Maggie's eyes passed from Lydia to me. Her shoulders tensed, but she managed a slight nod. She carried a yellow tray. On it were a couple of prescription forms, as well as two small paper cups containing pills. At the sight of the pills, the man lunged forward. Suzy clutched his wrists and held him back. His breathing grew rapid as he struggled like a mad dog on a chain.

Maggie slowly fed him the two pills. He slunk back into the corner and leaned his head face-down against the wall. Maggie placed the tray on the table and spoke to me. "By controlling their dosage we're helping cut down the number of unnecessary overdose deaths. We've never been able to make much progress with this-"

"—Enough," interrupted Lydia.

"Lydia, the more I know the better I can-"

She cut me off. "—Everything that's necessary will be provided when I come to your clinic on Monday."

"That leaves me no time to prepare."

"Patient data is considered restricted until the probationary period is over. You'll have to work without it."

The project hadn't even started, and I already had both hands tied behind my back. How many addicts would die unnecessarily because of Lydia's arbitrary rules? Rules that could sink the program before it had a chance to breathe?

"Fine," I said. "I'll handle it."

"I'm glad," Lydia replied. "Suzy you can let him go."

Suzy took the man by his elbow and guided him out of the room. I gazed into his cold, dead eyes as they drifted past me. A sense of dysphoria washed over me at the prospect of entering the man's memories. Anxious dread sat like lead in the pit of my stomach. My mind fled to the extirpation tablets in my desk drawer at the clinic. Would they be strong enough to wipe away his lifetime of pain from my conscious mind?

*   *   *

I threw my bag into the back seat of my old Honda Civic and sat behind the wheel, thankful the morning of meetings was over. The drive back to my office on Pender Street would take me through the busy East Hastings area. Midday traffic was always bad. I had a patient in an hour; there was no time to waste. I tore out of my parking spot. When my tires were about to crest the curb, a woman banged on my driver's side window.

"Maggie?"

"You're *that* Dr. Chambers!" She was out of breath.

"I guess I am," I said. "Listen I really need to get-"

"—You have to let me book an appointment with you!"

"Well, I'm not taking appointments right now and with this project coming online next week…"

"Please, I've got to come see you. I've put it off for too long. This might be my last chance."

Every loose end that needed tying floated through my head.

"I don't-"

"—I will tell you everything I know about that man, the mute. Please…"

If Lydia found out we were talking behind her back she could easily use it as an excuse to cancel the program. But I needed every advantage I could get with the nameless man. I dug in my purse and extracted a business card. "Call my office and book an appointment for later this week."

"Oh, thank you, thank you, thank you," cried Maggie. She held my card close to her chest.

"See you soon," she said.

"Goodbye." I smiled. I ripped a hard left onto East Hastings Street and was soon driving twenty clicks over the limit. Luckily traffic was light. I flicked on the radio.

A male DJ's soft voice came through the speakers. *'Here's a piece I love. This comes from the late Charles Chambers. The composition is called 'Pools of Ivory.' Enjoy.*

Soft piano twinkled through the car as padded hammers fell against the wires of a baby-grand piano. The piece was magical. I remembered it well. My body broke into a nervous sweat. My stomach wrung itself into knots. My foot tapped the brake as I worked my hands back and forth along the steering wheel.

Just as I reached to turn the radio off, a man stepped into the street in front of me. It was the mute from the rehab center. He stared down the hood of my car as impact neared.

The piano continued to play as my hands jerked the wheel. The motor stalled. The sound of fiberglass shattering overpowered the music as I went over the curb. The hood of my car ploughed into a light post. The sickly-sweet piano continued over the radio as the airbag smashed into my face and knocked me unconscious.

CHAPTER THREE

My world was replaced by a vision of a man with long skeletal fingers grabbing a young girl by the arms and pushing her hands back on the piano keys.

"If you screw this up…" he trailed off as he withdrew a pill bottle from the folds of his shirt. He poured out the tablets and spread them across the lid of the piano.

"I'm so-, I'm sorry," she said, "I'll try again." She squirmed herself from his grip and placed her fingers by middle C. The man walked around the piano and stood behind it. His long body was stretched and contorted, like an arachnid ready to pounce on his prey at its first wrong move.

Out of the keys sprang the soft pangs of Debussy's 'Claire De Lune'. The melody juxtaposed against the hot anger that wafted from the man. The top of the piano began to stretch out into the distance. The man's long body became quadrupedal as he crawled across the lid. His face was shrouded in shadow. Only his emerald green eyes pierced the darkness.

The girl's body tensed. The notes lost their soft beauty. Then, she hit an errant note. The room fell silent. The man gripped a pill between his fingertips, placed it in his mouth and swallowed.

"Again," he hissed.

She fumbled the notes again.

His fingertips took two more pills from the piano lid. "Again," he bellowed

The girl had barely completed a measure before a deafening error rang out. A handful of pills disappeared into the shadows of the man's face.

"I can't," she cried. "Please don't make me. I don't want to let you down."

He sprang at her. Out of the dark emerged dad's face with his heavy, dark eyebrows, angular nose, and narrow jaw. His thin lips curled up to expose his crooked teeth, and he snarled like an angry dog. "Redeem yourself," he said. "AGAIN!"

* * *

The sound of metal grinding on metal. My eyes ripped open. A man outside my window heaved on the door. As my vision cleared the door gave way, and he poked his head inside. His ears had big-gauge earrings; his head was shaved, and a tattoo crept out of his green shirt and along his neck. My hands yanked at my seat belt to get it free. It wouldn't unlatch. Adrenaline coursed through my limbs. I yanked at the belt with all my strength.

"Whoa, whoa, whoa," he said. "It's okay. I'm not gonna hurt you. You've been in an accident. I'm just checking to make sure you're all right. You were unconscious." He put his hands up and backed out the door. When my hands stopped trembling, I unhooked my seat belt and crawled out of the car.

"You feel okay?" he asked.

My neck ached, and I had a throbbing headache; otherwise my body felt fine. The clouds sprinkled rain. "Yeah," I managed.

The hood was completely crumpled around a lamppost.

"Looks like a write-off," he said.

The car had been a gift to myself when I completed my PhD ten years ago. It didn't owe me anything. "I loved this car," I muttered.

"Do you have someone you can call?"

Who didn't I have to call? The accident meant I'd have to call a tow-truck, the insurance company, my husband, and my clinic. I couldn't afford this setback. Not with the pilot project starting in a week. Nor with the sheer magnitude of work I had to get done.

After a long silence I finally spoke. "Yeah. Sorry for my awkwardness. I'm just so frustrated. This is the last thing I need."

"I hear ya." He nodded and wandered off into the heart of East Hastings.

The next hour of my life was spent on calls with a tow-truck and then the insurance company. Once it was all sorted and the car was on the hoist, I rang my husband Eric. By this point clouds had blown in and rain was pattering my head.

"Eric Fisher Realty," he answered.

"It's me," I said.

"Oh, hey, what's up? I'm with clients," he said. As a real estate agent in a hot market, Eric was always with clients.

"I was in an accident, car's a write-off."

"Oh, god! What happened? Are you okay?" His voice became shrill as he dropped his business manner. The sound of his footsteps echoed into the phone.

"Some guy walked in front of my car on East Hastings. Had to swerve to avoid him."

"Goddamn lunatics down there..." he trailed off. "Is he still nearby?"

I scanned my surroundings for the man that would be my first patient in less than seven days. "No," I said.

"Figures. I'm sorry, Cat. I know you loved that car."

"It's just a car. I do have good news though. I won the project with the city!"

There was a brief pause on the line.

"It's everything you wanted," Eric's voice became flat and emotionless. "Do you need me to do anything about the car or do you have it under control?"

"Well, uhhh, yes it's already towed."

"Good. I've gotta get back to my clients. See you tonight." The call went dead. Rain fell heavy now and ran in rivulets through my hair that hung in front of my face. Water dripped in my shoes, making each footstep slick and uncomfortable as I walked back to my office building.

Why did you expect anything different, Cat? You know he wanted your practice to fail. He thinks it's stealing you from him. The hell with Eric. You're not his property.

On the sidewalk was a sign for the nearby sandwich shop. I hefted my foot and kicked a hole through it, then ripped it off my leg and threw it into the street. It bounced off the front fender of a passing car. The driver slammed on his brakes. A middle-aged man leapt out.

"HEY!" he yelled.

"Get back in your car, asshole," I yelled back.

"Asshole?" His face turned red; rainwater streamed down his forehead.

I lowered my gaze on him.

He clenched his jaw and got back in his car, slammed the door and drove off.

My reflection in a shop window explained why he decided it was a fight he couldn't win. I looked like I should be admitted to a psychiatry clinic, not running one.

The wet, twenty-minute walk back to the office would take me through the worst of East Hastings Street. Skid row. It hadn't always looked like this. The expression 'skid row' originated two hundred years earlier when logging companies sent huge redwood trees skidding down oiled logs along the street towards the harbour. Later it would be the central thoroughfare for the city. Lined with tourist shops, it was Vancouver's most popular destination.

When the streetcars were removed in the sixties it went downhill. Every third building had a boarded-up window. Old hotels became drug hovels. The vagrants scared off legitimate customers. City council struggled to solve the problem. Clean injection sites and rehabilitation centres were not enough to fix the issue. Would my pilot project be the answer? The nameless patient's sallow, unhealthy face flashed through my mind.

"Layyyydeeee. Got some keys for you. Five dollars!" the man on the corner screamed in my ear. He waved around three computer keyboards that were at least twenty years old. Behind him was a shopping cart full of smashed-in monitors, sticks of ram, rusty hard drives, and dirty computer mice. Occasionally, I'd humour him and buy something for a couple bucks if I walked by. He wore a fraying Vancouver Grizzlies basketball jersey. His feet were covered in colourful wool socks with a swirled pattern. I would have recognized the design from a mile away. It was mom's signature knitting.

Mom and I had followed two different paths after Dad's death. Her penitence was providing warm clothes to the homeless of the Hastings area. I went into psychiatry to try to stop others from slipping into the depression and drug addiction that stole my father. My mother blamed the doctors and therapists. She saw my work in psychiatry as a betrayal. Over the years, the distance has only grown between us.

A stick-thin woman with short, black hair and tattoo-lined arms wove through cars on the street. She was yelling at the top of her lungs: "GO…GO," as each car swerved around her. She made it over to me and stuck her face in mine. Her teeth were yellow, her breath rancid.

"GO!" she screamed, then strode over to the man with the keyboards and kicked one of the relics out of his hand. The two got into a shouting match. I walked through more of the same for five minutes before turning off East Hastings onto Pender Street. A few minutes later, I was back at my office building.

Instead of taking the stairs to my clinic like I normally did, I slid like a drowned rat into the elevator. Another woman rushed into the lobby and called for me to hold the elevator.

I closed it in her face. As the elevator slowly ascended to my floor, I burst into tears. One step closer to making good on my promise to my late father, one step closer to losing my husband.

The elevator doors opened on my floor. I marched out, full of anger and confusion, and ripped open the door to my office. My technician Rhodes Walker and assistant Debbie Sullivan were at her desk sharing a laugh. Their eyes bugged out when they saw me.

"Dr. Chambers, I've been trying to reach you for over an hour," said Debbie. She had wavy, auburn hair, blue eyes, cheeks dotted in freckles, and a small nose. If it weren't for all the wrinkles lining her face, Debbie would be cute. At that moment all she looked was worried. Rhodes nodded along beside her. He was no taller than I was, and he was getting chubbier by the month. His face was a mess of bad-beard stubble, his hair no better. But his crooked smile was electric, and his endless nagging actually helped silence my own anxious thoughts. It didn't hurt that he was excellent at his job.

"There's a patient in your office who insists on seeing you," continued Debbie. She lowered her voice to a whisper. "I tried to reschedule him to tomorrow, but he's insistent. He says he might not make it to tomorrow."

A sick wave of anxiety pumped through my veins. It told me to run. But giving up on my patients was never an option. I pulled my hair back into a ponytail, hung up my wet blazer, and rolled up my shirtsleeves.

"Leave him to me," I said.

CHAPTER FOUR

The man on the office couch worked his thick, calloused hands back and forth across his thighs. His boots bounced up and down. He leaned back in to the couch and crossed his arms, only to sit back up a second later and resume running his hands across his thighs. He repeated the cycle. I quickly scanned his file on my desk. His name was Gavin Sparks. A commercial fishing accident claimed the life of his son. He'd been to several therapists in the past without success.

"The problem with conventional therapy, Mr. Sparks, Gavin, is that it can only address the issues the patient describes to their doctor. Our memories break down over time, making it impossible to reliably recall the past."

"What's your point?" Gavin walked to the door and tried to peer out the frosted glass.

"The technology I developed allows me to experience your memories, the events, that is, just like you did before time decayed their integrity. Details of the original memory are lost and replaced by bits and pieces of whatever our imagination uses as glue. A lot of horrible garbage gets in there given enough time."

"You can't fix me." His face was covered in black stubble. His eyes darted around the room.

"I don't think you believe that."

He wrapped his hand around the door handle. Seconds passed as he stared blankly at the back of the door. Finally, he let go. His shoulders sagged. He turned back towards me, looking to have aged ten years.

"The process will stop the feedback loop between your trauma and your everyday life so that you can leave the past in the past," I said.

"Just rip the goddamn memory out!" he barked.

"That's not how it works."

Gavin plopped back down on the couch. Sweat dampened the collar of his burgundy T-shirt.

"Let me show you PTER."

We walked down the hall, Gavin dragging his boots as if they were full of cement. The examination room was empty.

"This is where your new life begins," I said, waving my hand. The room itself was about three-hundred-square-feet. Along the wall to my left was a tabletop covered in the synthesizers used to produce the SLUMB-Rx sedative as well as my extirpation tablets. The walls around it were lined in cupboards filled with medical supplies.

The wall to the right held a wash station and a large change-room that housed the acusensory suits that the patient and I would wear. Computer monitors covered the opposite wall. Each monitor displayed a different vital diagnostic that Rhodes tracked during sessions. From the computer bank, a thick tube of cables sprouted up the wall and ran along the ceiling to my prize.

"What the hell is that thing?" Gavin's mouth hung open.

"Gavin, say hello to the device called PTER."

The metal plating of its black outer hull shimmered. PTER stretched twenty-feet-wide by seven-feet-deep and stood a further nine feet off the ground, nearly scraping the ceiling. On either side of its central console were two large curvilinear compartments that looked like a pill capsule with the bottom snipped off.

"The two outer sections are where you and I stay during a session. The compartments are sound and light-proof. Removing as much of your sensory experience as possible improves the depiction quality of your memories."

I pressed a button on the console and stepped back. PTER let out a hiss as the compartments decompressed. With a heavy clunking sound, each sheet of steel connecting the curvature of the walls slid together like a deck of cards. They retracted into the console along a track that ran around a circular platform that stood eight inches from the floor at the bottom of each compartment.

"Beautiful, isn't it?" said a voice from the doorway. We both jumped. Rhodes sauntered up.

"Gavin, meet my assistant Rhodes."

Gavin ignored him. "What are the drains in these platforms for?" he asked.

Rhodes said, "It's part of the sensory suppression experience. Once you're inside, the compartment fills with a salt-water solution. It makes your body feel almost weightless when sedated. That's why we have these." Rhodes extended one of the respirators towards Gavin.

"Nope, no way, not gonna happen. I'm out," he said putting his hands in the air. He made a beeline for the door. I stepped in front of him.

"I understand it's intimidating. But I want you to know I've been doing this for nearly ten years and that I've had success with close to a thousand patients. The technology has only gotten better over time."

"It's the water," he muttered. I took Gavin by the hands.

"Wouldn't it be wonderful if when you thought of the water you thought of nothing else?"

He stared at me and said nothing.

"You'll be sedated long before we shut the compartment. By the time you come around, you'll be safely out of PTER."

Gavin took another step back towards the door. I gripped his hands more firmly. "Please, Gavin. Only one thing is waiting for you if you walk out that door."

A childlike terror washed over his face. There was no fight left. It was PTER. Or it was the end.

"Okay," he mumbled.

Rhodes led Gavin to the change-room and helped him with the acusensory suit—a black and gray, form-fitting garment outfitted with rubber acupressure nodes that transmitted the patient's physiological response to their trauma through to my own suit. I felt what they felt. The suit was also a hot and uncomfortable skin wrapped around my naked body.

"Where's my sexy nurse?" said Gavin to Rhodes when he was dressed. Since deciding he wanted to get better, he had cheered-up remarkably.

"You didn't hear? British dudes with a little extra around the middle are the new thing," Rhodes quipped.

We all laughed; the levity was welcome.

"You'll feel a pinch," said Rhodes as he placed the transmitter around Gavin's forehead, down his neck, and then connected it to the back of his acusensory suit and the tiny injection site for SLUMB-Rx.

Gavin reclined against the black plastic seat at the rear of his compartment. Rhodes helped him place a respirator over his mouth and nose. Gavin's pupils narrowed to tiny dots. The color drained from his face.

I put a hand on his shoulder. "Count down slowly from ten to one. Your sedative has been administered, and you'll soon drift into an unconscious state."

Seconds later Gavin's head slumped to one side. Rhodes typed a sequence of commands into his computer.

I stood next to Rhodes in my acusensory suit, feeling every rubber node press against my skin.

Rhodes spun in his chair to face me. "I swear you get hotter every time you put that thing on," he said.

I blushed at his remark. He scrunched up his nose and pointed at a monitor.

"No, seriously, look at your body temperature. It's a good half degree higher on average than it was a few months ago." He gave me a stone-cold stare. My cheeks burned from red to crimson. The sensors in my suit kept no secrets. After a second, he cracked up laughing.

"I hate you," I said. With a smile I slid a wireless transmission band around my forehead. The band was outfitted with a set of ear buds so I could hear Rhodes while inside the machine. I snapped a set of goggles onto the transmission band so I could see under water, then clicked a button on PTER's console to seal the drainage system. Two small hoses would pump out water from the bottom of each chamber once they were closed.

"Forgetting something," Rhodes said. He had a pen needle in his hand.

"Oh, thank god you remembered." I depressed the needle into my bare neck. The injection inserted an inhibitor capsule into my bloodstream. It served as a landmark. When I consumed an extirpation tablet, the inhibitor released its contents to prevent extirpation from erasing any memories before the landmark. Without it, I risked forgetting pieces of real life.

"Ready?" Rhodes' voice rang through my earphones.

"Ready," I said as I slid my respirator over my face. PTER wheezed as the hydraulic paneling of the metal doors slid across the circumference of the platform and enclosed the chamber. With a heavy clunk, the panel sealed, followed by a hiss as air was vacuumed from my cell. The silence was absolute.

"Here we go," said Rhodes.

Water gushed out of the hoses at the bottom of PTER. Moments later my blood cooled as SLUMB-Rx carried Gavin's mind into my memory chamber. Like the ocean's undertow, the world was pulled out to sea, and I was left naked on the beach.

CHAPTER FIVE

The walls of my compartment burst into a spectrum of coloured lights. Gavin's lattice—a space between his waking mind and a vast neural web of memories floating in inter-temporal space, like giant stars in the night sky—was projected throughout my chamber. The curvature of the walls created a three-dimensional experience.

The sensory deprivation was so absolute that my mind and body lost their grip on the world. Sometimes I dreamt of never returning home. All around, orbs of memory begged me to relive their history.

Finding the memory that causes post-traumatic stress is the easy part. If the experiencing self is the gravitational pull of the sun that keeps the planets in orbit, the traumatic memory is another star entering the solar system. It is a force so strong it stops an individual from fully experiencing waking life.

A thick cord stretched into the darkness at the edge of the lattice. I pulled myself along its length. The lattice grew dark as I wandered into a nebulous, suppressed place. Gavin's trauma loomed immense before me: a black orb of epic proportions haloed in a ring of light. Its watery surface undulated, as if bodies were struggling to breach the memory for a breath of air. Long tendrils emanated in all directions, stretching for miles to wrap around the healthier parts of Gavin's mind.

A chill ran up my body as I tried to mentally prepare myself for entry. To enter is to breach the event horizon, to say goodbye to Catarina as she is, for I never exit quite the same. A piece of me is left inside the memory, a piece of my patient comes out.

I placed my hand against the orb in front of me and my acusensory suit grew hot as the edges of the memory opened. The lattice let out a low, rhythmic pulse. Negative energy rippled out of the trauma as the gates of Gavin's hell opened.

* * *

My eyes became Gavin's. Each swell lifted the fishing vessel up into the night sky. Then the ebb of the surf gave way, opening up a hole in the sea that swallowed the ship, only to spit its oiled hull into the night with the next wave. The chain holding the anchor groaned as it tested its strength, time and again. The sudden storm caused it to tangle around something on the ocean floor.

Gavin was alone with his thoughts as he stared at the ship's control panel. The window and console to Gavin's right were littered in black lines, fissures, tears in the memory. Floating elsewhere in my chamber were fragments of memory without a home. The gloves of my suit were coated in an electromagnetic substance that, similar to electroshock used in the fifties to treat anxiety, allowed me to unscramble a broken memory. One hand ran across the fissure while another plucked at the fragments and sewed them into the gaps. A man appeared out of the rips and tears. He looked out at the water and at the lights of a small coastal town that teased in the distance.

"She's not built for this Gavin," he said.

"I know Jim," Gavin replied.

"You know?" spat Jim. "When the hell was the last time you tried the radio?"

"Just before you got up here. Still nothing. The antenna is ruined. I've shot up flares, but it's three in the morning. Who knows if anyone in town is up to see them."

"We can use the raft to get away from the ship. Otherwise, we risk being sucked down with it. How could you let this happen Gavin?"

"How could *I* let this happen? You were the one who dropped anchor. And as for the raft, you forget what time of year it is?" Jim glared back at Gavin. Dark rings ran under Jim's eyes. He frowned, and pointed at the console.

"And what about the water we're taking on?" Jim asked.

"That's what the bilge pump is for."

"No shit. When was the last time you turned it on?" pressed Jim.

Gavin fell silent for a moment and pressed his lips together. Finally he said, "Just go speak with them, okay."

Jim sighed and went downstairs into the hull of the fishing boat. A moment later Gavin heard the deep tones of men's voices rising through the floor. The boat moaned as water splashed over its sides. Gavin stretched the muscles across his back, reached out his hand and clicked a switch on the boat's console. The hum of a motor died and the lights with it.

Gavin's heavy footsteps followed Jim's down to the crew quarters. The room was lit by a handful of flashlights the men had jammed between the bunks and the bed frames. The men stretched out in their beds, sipping cups of whiskey as they tried to keep their feet dry. The floor was swamped in several inches of icy water.

"Cap, drink enough of this stuff and the room stops smelling like your mom on a Saturday night," yelled a young man in an upper bunk as he tossed a bottle of Jack Daniels to Gavin. He caught it with one hand, unscrewed the top and took a long swig.

"Matt, my mother was a fine upstanding lady," said Gavin. He tossed the forty ounce bottle to a boy no older than nineteen. He wasn't expecting the bottle and it smacked into his forehead. The men roared with laughter.

"Fuh…" the boy groaned, rubbing his forehead. His features were remarkably similar to Gavin's.

"Well, you gonna drink it Tom or what?" said Jim with his arms crossed over his chest.

"Gimme a minute Jim, Jesus." Tom uncorked the bottle, took a swig and grimaced.

Jim scoffed, "Sorry we're out of vodka and orange juice, kid." He reached across the room and ripped the bottle out of Tom's hand.

"We can thank Jim for getting the anchor all fucking tangled," Gavin said. "Can't risk going up on deck to release the chain. The radio antenna is toast, but I've shot up a few flares, so hoping we can get the Coast Guard's attention. Not enough gas to keep the boat running all night. I have to save power to run the bilge pump to get rid of water. Could be a long night, boys."

The men said nothing. The boat heaved to the left and nearly knocked Gavin down. He thrashed his feet through the water on the ship's floor.

"Guess I'm going to have to pump sooner than I expected," he said.

The perspective shifted focus and turned back towards the bridge. I ran my hands along the little black micro fractures running up the walls and wove fragments of memory into place. Instead of returning to the bridge Gavin bypassed it and went down a hall to the engine room.

His flashlight inspected every inch. The bilge pump was nothing but a short cylinder on the floor next to the engine. It connected to a hose that ran across the bottom of the room and into other sections of the boat. Under the pump was a metal plate that attached it to the floor. Gavin leaned down and jiggled the plate. It was loose. He took a screwdriver from his belt and turned the screws at each corner of the plate to hold it down more securely. He jiggled the plate again; it didn't budge. He ran his flashlight across the engine to ensure it was still in one piece.

Back at the bridge, wind howled against the windows as the night sky bled inky raindrops. Swaying back and forth, Gavin cast his flashlight over the ship's console. He flicked on the generator and the lights came to life. The headlamp over the boat shone on a large outcrop of nearby rocks. Their cracks and crevices were etched in fissures. I pulled a pair of memory fragments from the air and swept them into the rock face.

In their stead was the town, much closer than before. *Was the boat drifting towards shore?* Instinctively I tried to grab Gavin's hand to stop him.

"The rocks! Gavin steer your boat, you've come loose," I screamed. The memory couldn't hear me. Gavin activated the engine and bilge pump. The boat jerked violently and was followed by the sound of tearing steel. Screams emanated from the crew quarters.

"Oh, god, oh, god!" yelled Jim. Gavin shut off the power and raced down into the crew quarters. The boat went dark.

"Tom? Where's Tom!" Gavin was breathless. The water was already up to his waist.

"Gavin, the anchor!" screamed Jim as he grabbed Gavin by the front of his shirt and shook. "... something cleaved a hole through the side of the boat. How... god, your boy!"

Gavin jammed his flashlight between his teeth and dove under the water. Fissures ran across the bottom of the boat. I massaged away the black cracks as Gavin swam through the darkness. Under the fissure was Tom, pressed against a jagged hole in the hull, trying to free himself. His arm was stuck in the twisted metal and bleeding badly.

Gavin heaved on the metal. It gave just enough for Tom to free himself. His wild eyes met Gavin's for a second before he made for the twisting surface. The boat swirled again as it took on more water. The ocean pulled him back through the hole. Gavin spun back to Tom and reached for his sleeve. But there was no strength in Tom's wounded arm. A wave lifted the boat. Gavin stumbled and cracked his head against a steel cabinet. Fragments of memory exploded on impact, filling my chamber and casting a blur of fissures across what was left. I scrambled frantically to repair the damage. I was only quick enough to watch the bubbles of Tom's last breath escape his lips before he was pulled into the black ocean.

"Nooooo," I moaned.

"Hang in there, Cat," said Rhodes' voice in my headphones. Hot tears welled up inside my goggles. My body started to sweat profusely inside the acusensory suit. The walls of my compartment felt like they were closing in as I drifted into the watery darkness alongside

Tom. Coupled with my own body's reactions to the memory, the acusensory suit mimicked Gavin's physiological response and it felt like my lungs were on fire as the suit's pressure nodes squeezed against my chest. Another wave tilted the boat on its side. A big hand grabbed the front of Gavin's coat and yanked him out of the water.

"Got him," Matt said. Jim stood in the sideways stairs, ready to give up on them both. His face was cracked and broken with little fissures. Through teary eyes, I waved a hand across the rips in the memory, and Jim was gone.

"What about Tom?" asked Matt. His flashlight was pointed on Gavin.

"Uhhhnnn," said Gavin, his head aching from smashing against the cabinet.

"Jesus Gavin, your head," said Matt. The boat listed upside down with the next wave. Matt yanked Gavin's coat and dragged him to the stairs. Gavin's head cracked off the edge of the stairwell as the boat heaved sideways. The memory disintegrated as Gavin was cast into complete unconsciousness. My chamber went dark. I took a deep breath and spoke to Rhodes through the microphone in my respirator.

"It's over," I said.

"Bringing you home," he replied.

CHAPTER SIX

I tucked my hands under my desk so Gavin couldn't see them shaking. He sat across from me on the couch in my office, hands tapping up and down on his lap, waiting for me to say something. I cleared my throat.

"How did you survive?" I asked. My voice was shaky. I reached into my bag and slid out the bottle of extirpation tablets. As silently as I could, I uncapped the bottle and pulled out a pill. I rolled it around my fingers out of Gavin's sight.

Gavin raised an eyebrow. "I don't remember. You couldn't see?"

"You went unconscious. The memory collapsed."

"A Coast Guard helicopter found us." Tears welled up in Gavin's eyes.

"Did they ever find Tom?" I asked, afraid to press too hard.

"No," Gavin choked. He broke into sobs, cupping his face in his hands. "He died, and for years I thought it was all my fault."

"And what do you think now?"

"That I should have never let him on that boat. I miss him so much."

"Gavin, did Tom choose to be there with you?"

Gavin closed his eyes and searched his memories. "Yes, it was our first trip on the water together. He wanted to be a fisherman like his dad. But now I'm not the man he wanted to copy. Now I'm nothing and he's dead."

"Gavin," I paused, "The tangled anchor came loose and the boat crashed into the rocks. The fact your hands were on the controls was an awful coincidence. You know that now and you need to stop blaming yourself. You insult Tom's memory when you despair, when you refuse to be the man he wanted to become. He admired you. He loved you. He wanted to be there. The rest is tragic luck. Tom would want to see you happy."

The image of the life going out of Tom's cold blue face flashed in my head. I took a deep breath in and a long breath out. It was my turn to hold back tears. I wrapped my hands tight around the seat of my chair and squeezed as hard as I could to pull my mind away from the pain of losing Tom. Tom wasn't my son, but Gavin's love was buried in that memory and bled into my own conscience.

Gavin stared at me at a loss for words.

"Did you ever give Tom a funeral?"

"There's an empty grave somewhere."

"Have you been recently?"

Gavin shook his head. He looked down at the floor with his hands cupped together between his legs.

"I want you to go there." I said. "It's going to rip your heart out, but you need to say goodbye."

"That's it?"

"How many years ago did the accident happen, Gavin?"

"Five."

"Do you think Tom would judge you for choosing to move on with life after five years of mourning. Five years of beating yourself up for something that wasn't your fault. For a decision he chose to take, in full knowledge of the risks?"

"Well no but-"

"—No 'buts,' Gavin. PTER isn't an instant cure. Look at it this way: the memory of Tom's death and the way you coped was like a broken bone that healed incorrectly. Whenever you put too much pressure on it you felt pain. What I've done is re-broken that bone and set it in a cast so that it can heal properly. Removing the distortion in your memory will help you gradually feel better."

Gavin stared at the far wall as he mulled over my words. Then he placed his hands on his knees and pushed himself up. His face had regained some of its color and the wrinkles around his mouth had softened. I placed the extirpation tablet under a sheet of paper on my desk and walked over to him.

"This is where it starts, Gavin, not where it ends," I said. We stared at each other for a moment. Gavin hung his head and sobbed. I gingerly wrapped my arms around his back.

"It's okay," I said.

"It's not okay," choked out Gavin.

"I know. But it will be."

*   *   *

Sitting back down at my desk, I slid the paper away from the extirpation tablet and put it to my lips. Wading through trauma on a daily basis was perilous to your mental health and PTER couldn't be used without the tablets.

When the pill was in my stomach, I closed my eyes and focused on recalling Gavin's memory. Like an ancient reel of film set ablaze, frames of the memory melted out of my consciousness. The pill took a minute to run its course. I opened my eyes. Debbie stood in the doorway, a file folder tucked under her arm. "Well," she said.

"Well what?"

"Your meeting this morning, how did it go?"

"My, god, Debbie! In all the chaos I forgot to tell you. We got it!" I exclaimed.

I ran over to her. She pulled me into a big hug and we whooped like teenage girls. The folder fell from her arm and spilled pages of bills and financial statements across the floor. Rhodes' footsteps barrelled down the hall. He careened into the room and jumped and giggled right along with us without even knowing what the hell we were celebrating. We just laughed harder. It was the happiest moment I had experienced in my practice in years.

"Boy or girl?" said Rhodes with a smirk. Both Debbie and I looked at him like he had two heads.

"No one is having a baby?" Rhodes said.

"We landed the pilot project with the city you idiot," said Debbie.

"Shut up!"

"It's the truth. No more of this scraping by bullshit," I said. I picked up the bills off the floor. "Fuck you!" I threw the ten thousand dollar utility bill over my shoulder. "And you." The fifty thousand dollar line of credit statement flew in the air. "And you." The five thousand dollar overdraft crumpled under my foot. Debbie and Rhodes grinned from ear to ear. Rhodes put his arm around my waist.

"One sec, I have a surprise I've been hanging onto for just this occasion." He ran from the room and returned holding three plastic wine glasses and a bottle of champagne.

"Baby duck?" Debbie asked

"Is that not good?" he replied.

"It's perfect," I said. Rhodes popped the cork and poured a glass for each of us. We sat in my office, reminiscing about the last ten years as we enjoyed the rest of the bottle.

"We have four days to get our act together," I said. The clock on the wall read seven PM. "But not tonight."

Debbie threw on her tan trench coat and pulled on a pair of tall boots. Her pay was modest, but somehow she always managed to look like a million bucks.

"Nice boots," I said, staring at the tear at the end of my own heels.

"Yeah, Debbie, nice boots," mocked Rhodes. He pulled up his pant leg to reveal a pair of old sneakers covered in grass stains.

"I let you wear those to work?" I said, and punched him in the shoulder.

His smile faded. "Almost forgot. We need to talk about PTER's deprivation chambers tomorrow."

"Why not now."

"It's late, and I don't want you thinking about it all night. It's just that with the project coming up, the old boy is going to need some work that we've been putting off. I can get into the details tomorrow."

"Sure. Goodnight, Rhodes."

"Night," he said and left.

Debbie was one step behind him. "Have a nice night," she said. "Oh, and just a reminder, you have an appointment with a woman named Maggie Hill tomorrow."

"Good grief, I told her to book *later* in the week. Well, thanks Deb. Night."

After finishing my end of day inspection of the clinic— switching on PTER's cleaning cycle and turning off the lights—I exited the clinic into the hall I shared with a dentist and an accountant. I stared at the letters printed on the frosted glass of the closed door: *Dr. C. Chambers - Psychotherapy and Exploratory Restitution, Est. 2010.* After ten years in the business, my work felt like a dream now more than ever. I shut my eyes and tried to remember what had happened over the past six hours. Nothing but a memory fragment of a boy's drowning face. A new ghost to visit my dreams that night. From behind me in the dark hall I heard the whisper of my father's familiar voice. "I expected so much more from you. I expected you to be perfect. Instead you screwed up. You let him *die*!"

I whirled around. No one was there.

"It wasn't my fault!" I screamed into the emptiness.

*   *   *

I walked home in the early autumn twilight. The rain had stopped. Streetlights glinted in the puddles. It was only nine o'clock when I got to my condo but I didn't think I'd be able to fight off sleep much longer. Eric was still out. He often worked late nights through the week. I didn't like to fall asleep without him, afraid that without a warm body next to me, I would never wake up. Trapped by a memory.

Listen to yourself, you're losing it Cat. I am not, it's under control. I just need some honest to goodness sleep. But not until Eric is home.

I dropped my head onto the pillow and tried to silence the voices in my head. Largo, our English bulldog was asleep between my legs. He was tired from a tight twelve hours of sleep earlier in the day. Whenever I closed my eyes, it was like someone cranked the volume of his snores and I would wake again. But as each minute passed my eyelids shut a little longer. Finally I let go, too tired to fight the inevitability of sleep.

* * *

My body was cast in pure darkness, floating in the warm salt water of PTER. Enveloped by infinite silence, my only company was the sound of my breathing through the respirator.

A pale white glow rose out of the bottom of my compartment. Below me emerged a girl, her skin ghostly pale. Long strands of her reddish brown hair flowed through the water. She was dressed in a tattered white gown. Her long slender fingers wrapped themselves around my ankle, around my calf, around my thigh. She crawled up my body in the black water.

My limbs were paralyzed. It was impossible to fight against her as she crept towards my face. Her hands wrapped across my shoulders and pulled her girlish face into my field of vision. I looked into the emerald eyes of my past self. The magnificence of her eyes, the only part of her still alive, contrasted against her pallid flesh.

She did nothing but stare; unmoving, unflinching. A second later she thrust herself away from me and faded back into the darkness of my compartment. My heart thundered against my chest. I tried to yell, *Rhodes, get me out!* but my voice faltered. It was just her and me. I flexed my limbs to wake them back up.

BOOM! The wall of PTER blew open. It was a mess of twisted steel. Yet the water didn't flow out. Instead young Tom's face appeared through the hole. His cheeks were bloated with the last breath he would ever take. I reached out my hand; he seized it. Suddenly it was me being tugged through the hole. His strength was monstrous. My body slammed into the side of the PTER compartment. I blinked and came face to face with Dad.

"How could you let me die," he screamed. Water plunged into his lungs as he wailed. His arm whipped up and ripped my respirator from my face. He retreated into the darkness with the respirator and disappeared.

I slammed my fists against the inside of the compartment. *Oh, god, I'm gonna drown, I'm gonna drown. I can't breathe-I can't. Let me out!* I kicked with every bit of strength I had. I felt around for anything that could save me.

My mouth spluttered and water leaked into my lungs. Each heave sent more water into my chest. The coughing turned violent. Every last ounce of oxygen was expunged from my body. Death's black inky tentacles reached out of the darkness and pulled my body down past the floor, down past the earth, down into a void so deep that my conscience would neve-

CHAPTER SEVEN

"CAT WAKE UP!" My eyes shot open. Eric was on top of me shaking my shoulders. His dark hair ran down his forehead. He relaxed when he saw me looking at him. He released his grip. The bed sheets were drenched with sweat. I was stick-straight on my back, staring at the ceiling. Eric's brow was furrowed, his jaw locked. Largo barked frantically at the foot of the bed.

"Cat, it's okay. You're all right. It was just a nightmare," he said.

My clenched teeth released and I found breath. "No, it was so real. It was… oh, god Eric, you don't understand. It was the worst it's ever been."

"Can you tell me what happened?"

"I was trapped in a prison that drowned me… he was there. He ripped off my…" I sucked in a deep breath, "Eric, I felt myself die!" I sat up from the soaked bed sheets.

Eric gritted his teeth as he searched for something to say. He clicked on his bedside lamp, stood up and crossed his arms. "Don't you get it, Cat? It's PTER. It's tearing your mind apart. I've laid next to you for too long biting my tongue. You can't keep it up. Something has to change."

Oh that's all Eric? I got out of bed and pulled off my drenched nightie. My pale skin broke out in goosebumps in the cool bedroom. I pulled my fluffy cashmere housecoat, an expensive birthday present from Eric, off the hanger on the back of the bedroom door. *No, these little comforts can wait.* Eric's insensitivity over my project approval made me too angry to wear his gifts. Instead, I pulled out a different nightie and slipped it on.

Eric went quiet.

"Well…" I said to him.

"Well what?"

"What has to change? You seem to be the expert on my mental health," I said.

"I just… I'm saying that your work, well, you're too dug in Cat. You need a vacation. A long one."

"That's impossible. I told you today that the program is a go."

Eric's shoulders sagged. "Something big is coming my way, too," he said. "Got someone promising sniffing around the Point Grey property. We could retire early Cat."

"Then enjoy the beach without me. These people aren't going to heal themselves."

"Goddammit Cat, who's gonna heal you? Where does your little crusade end? There's an infinite supply of anxiety down the street. Why do you embrace it?"

"Don't presume you know what I should or shouldn't do. Who made you the moral authority, Eric? I have the opportunity to make a real difference, and I'd never forgive myself if I didn't try."

I sat back down on the bed. The nightmare had left me without strength for further arguing. After thirty seconds of silence, Eric sidled over and wrapped his arms around my shoulders.

"I'm sorry. I've been a selfish prick for not celebrating your project approval. I know you've worked so hard for this. It's just that I don't want to lose you." The problem was that Eric was right. My work stole something from me each and every day. A bit of light drained out, and my patients' darkness seeped in. Their memories became my memories. But it worked. They got better. Every single one of them. *I can't give up now.*

Eric kissed me on the head.

"You won't lose me. I'm yours whether you like it or not," I said.

"Love you," he replied. He squeezed my shoulder. "It's four am. We're not getting back to sleep now. I'll change these sheets. Why don't you throw on some coffee, and then we'll migrate to the couch and watch a movie."

I leaned my head on his shoulder and said: "deal."

*   *   *

Our movie finished before I realized it even started. I tried to focus on the film but drifted to the persistent heaviness of the looming work day.

"I'm gonna hop in the shower," said Eric as he rose from the couch. "Care to join me?"

I gave him a wan smile. "Not this morning, hon. Besides, you can't handle a properly hot shower anyway."

Eric deflated. "That's true." He kissed me on the forehead before leaving.

I stared into the bottom of my empty coffee mug. The grinds

were my tea leaves; a prophesy of the day ahead. The dried brown constellation had no secrets to share.

I tossed our mugs in the dishwasher, poured myself a bowl of cereal and drowned it in milk. I sat down on the piano bench to look at the old photos running along the top of the instrument. A picture of Eric and his family at a reunion several years ago was prominently displayed.

Eric was the second of three children, born in short succession. He was the even-keeled one squeezed in between his control freak of an older sister Jill, and his Indiana Jones wannabe younger brother, Brian. Eric's parents were wonderful people, full of good stories and unfailing optimism. His father Tim met his mother Lei when he went to Shanghai to teach English as a second language. When his work visa expired he brought Lei back to Vancouver. Eric's half Asian heritage and fluency in Mandarin and Cantonese gave him an enormous advantage in the Vancouver real estate market. Our high end loft was proof of the spoils.

Next to his family photo was a picture from our wedding fifteen years prior, just kids straight out of university. Tucked behind the other photos was one of my favourites. It was a picture of a wild-haired man in his early thirties sitting at a beat-up grand piano. It was Dad as I tried to remember him. He could never sit still when he played. For a man who always hammered home technique when teaching me, he was a hypocrite. In this particular photo the chair had been kicked behind him and was lying on its side. He stood at the piano in a lunge, his hair hanging down around his face as his hands slammed out a chord. The photo was clipped from a newspaper. Under the photo was the caption: *Emerging talent Charles Chambers'* album, 'Blood and Ivory', breathes new life into a staid genre.

The piano was collecting dust. Its presence was a vain attempt at reconnecting with a life I'd left behind at university. Yet this morning the instrument beckoned. Almost in a trance I set aside my cereal bowl and folded back the lid of the keys. The fingers of my right hand ran over middle C.

I picked away at an old melody Dad had taught me. Despite the years it was easy as riding a bike. My left hand joined my right. I was never able to capture the same passion Dad poured into his playing. Each note was in its proper place, but the music felt stiff. For Dad, each new bar was like finding a piece of buried treasure. But he tainted his pieces with the odd bit of dissonance, as if to remind listeners the world had a dirty underbelly.

That dissonance which echoed out of my own fingers was also why his career in music never reached the big leagues. He impressed the critics, but the critics didn't pay. The public did, and they didn't always like what they heard. Over the years the increasing dissonance in Dad's compositions signaled a deepening problem with his mental health. We never picked up on it at the time. Then one day he was dead.

I stared down at the keys. My own playing was clumsy, the muscle memory had vanished. The shaking in my hands intensified. Mistake after mistake tainted the melody. I couldn't match his greatness. I would never be good enough.

"Goddamnit," I said after fumbling one of the final chords. I balled my hands into fists and pounded them against the keys. *What am I so afraid of?* I slammed the piano lid down. Largo growled. He was watching me from the arm of the couch. He cocked his head, the stub of his tail tugging his rear end back and forth. Clapping issued from the bedroom door. I could feel my cheeks turn red. Eric stood there applauding me in nothing but a towel.

"You are way too hard on yourself," he said.

"The piano is out of tune."

"I couldn't tell."

"I could."

"Who wrote the song?"

"Piece. It's called a piece. My father."

"You don't play much anymore. I miss it."

"I rarely have it in me. Besides there's no time."

"You'll have plenty of time if these bad dreams keep up," he joked. My temples pulsed at Eric's poor taste in words. I tossed my unfinished cereal in the sink and marched past Eric into the en-suite. *Idiot…*

Forty-five minutes later we were both at the front door. Eric wore a tailored, navy-blue suit over a light-blue dress shirt, a red and navy tie, and brown, pointed Italian leather shoes. He looked fantastic, as usual, and I hated him a little bit for it. Comparably, I was a ghost of my former self. Too many long hours at work, sleepless nights and a vanishing appetite left me feeling skinny and weak. My face was pale and sallow. Going out without make-up was no longer an option.

"You look nice today," said Eric.

"Do I not look nice other days?"

His eyes went wide. "No, I just wanted to give you a comple-"

I grinned at him.

"Very funny," he continued. "Sorry again about your car. Do you want a drive to work?"

"I feel anxious about getting in a car right now. I'm happy to walk," I replied. "Can you take Largo for a stroll though?" Largo smacked his chops at the mention of his name. I gave him a scratch under the chin.

"Sure," said Eric. "Oh, and before I forget, your mother called me yesterday. Wants you to get back to her."

"Umm, okay, I'll try. See you tonight," I said. I dreaded speaking with mom; it usually ended in a fight.

"See you. Love you," he replied. He leaned down for a kiss.

"Love you." I pecked him on the lips and grabbed my work bag. Once on the other side of the door, my mind drifted to Rhodes last words the night before. PTER was an old car with too many miles on it, and I shuddered over what it would take to get it working like new again.

CHAPTER EIGHT

The clinic was empty and quiet save for the sound of metal being hammered. The heavy exam room door resisted the push of my hand. When it finally opened it revealed pieces of my baby littered across the floor.

The great compartment door panels of PTER were piled in a heap. The metal grating of its dual platforms was removed and the floor was strewn with nuts and bolts. Rhodes head and arms were buried in the drainage pipe under the platform. The only part of the machine that was still in one piece was the console in the center.

"What in god's name have you done?" I said. Rhodes lifted his head out of the hole, knocking it on the edge of the platform. His wrench clattered to the floor.

"Motherfu-" he said as he rubbed the back of his head. He looked at me and then back at the pieces of PTER lying on the ground.

"The saline solution we're using in the water is creating a rust problem. Had to install some metal flashing to cover up holes so water didn't leak out all over the floor. No idea how long it'll hold."

"And the compartment doors?"

Rhodes kicked a can of industrial black paint towards me. "That's what this is for. Same problem with rust. Why you built them out of metal is beyond me. There's a serious risk of them jamming. If that happens, I might not be able to get you or the patient out of the machine."

A chill ran down my spine. Trapped in one of PTER's sensory deprivation chambers? What could be worse? PTER had fail-safes to control emergencies, but I had zero faith in them. Dismantling and reassembling the device once a week to solve a different problem was costly. And we were running out of money. Rhodes was a capable guy, but his MacGyver approach made me anxious.

"We have a patient this afternoon. Can you get this all put together in time?" I asked, thinking about rescheduling Maggie, but how that would only delay getting information about the mute. It was a catch twenty-two.

"Good lord, when did she go into the schedule!"

"Late yesterday."

"I'll have to scramble. The machine isn't exactly up to code though, Cat. I wasn't finished rhyming off all our problems. We've got eroding respirator hoses, sensor failures in the suits. Hell, I'm even straight-up running out of hard drive space to maintain our records. The cherry on top is that Debbie tells me there's no money for repairs."

"None?" I exclaimed. *Was I that out of touch?*

"Not enough to make a dent. I've got a little bit I can contribute to the cause but it's peanuts."

"Coming up with capital is my problem, not yours," I said. "How much do we need?"

"Like twenty grand. If this Lydia Qiao is half as bad as you tell me she'll find a problem if we cut any corners and try to get away with less."

The dollar figure made my head spin. I put my hand on the counter and eased myself into the chair next to Rhodes. He studied me.

"Don't go all faint on me, Catarina. You don't have the money, do you?"

My mouth felt pasty. "Not exactly. I'll have to speak with Eric." The idea of broaching the subject with him made me sick. I drank the full mug of water on Rhodes desk in two gulps. Rhodes put his hand on mine.

"That bad, eh. It'll be okay, Cat. You'll see." I squeezed his fingers. Rhodes awkwardly uncrossed his legs and re-crossed them. I burst out laughing.

"Are those skinny jeans? How did I not notice them earlier?"

"As a matter of fact, they are, and I was kinda hoping we could wrap this day up early so I can go ice myself. But now that I know we have a client I might have to call in sick tomorrow." Rhodes took a long inhale, stood up and adjusted himself in front of me. We had been working together long enough to become like an old, chaste married couple.

"I don't think the sick leave policy covers testicular torsion," I quipped.

"We have a sick leave policy?"

"Can we just get this thing back together as best we can before our patient shows up," I said. We spent the next three hours rebuilding PTER, which left me almost no time to prepare for Maggie.

Back in my office I used the few minutes I had before our session to check Maggie's file. Outside of our intake form, it was empty. Not nearly enough time to collect all of her previous medical records. She was unmarried, no children, parents divorced, and one brother. She was twenty-eight-years old, born and raised in Toronto, but moved to Vancouver six years ago after witnessing a suicide in the subway system. *And there it is.* A wave of nausea hit me. I hated memories that struck too close to home. Debbie popped her head in the door to tell me Maggie had arrived. I took a deep breath and rounded my desk.

"Maggie," I called from my doorway. She lifted her head from her phone. Her eyes were wide. She rose on shaky legs.

"Please have a seat on the couch," I said. She sat in the corner while I sat on the opposite end.

"Now that I'm here I'm not sure I want to be," she said.

"Everyone feels that way. It takes courage to relive our worst memories. Can you explain what's haunting you, Maggie?"

She folded her hands on her lap. "There was a train and a woman, and she was pulled under, and I could have done something about it, but I didn't and I can't get the image of her face out of my head."

"This is an opportunity to be rid of your suffering. You don't need years of therapy. Do you trust me?"

"I barely know you. What was going on in the center bathroom when we first met? You were in a way."

"It was just nerves."

She crossed her arms. "I've been crushed by anxiety so badly I can barely breathe enough times to know what I saw. I should have known this was a bad idea." She started to rise.

I grabbed her by the wrist. "Maggie, I'm sorry. You're not alone. I'm haunted by my own ghosts."

Her face softened and she sat back down.

"But your life looks so perfect. You're an accomplished woman who owns her own clinic helping people no one else will. You're tall and beautiful and have a sparkling diamond on your left hand."

"You know it's not that simple," I said.

"Maybe, maybe not." She took a deep breath. "How much does the PTER procedure cost, Dr. Chambers?"

"A session costs twenty-five hundred dollars."

Maggie swallowed. "I don't have that kind of money," she said. "But I can tell you everything I know about the man from the rehab center if that makes a difference."

Horse trading with Maggie was dangerous. If Lydia somehow found out, the consequences could be worse than just the project being shut down. Fines, legal trouble. Who knew what kind of wrath she was capable of. But to solve the mute's trauma I would need every advantage I could get.

"Pay what you can," I finally said.

Maggie hugged me. "Thank you, Dr. Chambers, thank you!"

"Okay, Maggie, Debbie will settle you up when we're done. Let me introduce you to Rhodes, my assistant and technician, who will get us ready. You can tell me what you know later."

The clack of our shoes alerted Rhodes to our entry into the examination room. He wheeled around in his chair and pushed his glasses back up his nose. He rose awkwardly.

"Rhodes wore his tight pants today," I said without thinking. He didn't skip a beat.

"I like to dress up for new patients," he said. "What do you think?" Rhodes pivoted on his toes to give her a full view of his skinny jeans. A smile crested Maggie's lips as her dark eyes widened.

"All jokes aside, you're in safe hands, Maggie," said Rhodes. Rhodes was a master at taking off the edge. I almost forgot I was about to witness Maggie's most traumatic memory. Almost. He ushered her over to the changing area and pulled down an acusensory suit.

"You'll need to undress and put this on. Don't worry, if I could slide into these pants today, you'll be able to get into the suit. It will help Dr. Chambers feel what you feel as the memory plays out."

She took the suit and stepped into the changing room.

"Nervous?" whispered Rhodes to me.

"She is, but she'll do fine," I replied.

"No, I meant you," he said. "You've been standing there like an idiot when you should be getting dressed." He punched me in the shoulder. I pulled down my own suit and took it to the bathroom to get dressed to save time. The thing made me look reptilian—a cold blooded shell walking towards disaster. In the examination room, Rhodes was finished getting Maggie prepared. The wires and hoses extending from the top of PTER made her look like a marionette. I injected myself with an extirpation landmark then stepped onto the platform of my chamber. It was my turn to become a puppet.

"Time to get started, Maggie," I said. "Rhodes, let's go."

Rhodes pressed a button on his keyboard to start Maggie's sedative. I heard her small voice through the microphone in her respirator.

"Dr. Chambers, I'm sorry." The metal-plated doors unfolded and shut me into sensory deprivation. The darkness was complete. Warm water inched up my body. Rhodes voice crackled in my ears.

"We haven't even started and your heart is already racing. You sure you don't need that vacation?"

To be honest, I was feeling claustrophobic. Completely isolated, enveloped in water, with no sense of up or down, left or right and no way to escape without help. The silence was a vice-grip and the darkness a curtain that seemed to separate life from death.

"I'm fine," I said to Rhodes.

"You promise?"

"I promise."

CHAPTER NINE

My feet planted hard on a sheet of ice that was wrapped around a frozen memory, metastasized to a cryogenic point separating Maggie's life before and after the event held inside. Rhodes was getting good. Spending time searching for the trauma left less time to do the real work, and I was thankful he spotted the landing.

Was it possible for me to watch one of Maggie's interactions with the mute? A first-hand account would be ideal. Stretching in all directions were millions of sparkling memories. Trauma had its own gravitational pull inside the lattice. That's why it was easy to find. A vanilla memory was like searching a beach for a specific grain of sand. I would have to give up on the notion of searching her mind and trust she'd make good on her promise.

Like crawling across thin ice to save someone who fell in, I reached a hole in the memory where Maggie disappeared. Under the surface was hypothermia, paralysis, and death. I took a deep breath and plunged face first to see for myself.

Maggie stood at the edge of the platform, pen in one hand, sheet music in the other, and headphones planted over her ears. One of my father's most famous compositions on solo piano drifted through my head. For an instant, the walls of PTER went dark and my father's face flashed huge against the wall, like an errant frame spliced into a reel of film. Maggie's memory resumed.

"What was that?" said Rhodes.

"Nothing, please be quiet, I'm working." It wasn't nothing. It was a problem, but not one I could solve as Maggie's memory unfolded. Maggie scribbled notes on her sheet music. The title across the top read *'Tickling Ivory,' by Charles Chambers.* The sound of the notes in her earphones invaded my conscience. The thudding and persistent rhythm was overlaid by a melancholic melody. *Why do you follow me, Dad?*

The same four notes beat faster, louder, harder. D minor, E minor, A minor, D minor. Faster, louder, harder. Faster. Louder. Harder. FASTER. LOUDER. HARDER.

As the song pounded through Maggie's mind, a woman further up the platform pushed through the distracted commuters. Her frizzy red hair stuck out in all directions. Her black blazer and white pants contrasted against her gaudy green costume jewellery. Her eyes pressed into narrow slits as she walked.

FASTER. LOUDER. HARDER.

Get out of my way, mouthed the woman, her voice competing with the composition playing in Maggie's head. The woman had a large dangling purse strung around one shoulder. Her feet pressed one in front of the other as she angled down the only clear path, inches from the edge of the platform. As she closed on Maggie, fissures rippled up from the subway tracks and split through the platform. Through the cracks she made eye contact with Maggie. My fingers tingled as I clutched at fragments of memory and massaged them back together. Maggie shifted to get out of the woman's way. But the platform was crowded and her shoulder caught the woman and threw her off balance. Fissures shattered Maggie's field of vision like a broken pane of glass.

FASTER. LOUDER. HARDER.

Whoosh, a train hurtled into the station. The window frame of a train car hooked around the strap of the woman's purse and smashed her body against the coach.

Time slowed to a crawl. Her face contorted in pain, but her wide terror-struck eyes never left Maggie's. Echoes of my father's composition was the soundtrack to this unfolding nightmare. I could barely concentrate. My body was slick with sweat. Errant fragments of memory floated off in the distance. I swam through my chamber to grab at them and piece together the trauma.

The woman's legs were caught in the gap between the train and the platform. She let out a blood-curdling scream. A thousand heads rose in unison from their smart phones. As each millisecond stretched on, the woman's emerald green eyes pleaded with Maggie to make it stop. Green like my father's. A spray of blood caught Maggie square in the chest, soaking her clothes and sheet music. The woman was gone.

"Rhodes, give me a SLUMB-Rx boost of ten percent. Short injection. Just need to catch up." A moment later the breakneck pace of the memory slackened. My hands plucked fragments of memory out of my chamber and wove them back through the fissures.

Maggie's eyes watched the woman get caught on the speeding subway much further up the tracks. In less than two seconds, her body disappeared under the train near Maggie's feet. She hadn't knocked the woman into the train after all.

The platform erupted in the deafening screams of men and women as bodies jostled against her. Maggie's joined them. The weight of a thousand glaring eyes fell on Maggie's body. But the visages of those on the platform were torn asunder by thick black cracks that disappeared into a void where their face should have been. The details were so hopelessly eroded, even PTER wasn't strong enough to piece them back together.

A hand rested on Maggie's shoulder. A man knelt down beside her. His bushy dark eyebrows were streaked with gray hair. His thin lips were pulled tight by his clenched jaw. He wore a light-blue striped shirt with a badge on the chest pocket: *William*.

"Miss, you need to leave. You're blocking the platform." The words reverberated out of the fissures running along his face, each crevice serving as another mouth. As I sewed them back together to reveal a genial face, new fissures emerged to make him monstrous once again.

"Didn't you see?" said Maggie.

It was hard to peer through the tears welling up in her eyes.

"We all saw," he said, "we just don't want the trains to be late." The fissures leeched down his body. The man looked like crumpled newsprint.

"Go clean yourself up. We don't want to scare anyone, do we?" he said. Without asking, he yanked Maggie to her feet. The bloodied sheet music dislodged from her hands and floated down the platform.

"Wait, my music," said Maggie.

"It's not important, they've all stopped listening to you," William said as he pulled Maggie roughly to the stairs. At the steps leading up to the station he let go. Maggie turned back to him.

"Go!" he yelled, pointing up the steps. His outstretched arm was covered in fissures like his veins had been injected with ink. William looked two-dimensional against the backdrop of the memory.

"Go!" he demanded again. As he gesticulated at the stairs his arm cracked in half along one of the fissures. Maggie backed away from him up the stairs as his entire body crumbled to pieces. She turned and ran as the pile of fractured body parts continued screaming "Go. Leave. You're not wanted."

"Need ten percent more SLUMB-Rx, Rhodes," I said into my microphone.

"Roger," he replied.

My hands worked overtime to catch all the errant fragments in my chamber. I swam to the bottom and scooped them in my palms and worked them like building blocks into William's face and body. He became human.

"Are you okay?" said the older man. His face was a couple feet away from Maggie's. She didn't answer.

"What's your name, dear," he said.

"Mmm...Mm, Maggie" she managed.

"Maggie, my name is William. You've witnessed something awful. We all have. Do you have a safe place you can go?" He withdrew his hand from her shoulder and folded his hands together.

"I, I don't know," she replied. She looked down at her shirt. It was clean of blood.

"Will you let me help you up?" William asked. She held out a limp hand. He pulled Maggie up with him. I washed away a sea of fissures, and the cone of silence surrounding Maggie and William lifted. The rush of sound was furious as the mob scurried about, everyone trying to remember if they actually saw what happened to the woman pulled under the train. The hat of a police officer milled over the crowd.

"Do you want to speak with him?" asked William. Maggie shook her head.

"That's what I thought," he said. He pulled her by the hand in the opposite direction. No one paid attention to them. Maggie reached a seemingly endless flight of stairs. I rubbed out a pair of fissures and watched as half the staircase, one step at a time, withdrew into the collapsing crack.

"Thank you," said Maggie.

William smiled. "Goodbye," he said.

Maggie turned and walked slowly up the stairs. With each step the walls of PTER faded to black.

"Get me out of here Rhodes."

"Connection severed. Welcome back."

CHAPTER TEN

The water flushed out of my compartment and light finally entered as the walls folded into the console. I ripped off my respirator and took a deep breath of fresh air. Rhodes stood on the other side of the wall. He scrunched up his nose.

"What?" I asked.

"Your vitals were all over today. What's going on?"

I paused to come up with an answer. "Hard to explain."

"Try me."

"I can't remember. Anyway, how did our patient do?"

Rhodes sighed. "Nothing too unusual. She should be awake in about ten minutes, do you wanna look at her charts till then?"

"Let me use the washroom first," I said. My legs felt like anvils as I trudged out of the compartment. My heel caught the edge of the platform as I stepped down, and the metal panel that wrapped around it dislodged and rattled on the floor. It exposed the drainage system underneath.

"Damnit," I sighed. "Rhodes, fix that before she wakes up." He grabbed a screwdriver off his desk. "I'll do my best." Oblivious, Maggie lay listless on her chair.

In the bathroom I squirmed out of my acusensor suit. Suddenly I became acutely aware of every organ in my body, every little twitch and pain as they churned and pumped. A layer of sweat sprouted across my skin and a pit grew in my stomach. I got to my feet and closed my eyes. *For God's sake Cat, really?*

My eyes snapped open and the red-haired woman from Maggie's memory stared back at me in the mirror. The pupils of her green eyes narrowed to a tiny point so that all I could see were a pair of massive emerald corneas in her wide sockets. Her head was barely attached to her body, hanging by threads of flesh sliced across by the wheels of a train. A similar line ran across the top of her legs. The congealed dark red blood was all that held the macabre corpse together. She opened her mouth to speak and my own voice emanated from her throat, "It's your fault. It's all your fault."

BANG, BANG, BANG. The door to the bathroom shook. I ripped my gaze away from the mirror.

"She's awake," said Rhodes.

I looked back at the mirror. My own face, brow beaded in sweat, looked back at me.

"Be right out," I said, pushing my hair away from my eyes and tucking it behind my ears. I ripped off a paper towel and mopped up the sweat as best I could. I blinked repeatedly. Each time the world came back just as it should. But the red-haired lady, Maggie's gift, wouldn't be far. It was too soon to take an extirpation tablet. There was still work to be done. I slid back into my dry clothes.

Slowly I opened the bathroom door. Rhodes had already gone back to the exam room. I smoothed out my blouse and collected myself before joining them.

Maggie stood on her platform chatting to Rhodes. She giggled at a joke but stifled her laughter when she saw me enter the room.

"You're in good spirits," I remarked.

"I feel... lighter."

"Maggie, why don't you get changed back into your normal clothes and we'll talk in my office," I said.

Rhodes handed me a manila folder with the statistics from Maggie's session inside.

I sat in my office chair and stared at the wall. Each breath was laboured. *Dad why won't you and your little reminders of what a failure I am get out of my head. Maggie wouldn't be the patient that allowed me to redeem myself.* A moment later, Maggie walked into the doorway.

"Please close the door behind you," I said and gestured for her to take a seat on the couch. I spread her file out in front of me and gave it a quick glance. The charts on the left were Maggie's; on the right, my own.

You wanted to see somatic empathy. If my heart rate moved up the same number of beats as Maggie's at the same time, it meant a perfect correlation. That never happened. Anything greater than fifty percent was a serious win. Maggie was a seventy five.

"Anything... unusual?" asked Maggie.

"Nope. A couple of spikes in your heart rate and cortisol levels, but that's to be expected when someone's prodding into a memory you'd rather keep buried."

"What did you see in there?" she asked. The image of the disembodied corpse of the red-haired woman, cut in three by the train wheels flashed through my mind. My hand slid open my desk drawer and found my bottle of extirpation tablets.

"Everything," I replied. "The woman on that platform made the choice to walk so dangerously close to the edge. The train caught her well up the platform. She went under in front of you. You can't unsee that image, but there's nothing you could have done to change her course."

"So that's it?" asked Maggie.

"For me. This is just the beginning of your healing. But changing your relationship with your trauma is essential to starting over," I said. "Remember that you can only control the decisions you make. You can't put the responsibility of everyone else's choices on your shoulders."

"Thank you, Dr. Chambers. I feel optimistic for the first time in a long time." She got out of her chair.

"Maggie, aren't you forgetting something?"

"Oh, yes, of course." She sat back down. "Ummm, what do you want to know about him?"

What didn't I want to know? What happened to the man? Where did he come from? How did he spend his time? What is his medical history? Experience with therapy? The list was endless.

"Besides the fact he's mute, what stands out about him?" I slid a notepad in front of me. There would need to be notes. I was kicking myself for not getting this out of the way before our session. Extirpation would vaporize my recent memories and I wouldn't remember what Maggie had to say otherwise.

"It's like he's never coming or going," Maggie said. "Seems like he's not all there but I don't believe it. I've never spent more than ten minutes with him at a time but it's like he's disconnected from everything. He remembers nothing and behaves as if the future is non-existent. What you might mistake as an absent mind is a man who exists solely in the moment."

Fascinating. If it wasn't for the violence and the drug addiction it was almost like he had achieved a state of pure mindfulness.

"Why the aggressive reaction to the sight of drugs?" I asked.

"If you couldn't speak, how would you react if every bone in your body told you that you needed something?" Maggie stood up from the couch. "I'm sorry Dr. Chambers, I don't know anything else."

"Thank you for your time," I said, rising from my desk. I tucked an extirpation tablet in my back pocket.

"No, thank you. When I think back on my past it comes back clearer. I'm hoping I can let go now."

"You will," I said. We shook hands and she left my office. I could hear her murmuring with Debbie behind my closed office door. The extirpation tablet was down my throat a second later. *Goodbye Maggie.* Black oily tentacles pulled my eyelids shut and sifted through my memories. They latched onto the recent past and pulled Maggie into the abyss where I thought nothing could return. Nothing but Dad.

CHAPTER ELEVEN

The glass on the kitchen island brimmed with red wine. It was my second of the evening. The first had been no smaller. The words I was going to say to Eric ran through my head. A set of keys jingled in the lock. Largo lifted his head from the couch. When Eric stepped through the door, Largo barked and ran for him, wagging his stumpy little tail as he scurried across the hardwood. A wide smile spread across Eric's face as he leaned down to Largo's level. He scratched Largo behind the ears, and then looked from me to the wine on the island.

"That kinda day?" he said.

"That kinda day."

He took a wine glass out of the cupboard. "Well, if it makes you feel any better, I just arranged for a potential buyer from Hong Kong to come visit the Point Grey property. You don't fly across the Pacific if you aren't serious."

"What does that mean for us?"

"The commission would be over a million dollars," said Eric with a huge smile. He tipped the wine bottle into his glass, but only a dribble came out. He raised an eyebrow at the bottle and set it back on the table.

A million dollars! Maybe this conversation with Eric would be easier than I thought. We were only in our late thirties. What luck!

"That's amazing, Eric!" I took a big sip of wine.

Eric leaned against the counter. "We shouldn't get too ahead of ourselves. It's not a done deal, but it's the most promising prospect I've seen since the seller brought the property to my office. Mansions like this one can make an agent's career."

"I'm so happy for you. Listen I need to ask you something," I said.

The smile evaporated from Eric's face. He pushed away from the counter and drank the little bit of wine that was in his glass.

"What is it?"

"Ummm, well, the project starts Monday and..." I was already floundering. "And PTER is getting old right, so... Uhhh, well, it's going to need some work." I took a deep breath. "The clinic needs money."

A shadow passed across Eric's face. His voice fell. "How much money are we talking about?"

"Twenty thousand," I said.

"TWENTY THOUSAND!"

"I know it's a lot of money-"

"-A LOT OF MONEY? Do you think we're just sitting on seas of cash?" Eric loosened his tie.

"We have our savings," I said.

"Which is meant for retirement. We aren't getting any younger. That money needs to stay there."

"You just said you were close to closing Point Grey. What does twenty thousand matter if we're going to be getting a million dollar commission?"

"I never said it was a done deal. Besides, you were planning on asking me this question long before I ever told you about the sale."

"I'll be able to square everything up by the end of next week when the probationary period is over."

"Probationary period. You're talking like everything is a certainty, Cat."

"Don't lecture me. I'm going to get torn to shreds by the city's auditor if I don't get PTER working like new. Do you want Debbie and Rhodes to go without paychecks if the business fails?"

"CATARINA, I AM DONE THROWING GOOD MONEY AFTER BAD!" He yelled.

I rounded the island to stand toe-to-toe with Eric. "What the hell is that supposed to mean?"

"Exactly how it sounds. I must have given you two hundred grand by now to keep that business afloat. I'm done. It's stealing you from me Cat. Maybe *you* don't notice, but I've watched it take pieces out of you for years. And it's only gotten worse lately. Why would I keep throwing you into that fire?"

"Because you love me, Eric, and it's important to me. I love what I do. The look on someone's face when they actually start to have hope for the future for the first time in forever... that look. It's such a gift."

"What happens the day you're the one who needs PTER. Who will be there to help you?"

I glared into his dark brown eyes. They were glazed with tears. My eyes were welling up, too.

"I have it under control, Eric."

He took my hand. "Maybe you do. But I don't. I worry about you every day." He squeezed my hand and then let go.

"Listen," he continued. "It doesn't matter what you tell me. I'm never going to agree to withdraw the savings for your clinic."

"WHAT?! Just like that? You're just shutting the door?"

Eric walked away from me towards the front door. He put his shoes back on.

"Where are you going?" I demanded.

"I'm taking Largo for a walk. There's nothing left to be said. I've told you exactly how I feel about this. I don't want to argue all night. I need some air." He clamped a leash on to Largo's collar and went out the door without saying another word.

I stared blankly at the door and gripped my glass of wine.

* * *

Eric and I didn't speak the rest of the evening. My mind skittered through the night on snippets of sleep. The fighting didn't stop in my dreams. Finally, I gave up. I lifted Largo off the bed and carried him with me to the living room.

In the predawn hours trying to stay productive with research kept my mind from drifting in to an anxious tailspin. As the memories of my father grew more troublesome, I revisited my PhD thesis. Was it possible to make my extirpation tablets more effective? Was there a way to engineer the compound so that it targeted a specifically identified neuropeptide and vaporized a single memory? It went against everything I professed to patients.

Catarina, you reek of desperation.

I scribbled some notes around a chemical formula in my notebook.

In theory there is no difference between theory and practice. In practice there is. The Yogi Berra quote was pasted on a piece of paper inside the lid of my secretary desk as a reminder to refrain from doing anything stupid. It was why there were no other lab rats but myself for my cocktail.

"Morning," said Eric standing next to me.

I jumped out of my skin. "Dear god Eric, you scared the crap out of me!" I said. I quickly shut my research notebook and jammed it into my work bag next to the desk. Eric ran a hand through his thick dark hair and scratched the back of his head. He was already dressed in a gray pinstripe suit with a light pink dress shirt and a blue tie.

"Making any progress?" he asked, as if the prior night hadn't happened.

"None," I said. I closed the secretary desk over my work. The reams of chemical compound equations splayed in front of me had turned a mild headache into a full blown one.

"What time is it?" I asked.

"Six thirty."

"Hmm, probably time to grab a shower."

"Of course," said Eric, pecking me on the cheek as I passed.

I lingered for half a second. Eric took the opportunity to wrap his arms around me. I recoiled. "Sorry, I've had too much coffee and still haven't brushed my teeth. It's for your own good," I said.

Eric slowly let go. "Fine," he said, turning for the kitchen.

Our love life wasn't what it used to be. After a bad fight Eric was usually first at reconciliation. But he was growing less understanding. The tension simmering between us was on the verge of boiling. Last night was just a teaser.

Ten minutes of hot water passed over my head in the shower before I finally got around to washing up and getting out. The bathroom was filled with steam. After towelling off, I ran my fingers along the foggy mirror, cutting five lines across it and dotting the staff with music notes. There was a knock on the door. *What now...*

"What is it?" I said.

"Just got an email from a client trying to buy a detached in Kitsilano," Eric said. "Apparently the bank turned them down for financing, whole deal just went upside down. I have to run. Want me to drop you off at work?"

"No thanks, I'm fine," I said.

"Okay, I'll see you tonight. Love you."

I turned back to the mirror and applied foundation to my cheeks and under my eyes then drew black eye-liner across the bottom of my eye lids. My green eyes nearly sparkled. Nearly.

I pulled on a pair of comfortable underwear, a soft bra and slid into a pair of loose gray dress pants, then donned the white sleeveless blouse that was my staple. I slid on the accompanying gray blazer. Largo looked up at me with his big dark eyes. He was curled up in his bed next to my dresser. His tail wagged as I chose a pair of earrings from my jewelry box. He let out a low whine.

"Oh, fine," I said. "Does someone miss his mom?" I scratched him behind the ears. In a display of agility unusual for a bulldog, he flipped onto his back and exposed his belly. I gave him a good scratch across his chest. He tried to look at me from his back, but he couldn't see past his big tongue hanging across his face. He rolled back onto his feet and pressed his front paws on my leg.

"Do you need to go out?" I asked him.

He let out a low humph and walked to the front door.

"Well, okay then."

The walk with Largo took us through the heart of Gastown and up to Burrard street. After grabbing a coffee and a scone I started for home. As I stood waiting for a crossing light to change I saw my bank branch, Columbia Trust, on the opposite corner. Was there a way to make something work? My credit was shot to shit, and the clinic was up to its eyeballs in debt. Getting a short-term loan would be next to impossible, but maybe, just maybe, there were other options.

CHAPTER TWELVE

Two hours later I was sitting in the lobby of the branch. It was a short walk from there to my office, and I needed answers before sending Rhodes on a wild chase to find everything we needed to get PTER fully operational. Wendy at the front desk arranged an appointment with a banker named Brian, then ushered me to the seating area.

Harold, the branch's small business banker, waddled across the lobby and made eye contact. *Damnit.* The ceiling lights glared off his bald head. His gut protruded over his belt. I was surprised he hadn't asphyxiated himself, given how tight his tie was wrapped around his bulging neck.

"Dr. Chambers!" he said with a big smile.

"Hello Harold."

He gave my hand a big shake and sat next to me. "We don't see you much these days," he said.

"I let Debbie take care of most of my affairs. I've been incredibly busy."

"What brings you to the branch?"

"I need to take care of some personal banking."

"Hmm, how's business?" he asked. His smile vanished.

"Just landed a big contract with the city. First payment should come through end of next week. Will square me up with you guys."

He nodded like he had heard this story one too many times. "What are the chances I could get a twenty-thousand-dollar bridge loan till then, Harold. Need to do some repairs to make sure the probationary audit goes off without a hitch."

"Well, I don't know. I'd have to look at the figures. It's a big number, Dr. Chambers. Probably have to send it up to my risk management department. Not sure when I'll hear back."

I needed an answer the same day, not next week. "Is there a way to expedite an approval?"

I could almost see the gears turning in Harold's head.

"Mrs. Chambers," said a younger man, who came around the corner. He couldn't have been out of university for more than a few months and was barely old enough to have washed off the placenta. He wore a cheap black suit that was too big for his skinny frame. He would need a few more years of nothing but sitting behind a desk like Harold to fill the thing out.

Harold looked relieved to see the young man.

"Brian?" I said.

"Yes, pleased to meet you, my office is this way."

"Call my clinic later today, Harold," I said.

"Sure thing, Dr. Chambers," he said. Harold and I both knew he'd call later with some bullshit excuse about why he couldn't make the figures work. My chips were on Brian.

Inside his high sided cubicle I could hear the faint murmurings of other bankers and their clients in the adjacent offices.

"Gorgeous day outside, isn't it," said Brian. His voice had a nervous edge.

"I hadn't noticed."

"Oh... well, umm," he paused. "How can I help you today?"

"I need to make a withdrawal from my retirement account."

Brian's shoulders slumped. He wouldn't be getting a sale. "Can I ask why you need to withdraw the money?" he said.

"Does it matter?"

"Well, if you just need the funds for a short period of time perhaps a line of credit would be more appropriate."

"I'd never get approved. I'm self-employed and my credit shows it. I just want to withdraw the savings."

Brian nodded along. "How much did you want to withdraw?"

"Twenty thousand," I said.

He clicked from screen to screen. "Oh, I see here that this is a joint account. To authorize the withdrawal I'll also need your husband's signature."

Brian's words felt dirty. It never occurred to me that I'd need Eric to sign. It was obvious in hindsight. A wave of guilt washed over me.

"Mrs. Chambers?"

"The funds are going from my personal accounts to cover debt payments my business owes your bank. It's going from one pocket to the other. You should be happy I'm doing this."

"I'm sorry, I really need your husband to be here so I can check his identification and so he can sign the paperwork."

"He's a very busy real estate agent. A lot of his clients take mortgages from your bank. Ask your colleagues. They know him."

"Well I-"

"—Come on, Brian. I don't have a lot of time. I just wanted to come in and get this straightened out quickly. I have to get back to work."

"Mrs. Chambers, you have to understand there are rul-"

"-I'm tired of this crap. You hide behind your rules to avoid good service. It's my money and I want it. There's always something every time I come here." My voice was now loud enough to be heard over the cubicle walls. My chair scraped loudly across the tiles as I hastily stood. "I'd like to speak to the manager."

"Mrs. Chambers, I'm sorry. I think we can fix this. Please sit down." Brian's face had gone pale. He stuck a finger between his neck and shirt collar. I regretted pulling Brian into my mess. I was almost twice his age and preyed on his lack of confidence. Whispers of my father's voice danced through my head. *This is sickening Catarina.* Brian took a few sheets of paper off his printer.

"You'll both need to sign here," he gestured to the final page of the withdrawal form. "Can you please get him to sign this and get it back to me today. My compliance officer will kill me if my paperwork is out of order." Brian fidgeted in his chair. "I'm still in my probationary period," he added.

You could get this poor kid fired because you put your needs above his.

"I don't think my husband is too far from here. I'll be back ASAP." My hands reached across the desk and took the paperwork from Brian. I rushed out of his office. Eric would never agree to sign, and I had no intention of getting him to. Instead, I ran the twenty minutes it took to get home. Somewhere in the condo would be some paperwork with Eric's signature. Largo was excited for an early visitor and hopped around the floor when I entered through the front door.

"Sorry, boy, no time to play," I took a treat out of a container and threw it on the floor. I tore into the drawer of my secretary desk where we kept our documents. After five minutes of searching Eric's haphazard filing system, I found a piece of paper with his mercifully simple signature. I laid it beside a piece of blank paper and began tracing it over and over. When I was finally satisfied I had it figured out, I wrote a copy onto the bank paperwork. My skin crawled with guilt as each curl of his name spilled out of my pen. Largo was at my feet, watching me with his dark brown eyes. It felt like even he was judging me. I scratched out my own name in the other signature box and then folded up the paper.

"I had no choice Largo," I said.

A half hour later I walked back into the bank. Wendy smiled at me from the front desk.

"I just need to drop something off for Brian," I said. I stepped into Brian's doorway. He looked up from his computer.

"That was quick," he muttered. I handed him the paperwork. He took it from me and compared the signature to existing documents in our file. The seconds stretched on as his eyes went back and forth from the files to the forged signature. Eyes tick left. Eyes tock right.

"What account would you like me to deposit the funds?"

"My personal account, not the joint checking."

He raised an eyebrow.

"It's linked to my business accounts," I stuttered.

"It takes a day for the funds to settle so you won't see them there till tomorrow morning."

If I were lucky Eric wouldn't look at the account for at least a few days. Hopefully a few weeks. Long enough for me to figure out how to settle everything.

"Thanks for your help, Brian," I said. He could only manage a nod. He didn't get out of his chair or offer a handshake. It wasn't often I made people hope they'd never hear from me again. My stomach gurgled, and a faint wave of nausea hit me. I scurried out of the branch. Ten steps down the sidewalk and my stomach heaved. I plunged my face in a nearby garbage can and threw up. I lifted my face out of the trash, my skin burning scarlet as people eyed me. I put my head down and walked to the clinic, completely ashamed with myself.

*   *   *

"You'll have your twenty thousand tomorrow. What can you get done in the meantime?"

Rhodes swirled around in his chair. There were bags under his eyes and a coffee stain on his shirt. The guy poured his heart into the clinic. Where else could you work on something like PTER? But he could do a better job of taking care of himself.

"Plenty," he said. "I'll shop the small stuff today and put in orders to pick up all the bigger items tomorrow."

"How long do you figure it'll take to do all the work?"

"With your help, we'll be lucky to get a shred of the weekend to ourselves."

Walking into day one without rest wasn't ideal but what choice did I have. "Make your calls. I've got my own things to straighten out. I'll be back to help you tomorrow. Don't stay too late, you look like hell." Pushing Rhodes too hard would backfire. Without him

Dr. Catarina Chambers' clinic was nothing. As dedicated as he was, he wasn't a slave, and years ago he nearly left. I had to give him some equity in the business to keep him with me, promising to deliver on a project as big as the one we just landed. His fate was bound to mine. We had to make this work.

Back in my office I scanned the shelves lined with psychology, psychiatry, and pharmacology journals. What Maggie told me about the mute had left an impression. The reduced expression of emotion, the poverty of speech, the diminished capacity to experience pleasure, and the withdrawal from social interaction were all symptoms of schizophrenia. The cognitive impairment, being unable to process consequence, disconnection from the past; it all pointed to the neurological disease. So why didn't it feel like the right diagnosis?

The mute was likely in his mid sixties. Male schizophrenics with substance abuse problems were at a heightened risk of suicide. That he had made it this far in life made me even more sceptical of the diagnosis. I pulled a journal off the shelf and sifted to page one hundred. *Neural Imaging and Exploratory Therapy Techniques by Dr. M. Dietrich.* Would the creator of PTER have answers for me? It often felt like where I was about to tread, Dr. Dietrich had walked first.

I scanned the pages for any mention of schizophrenia but came up blank. Browsing for other keywords also yielded nothing. Just when I was about to give up, my eyes locked on the word 'mindfulness' in a footnote.

Successful patient MRI scans showed neurological activity synonymous with a state of mindfulness. The brain would resonate a deep blue across both hemispheres as the present waking self disconnected from all internal and external stimulus. The purity of their peace was remarkable.

Debbie walked into my office. I snapped the journal shut.

"What would you like me to do to get ready for next week?" she asked.

"Pretend you're someone who would leave no rock unturned. Whatever you think is good enough Lydia Qiao will pick to pieces. I hate putting you guys through this exercise, but we have to be as perfect as humanly possible. Can you do that for me?"

Debbie looked sick. "I mean, I can try. How will I know if I've gotten it all?"

"If you think you're done, triple check. If we don't have a checklist for it yet, make one."

"Umm, okay." She closed the door to my office. For the remainder of the afternoon I read as much research on schizophrenia and mindfulness as possible. With each word that passed my eyes I felt the knowledge I was gaining on the mute's possible condition release the binds from one of the hands Lydia had tied behind my back.

CHAPTER THIRTEEN

When I got home my skin was crawling. I needed to wash away the day, so I took off my clothes and started up a hot shower. A solid ten minutes of shampooing and soaping up had passed by the time Eric arrived home.

"Heyo," he yelled from the bedroom. The water on my naked body felt like a thousand drops of guilt. I stuck my head out from around the curtain.

"Eric, come here," I said. He walked into the bathroom, still in his suit.

"You're not going to get in here with me with that on are you?" I said.

Eric's pants dropped faster than a Japanese bullet train. He tossed his blazer into the bedroom and fumbled his way out of the rest of his clothes.

"Easy there boy," I joked. He jumped into the shower with me.

"Jesus, it's hot," he yelped.

I put my arms over his collarbones and wrapped my hands around the back of his head. "You'll live," I said and pulled him in hard and pressed my lips against his. He ran his hands over my hips. I wrapped a leg around his thigh and pushed against his body.

We hadn't been intimate in at least six weeks. The last time was only memorable because it was the first time it had happened in over a month. *This time would be different.*

He opened his mouth to say something, but I put my finger over his lips. I pulled my face away from his and watched a devilish grin spread across his face. I turned my back to him, putting one foot on the edge of the tub while I pressed my other hand against the wall. I guided him inside me. He was a rock.

After five minutes Eric finished. We quickly rinsed off as the water started to cool. I wrapped the lone towel around me and left. By the time Eric emerged from the bathroom, I was already half dressed in my pyjamas. He looked pleased despite being covered in water, holding nothing but a hand towel in front of his privates.

"What was that all about?"

"You're welcome," I replied.

He chuckled and made his way towards the linen closet. "I'm not sure I can think of a better way to end my day," he said as he dried off.

"Neither can I," I lied. Despite my efforts to put it out of my mind, the nagging guilt about what I had done earlier that day crept back.

"Maybe tomorrow we can try that again," he chirped.

"Easy there. Don't get too ahead of yourself."

Eric pulled on a pair of sweat pants and a tank top. "So what are we going to do tonight?" he asked.

"Considering we're in our PJ's we're going to have to convince Largo he doesn't need a walk."

On cue Largo marched into the room with his leash in his mouth. He cocked his head from Eric to me and back again.

"Fine, just a quick one," said Eric smiling. Largo wiggled his stumpy tail. Eric turned to me.

"Do we have any red wine?"

"Do we have any red wine?" I repeated mockingly. "Who do you think I am?"

"Right… well, open a bottle, would ya? I'd like a glass or two when I get back."

I winked at him.

When Eric smiled the churning feeling in my gut subsided. "Be quick," I said.

"I will," replied Eric.

The front door closed. I uncorked a bottle and filled a pair of glasses. I sat on one of the stools next to the island, staring into my merlot, pondering tomorrow. Always tomorrow. The promise, the threat. I took a long sip.

*   *   *

Over the remainder of the week, I was home so little Eric was barely more than a warm body in my bed.

The clinic became my prison. More than once I caught Debbie wiping away tears at her desk. She had to revamp our patient intake system from top to bottom. There could be absolutely no holes in our documentation or Lydia would skewer us. My encounters with the anal retentive monster were enough to turn me into a similar creature. Every barked order made me hate myself a little more each day, but I didn't see another option. Debbie would enjoy a nice pay raise once the money started flowing in, but it was still cold comfort.

Rhodes got it the worst. I forced him to stress test every aspect of PTER. Every time I turned around something was broken. Our original list of malfunctions spiralled out of control.

"Catarina, the saline is clogging PTER's plumbing."

"There are leaks seeping out of the door panels."

"The console cooling fans have failed."

The twenty grand barely had a chance to hit our account before we'd spent it all. Rhodes had to rent a trunk to get everything back and forth from the office. After the next set of paychecks, we were broke.

When I wasn't bossing around the other two, I prepared a new batch of SLUMB-Rx and a dozen extirpation tablets. And I cleaned. Top to bottom. I cleaned every damn corner of the office until it shone.

On Sunday night I offered to buy us all take-out. The looks on Debbie and Rhodes faces told me they just wanted to go home. After another survey of anything that we could have possibly missed, I gave up trying to find flaws and let them leave. I hung back another ten minutes, shut everything down and turned off the lights. Every inch of my body ached and begged for a night's sleep. With day one starting the next morning, I was confident my mind wouldn't let rest come easily. But I had to try. *And tomorrow… tomorrow I had to win.*

CHAPTER FOURTEEN

Eric and I shared a silent drive to work Monday morning. He stopped the car opposite my building and shut off the engine. Behind his eyes, the gears were working full tilt. He finally spoke up.

"Cat, I'm sorry I haven't celebrated you winning the project. It's been for purely selfish reasons. So," he paused. "Good luck today."

"Uhhh, thank you." He pulled me in close. He pressed his lips against my forehead. His other hand squeezed my thigh. His kiss lifted a heavy weight off my shoulders.

"Promise me you'll be careful today," he said.

"You have nothing to worry about." I gave him a quick peck, and then got out of the car. It was five minutes to eight at this point. I skirted across the street, into the lobby and up the three flights of stairs to my floor.

There she was. Standing stick-straight with her arms crossed and a large work bag slung over her shoulder. In one hand was a clipboard. She wore black pants, short black heels, a peach blouse and a black blazer. Her ears were emblazoned with large diamond studs. Her black hair was tied back into a tight bun behind her head. She wore a burgundy shade of lipstick and a hint of eyeliner.

"Mrs. Qiao, you're early. I wasn't expecting you for another hour."

"There needs to be an inspection before the patient arrives," she said.

I was grateful I left no stone unturned the night before. From my prior encounter with her, I'd suspected she'd pull something like this.

"Is there a problem, Dr. Chambers?" she pressed.

"No, please come in." I unlocked the office door and flicked on the lights, half expecting the place to be torn apart by rats. That would be my luck. Miraculously, it was just as I'd left it the night before. Lydia pushed past me and scanned the waiting area. She ran her fingers over the chairs and pulled on a fray in the upholstery. She marked something down on her clipboard.

"I'd like to see PTER," she said.

"Can we wait until my technician Mr. Walker arrives?"

"Something to hide, Dr. Chambers?"

"Of course not," I said. Every word out of her mouth was designed to keep me on the defensive. "He is just the most well-versed in the intricacies of PTER's mechanics. I figured you'd want to go over it inch by inch."

"There can be absolutely no risk to the patients and by extension, the city."

"You can see in my reports that I've never had any patient complications."

"I'll be the judge of that," she said, tapping her pen on her clipboard and narrowing her eyes. *And jury, too, I bet.* As I started down the hall to the examination room I was saved by Rhodes entering the office door.

He wore a pair of khaki's, a blue dress shirt, and a white and blue checkered tie that squeezed his neck. He had managed to tame his wild curly hair. I gave him a nod to show I appreciated the effort.

"Rhodes, this is Lydia Qiao from the city."

"Pleasure," said Rhodes extending his hand to Lydia.

She simply nodded and clasped her arms around her clipboard.

Rhodes slowly put his hand back down by his side. He glanced at me. All I could do was shrug.

"The examination room," pressed Lydia.

"Of course. Rhodes, can you show Lydia around and explain to her all of the safety precautions we take with PTER."

"No problem," he said. As we walked into the examination room I examined Lydia's face. It betrayed nothing. She appeared entirely unimpressed with the hulking machine and its glimmering oiled black hull. It looked almost as pristine as the day we constructed it ten years ago. Despite our best efforts, beneath the surface it was all duct tape and Band-Aids. I prayed they held together long enough for me to walk away with an instalment payment from the city.

"Ms. Qiao, what you see here is one of the most sophisticated pieces of psychotherapy equipment in the world," said Rhodes.

"Mrs.," corrected Lydia.

I rolled my eyes.

"Huh?" said Rhodes, his mouth hanging open.

"It's *Mrs.* Qiao."

Hard to believe someone had married this ice queen. I pictured a short, soft weakling who responded to her every beck and call. I bet he even gives her a nightly foot rub. A smirk spread across my face. It took a couple seconds, but Rhodes finally recovered.

"Right, anyway, PTER is a highly advanced sensory deprivation chamber. It completely eliminates both Dr. Chambers and the patient's attachment to the real world. From out here I produce a memory map called a lattice. My job is to help Catarina navigate this lattice. Once we've identified the traumatic memory, our acusensory suits and projection chamber lets Dr. Chambers see and feel the memory in the same way the patient felt it when it was originally experienced."

"Yes, yes, I've read all the documentation. What I want to see are the safety features. These chambers fill up with water, do they not?" Rhodes clicked a button on the console; the chamber doors folded open. He showed her one of the respirators.

"What if the respirator malfunctions?"

"There is a sensor that will immediately purge the chamber of water out of the drain at the bottom."

"And if that malfunctions?"

"The patient vital signs are transmitted through the acusensors via these cables to my monitoring systems. I'm watching them the entire time. Any hint of trouble with the patient and I abort."

"What about a power outage?" asked Lydia.

"You've thought of everything," remarked Rhodes.

"It's my job to guard against every contingency."

"If there's a power outage, the backup generator kicks in. It has about five minutes of power, which is enough for the water to be expunged and the chamber doors to be released. I can assure you, we've thought of everything, too."

Lydia scribbled notes furiously across her clipboard.

"First aid?"

"Both certified," I said.

Lydia chewed the end of her pen and stared down at her sheet. Then she raised her head and looked me square in the eye.

"Where can I set up while the session is underway?" she asked.

"I can put you at the table in the kitchen," I replied.

"I should be here, observing the process."

"That's impossible," I said. "Mr. Walker needs to maintain his full attention on the safety of me and the patient throughout the session. I can't risk you distracting him."

"I'll be quiet," she said.

No way I was giving in on this one. "If you're going to insist on this, then we should just wrap this up right now," I said.

The look on her face told me she wanted to call my bluff but knew she couldn't. Instead she said, "Fine. But I'm not sitting for four hours at a kitchen table. I'll take your office."

And go through all of my things I'm sure, I thought. "Whatever works best for you," I said.

We had been chatting in the examination room for at least fifteen minutes, and we hadn't notice that Debbie had drifted into the doorway.

"Dr. Chambers." Her eyes darted between each me, Lydia, and Rhodes. She looked pale. Was she scared?

Debbie cleared her throat. "Your first patient has arrived."

CHAPTER FIFTEEN

In the waiting room Debbie looked frazzled as she asked for information from the bull of a nurse Suzy who was unwilling to help fill out an intake form. I looked past her at the mute standing in the doorway. His hair hung long and limp around his face. His beard was no less tangled than on our prior encounter. His long arms stuck out of a black t-shirt. His blue jeans were ripped and frayed at the bottom. His sneakers were ancient.

Lydia tapped her pen. "Dr. Chambers, as I've made clear, during the probationary period there will be no identifying information, which I would have thought you'd have told your secretary."

At the mention of my name the man raised his head and looked at me. His pale blue eyes were like ice on a frozen lake.

A shudder ran up my spine. Each step across the room felt like a lifetime. I extended my hand to the man, hoping to get something out of him. He didn't react, though his eyes never left mine. Like a drill they bore deeper and deeper into me until I had to look away. My stomach wrapped itself in knots. *You're not ready for this Catarina. You know that, don't you? Run Cat. RUN!*

"Dr. Chambers, let's not waste any time," said Lydia. She set her bag down inside the door of my office and then ushered the nurse and the man to the examination room. My feet followed them while my mind strained to escape out the clinic door. Each step the man took stretched as far as two of my own. Lydia pushed the exam room door open. The mute had to stoop under the frame to get inside.

Rhodes pushed his chair back. "Whoa," was all he could say.

"Is he able to dress himself?" I asked Suzy.

"Yes, he's quite capable," she replied.

I went to the collection of acusensory suits and found the biggest one we had. Mercifully, they had some stretch to them.

"Can you put this on please," I said, "It will help me feel your memories the way you once did." None of the situation felt right. There was supposed to be a consultation first. I was supposed to have background information. The patient was supposed to agree to the procedure. While the man changed, I whispered into Lydia's ear. "I don't like this. How do I know he's agreed to take part in the procedure?"

"It's been taken care of, Dr. Chambers."

I gritted my teeth. "Does he at least have some initials I can go by?"

Lydia tapped her pen on the top of her clipboard.

"Call him whatever you want," she finally said.

A moment later the mute emerged from the change room in his acusensory suit. The tightness of the suit made him look even more skeletal than he had earlier. He wasn't abnormally tall, but the length of his arms and legs gave him an arachnid-like quality as he quietly moved into the center of the room. Despite his appearance, there was strength to his movements. He stood in front of Lydia and me and stared down at us with those pale blue eyes. Every millisecond looking at him made me anxious. *Do I want to know what's inside this man's head?*

"Ummm, Rhodes... can you get our patient prepped?" The lack of a name seemed objectifying, but I certainly couldn't call him the mute out loud. Rhodes moved over to the mute and asked him to sit on the seat in his PTER compartment. He obliged without issue. The man was remarkably placid about the entire experience. But his eyes suggested something burned beneath the surface. My legs were wobbling. I tried to hide my nerves by skirting into the change room and putting on my own acusensory suit.

By the time I was dressed the mute was ready. I stepped on to my platform and made eye contact with Lydia.

"This is where I need you to leave," I told her.

"Just a moment, Dr. Chambers." She scribbled more notes on her clipboard.

"Lydia, please."

She studied my face. "Fine," she said.

Once she was out of earshot, I let out a sigh of relief. From around the other side of PTER, I heard Rhodes telling the mute that he would administer his sedative. After thirty seconds I heard the familiar sound of the compartment door folding closed.

Rhodes came around the console and started prepping my sensors. He looked me straight in the eyes as he worked. "I'm not sure whether he or she bothers me more," he said.

I let out a nervous laugh. "We've got our work cut out for us."

Rhodes clicked the last parts of my sensors in place. "You look more nervous than usual, Cat?"

"I'm fine," I lied.

"Cat…"

"That man. I don't like not knowing anything about him. I have no idea what we're walking into."

"It'll be fine."

"How do you know?"

"Because you've always handled it in the past."

"I wish I felt that confident," I said.

Rhodes was done working and stepped off the platform. "It's time Cat," he said.

"I know." I put the respirator over my face and gave him a thumbs up. He clicked a button on the console and PTER's door closed around me, one metallic clunk after another, until I was shrouded in absolute darkness. The only sound was my own breathing echoing in my ears. The compartment started filling with water. Within a minute it was under my chin. A few seconds later I was completely submerged. The walls felt like they were crushing my chest. I closed my eyelids and willed my mind to retreat into a safer place, but Rhodes' voice ripped me from my meditation.

"Cat, I can't find his lattice!"

"That's impossible. He's still breathing, isn't he? There must be something there."

"It's like nothing I've ever seen before. I can't be sure I'm landing you anywhere close to his trauma."

"What can you be sure of?" I said.

"It's like …" he paused.

"Rhodes?"

"It's like all of his memories have disappeared into some kind of black hole."

What choice did I have but to press on? I cleared my throat. "Then we follow the dying light."

*   *   *

The sounds that filled PTER were cacophonous: snarling, slashing, the yelp of dogs, and the wails of dying men. The walls of my compartment turned a brilliant orange as flames licked up and down my body. My skin felt like it was peeling away from my muscles. From behind me a deep voice bellowed. I spun around. There was a glint of steel. Instinctively I ducked my head. A massive blade cleaved through my collarbone and PTER was instantly cast back into darkness.

"What the hell just happened," yelled Rhodes.

My hands ran along my body. "I don't know." My voice shook. "It all moved so fast."

"You flatlined for a couple seconds there."

I bobbed up and down in the water. "Must have been a sensor malfunction," I said.

We had spent so much time on the weekend tinkering with PTER it wouldn't surprise me. I rubbed my collarbone. It didn't feel like a malfunction.

"Do you want to try that again?" asked Rhodes.

"Is there any way you can land me a little further away from the center of whatever it is you're seeing?"

"Like I said, there's nothing to coordinate. It's like I'm dropping you into the bottom of a giant well."

"Okay, just do your best."

An instant later images flashed across the walls of PTER, images that made me feel like I was falling into a pit. My stomach lurched. Then the wind blew out of my lungs as my body seemed to slam against the ground. *What in god's name is happening?* I rolled onto my back.

Lying there, I looked up at a man who was at least eight feet tall. He wore a suit of gleaming armour. His chest and shoulders were as broad as a car. A helmet masked his face with a single slit for eyes. The pair of frosty blue irises looking at me were unmistakable. The sky over his head was a swirl of orange and black as flames licked up into the night. Each of his giant feet straddled the bottom of my legs. He lifted a great sword nearly as tall as him over his head.

"GET OUT!" he bellowed.

*   *   *

He swung the sword down with all his might. I threw my arms up in front of my face. Slicing hot pain seared through my body just before PTER went black again.

"Another malfunction. Everything flatlined again," said Rhodes.

I wasn't so sure. My body felt normal, but I couldn't convince myself everything was in one piece. Never had a mind worked so violently to keep me out. Inside PTER it was impossible to distinguish between sensory deprivation, sleep and… death. Rhodes voice was the only thing keeping me grounded.

"Keep talking," I said.

"Huh?"

"Tell me what you see," I still couldn't figure out what to do next.

"Umm, well the patient's vitals are totally stable. Yours are erratic.

Like normal and then they go crazy for a few seconds and then PTER cuts out and then you're back, normal again."

"Can you test my sensor connection?"

"Not while you're still in there."

If we aborted now we might as well get Lydia to tear up the check from the city herself. "Rhodes, I need you to locate his lattice. I'm landing somewhere I'm not supposed to be. But it all ends too quickly for me to tell what's happening. I don't have time to go searching around in there."

"And I told you before, Cat, he's like a ghost. His mental map doesn't exist."

"Don't start with me, Rhodes."

"Then stop asking me the same question over and over."

I gritted my teeth. This problem was bigger than him or me. He needed to be on my side. "Could it be another malfunction?" I asked.

"Unlikely. All of his monitors are feeding the computer properly. There's something there. It's just like a, like a vortex."

"Then I need you to increase his SLUMB-Rx dose." I hated the idea of pumping a drug addict with any more of our tonic than absolutely necessary, but it was my only chance.

"It'll go into the log, you know?"

"I know," I said.

"Okay, I'm upping his sedative ten percent."

"Better make it twenty."

"Twenty percent," he continued. "Time to try again, Cat."

"I know."

CHAPTER SIXTEEN

The walls of PTER turned orange and crimson. The howls of pain, the clash of steel, the crying of horses, the snarl of hounds. Hooves pounded thunderously across the ground. But instead of slamming hard on my back, I floated down like a feather.

A knight on a massive black stallion wheeled around when he spotted me. He put the horse into a gallop. But the SLUMB-Rx slowed his movements. A sprint became a jog. I was still in danger.

On the ground near his horse a spear protruded from the carcass of a giant dog. He grabbed it with one hand as he passed and wrenched it free. He hefted it up over his shoulder and heaved it directly at me. I watched its metal tip spin over and over. When it was no more than two meters away, I spun to my left. The spear seemed to sink deep into the wall of the compartment behind me. Bits of dirt spluttered up into the air. My heart pounded. Normally Rhodes would be asking what was wrong, but the only sound in my ears was the unfolding battle.

My body was next to an embankment. I scurried up the side, slipping on a wall of mud. The knight was nearly on me. He took a slow, lunging swipe at my legs, but I was able to pull them up over the lip of the hill before he could hit me. He leapt off his horse and pursued me on foot.

I was about to run when something warm and heavy pressed on the middle of my back. A second later it was gone. I whirled, expecting the knight to have crested the ridge. Nothing. Moments later a man's tortured screams echoed over the embankment.

Down the ledge a massive hound was savaging the knight with hundreds of razor sharp teeth. The hound's body was covered in black and green scales and tufts of coarse black fur. The beast yanked the knight's entrails from his gut. I crawled away on my hands and knees. The ground was dry and ashen. I pinched the dirt between my fingers and felt every granule as I rolled it back and forth. *How could it be so real?*

When I looked up I saw that I was crawling away from the chaos. The hard packed earth gave way to darkness. Periodically another hell hound would emerge from the black curtain and race past me into the fray. They seemed uninterested in me, and I was thankful to be spared the knight's fate.

After another minute I finally felt confident enough to stand. I turned back to the battle and marvelled at the epic sight.

*   *   *

Stretching for miles was a battlefield littered in death. Thousands of corpses were strewn across the ground. Thousands more fighters danced in spilled blood as they clashed with waves of demonic creatures that spewed from a great crack in the earth. Behind the crevice was a wall dotted with tunnels. The recesses glimmered.

Opposite the wall stood a colossal fortress. At its center was a tower that flirted with the clouds. Lightning ripped from the sky and struck its peak. Its apex shimmered with a bluish haze. Each stone used to construct the monolith was at least one hundred feet wide and fifty feet tall. Yet the vast tower was completely windowless. Nothing in. Nothing out.

At its base stretched a two hundred foot high wall that I guessed enclosed an inner courtyard. Along the wall's length stood hundreds of men. They wantonly fired a hail of arrows into the battlefield. The arrows pierced through man and beast alike. Hundreds more men along the wall poured great vats of burning tar down on the creatures slithering up the ramparts.

In the center of the wall was an open drawbridge. Out of it paraded men on horseback. As a man on the battlefield fell dead, a new knight took his place. The fight was tireless and infinite.

Behind the castle stood a mountain. From its peak, great boulders fell in a never-ending avalanche. They collided with the far wall of the castle, sending cracks up and down its foundation. As each boulder broke upon the wall, men would emerge from somewhere in the courtyard to mend the seams. They built the wall higher and higher, lifting it another foot into the sky as each minute passed, trying to keep the rocks out. Periodically a boulder would topple over the side and land in the courtyard. A chorus of screams would erupt each time one fell.

Exhaustion consumed me as I watched the endless assault. How could one man contain this struggle in his head? And how could I possibly help him?

Go into the heart of danger for there you will find safety. It was an old

Chinese proverb. My feet carried me to the battlefield. I called out to Rhodes but received no answer. No turning back. There was too much at stake.

When I returned to the fray, the battle shifted in my direction. The gaze of each knight fell heavy on my body. Regret simmered in my belly as I closed on the men. Spears and arrows dotted the sky. I bobbed out of the way. My manoeuvres did not pull me towards the chaos, but towards the wall dotted in tunnels. I drifted into a pack of hounds. In the mouth of the enemy I was safe.

With each step I angled closer to the black tear in the earth from which the creatures gushed. Over its edge was an onyx void that yawned into oblivion. Goosebumps covered my skin. *What broke this hole open?*

The only place left for me to retreat was the tunnels. I climbed up a brick wall and stood on a platform that curled around the bowl of the valley and out of my line of sight. Every brick of the wall was immaculate, spared from battle. The tunnels were laid out in perfect symmetry. They ran as high and far as the eye could see.

A tunnel beckoned; it emanated a crimson hue that endlessly shifted direction. I stepped closer to the tunnel and put my ear next to the opening. The faint twinkle of a familiar piano piece emanated from its depths. The hypnotic music pulled me, step by step, into the red glow of the memory.

CHAPTER SEVENTEEN

The mute stood over a large steel sink and soaped up his hands and forearms. He looked up from the sink at his reflection. The beard and gray hairs were gone. His short hair was tucked under a surgical cap. A medical mask hung under his chin and matched his light blue smock. His youthful face was angular and striking. He had high cheekbones, a square jaw and prominent chin. His powder blue eyes were vibrant. He stared deep into the mirror and flexed his muscles. Through the acusensory suit I felt the tingle of his skin. He rubbed his right hand with his left to massage out a sharp pain.

"Let's do this," he said to himself. He used an elbow to push through the prep area door and into the operating room. On the table, covered up to her chin, was a young girl. Her hair was shaved. There was a red hole in her upper right forehead. Tension cut across my chest at the sight of her. I hated traumatic memories involving children. They were the hardest to shake. Eric and I had no children of our own for a reason.

The anaesthesiologist wheeled back in her chair at the sight of the mute. Her face was haloed in fissures. I ran my hands across them and was able to stitch them back together. A twinkle came to her eye when she saw him.

"We need to work fast, Mason. Eight-year-old girl, gun shot to the head. She's stable for now. It's a miracle she's still alive."

Mason? That explains half of the name.

"Where the hell are my residents, Sophie?" Mason's voice was deep and commanding.

A moment later two resident doctors, a man and a woman, burst into the operating room. The man appeared to be from somewhere around the Pacific rim, with smooth skin and almond eyes. The woman was Middle Eastern and had dark features, heavy eyebrows, and long curly hair that poked out of the back of her surgical cap. They were both breathless.

"Sorry we're la-" she tried to say.

"—We need to hurry," barked Mason. "Nirali, put the X-rays up. Yong, I need you to use the bone saw to give me more space to work. Get the incision markings done. Sophie, music please."

Thunderous was my heartbeat. Dad's music followed me into Mason's memory. It was one of his better paying compositions—a film score on solo piano for a movie that debuted at the Cannes festival. Despite my vitals going haywire, Rhodes comforting voice was absent. Every muscle in my body flexed as I attempted to steady my nerves.

Mason pulled on latex gloves. Another sharp pain ran through his hand. He turned his back on the rest of the room and rubbed at the tendons. A few seconds later the three of them were standing around the little girl. Nirali was on Mason's left. Yong was across the table. Mason looked at the large X-rays on the wall behind Yong.

"A bullet passed through the top of her skull. From the size of the hole, probably only a .22 calibre. It exited the back of her head, which is good. If she's lucky the bullet didn't travel much lower than the meningeal layer. We need to create space for swelling, regardless, to give her a chance if it's worse than I suspect. Yong, we need to remove the left side of her cranial plate." Mason surveyed the incision markings. "Looks good, Yong, you can proceed."

Yong chose a small circular saw off the table of tools and turned it on. Its loud whirring filled the room. He lowered the saw over the girl's head, right next to the incision markings.

I shut my eyes. After years of PTER I had developed a strong stomach. But this was too much. Blindly my fingers crawled at the inner walls of my compartment. The whirring continued unabated. Finally, after five minutes it stopped.

"Nirali, please remove the cranial plate," said Mason. I opened my eyes and watched as Nirali used a small tool to pull the skull away. Underneath was the gray cerebrum. The girl's head was covered in fissures. I washed them away, cringing. So began an hour-long process of the three of them sewing parts of the little girl's brain back together.

Finally Mason spoke. "There's a tiny bit of bullet fragment near the exit wound," he said, pointing his scalpel at the back of her brain. "We need to cut a small fold to reach it. Yong, please take care of as much residual bleeding as possible." Mason passed the scalpel from his right hand to his left. He flexed his free hand multiple times.

"Everything okay, sir?" asked Nirali.

I felt the pain in Mason's hand subside. My heart rate did not. My muscles tightened alongside Mason's as tragedy loomed.

"Everything's fine," he said passing the scalpel back to his right hand. "I'm perspiring, please wipe my forehead." Yong exchanged a glance with Nirali. She did as Mason said.

Mason lowered his scalpel towards the incision point. When he was only millimeters away he withdrew his hand. He reached up with his left hand and flicked his magnifying glasses down over his eyes and leaned back over the girl. He lowered his hand again and deftly cut a small incision above the bullet fragment. Nirali clamped onto the loosened fold and peeled it outward as Mason cut in behind. Seconds seemed to stretch to hours as he worked.

The tendons in Mason's hand locked. The scalpel thrust forward. The blade sliced past the fragment. He withdrew the blade a split second later. But the damage was done. Dark red blood oozed quickly from the wound. Yong mopped at it futilely. The color drained from his face.

"Her heart rate is falling rapidly," said the anaesthesiologist. Mason stepped back from the table. The scalpel fell from his hand and clattered onto the floor. Yong dabbed at the bright red blood oozing out of the hole in the girl's head. He looked back at Mason for direction. Mason could only stare.

"Out of my way," said Nirali, elbowing Mason in the stomach and pushing him back from the table. "Her motor strip has been slashed. Yong, you need to staunch the bleeding on the right side so I can see enough to repair the wound."

"Heart rate is still falling," yelled Sophie.

"What's going to happen to her?" said Yong.

"If we don't lose her, she'll be lucky if she ever walks again." Nirali shot a glare at Mason who was nothing but a statue filling space in the room.

"She's entering cardiac arrest," said Sophie as she pressed an emergency button on the wall. Moments later two nurses burst into the operating room.

"Get the paddles," said Nirali. "Yong keep working."

The nurses wheeled the defibrillator over to the operating table. One of the nurses pulled the cover off the girl and pressed the paddles on her bare chest. Her small body lifted into the air violently, then fell back on to the table.

The room became a flurry of chaotic movement and black fissures. They encroached in around Mason's field of vision. I worked against them, but when one was sewn up, two new ones took its place. The room became a cacophonous blaring of vital sign monitors and shouting.

Finally, I was able to wash away the black cracks that filled his field of vision. Mason was sitting in a chair on the far side of the room. One of the nurses pulled a cover over the girl's head. Everyone looked sombre. They removed their latex gloves. All of them except Nirali shuffled out of the room. She walked over to Mason and knelt in front of him. She pulled the medical mask covering her mouth down under her chin.

"This was entirely avoidable," she said.

Mason wasn't even able to nod. He looked down at his hands.

"I used to admire you. Now all I see is an egomaniac who couldn't admit to his own weakness. A girl is dead who didn't have to die." She sighed, threw her gloves in the nearby garbage can and walked out.

Mason was left alone with the girl's body. The operating table held his gaze. It was still illuminated by a bright overhead light; the rest of the room was cast in shadow. As he stared, dark cracks formed in the corners of his vision. They encroached on the table like a den of snakes, spinning and snaring the girl's body. The fissures twisted and pulled the image apart. Tiny fragments of the memory fell into the seemingly endless depths of my chamber until the world went dark.

CHAPTER EIGHTEEN

My eyes opened. I took off my respirator, disconnected the sensors and stepped off the platform into the examination room. The other PTER capsule was open and Mason sat placidly, eyes closed, on his chair.

Rhodes got up to speak, but I ignored him and marched to my office clad in the acusensory suit. Lydia was inspecting the books and journals that filled the shelves behind my desk. She turned to face me. "So is he fixe-"

"—You need to tell me who Mason actually is," I demanded. "He was a goddamn neurosurgeon, for Christ's sake."

"Watch your tone with me, Dr. Chambers," said Lydia. "We are still in the probationary period of this project. Patient confidentiality trumps whatever your needs might be. If we don't approve the project, there can be no residual exposure to the city from a confidentiality breach."

"What in god's name do you expect me to do, steal his social insurance number?"

"Your technology is dangerous, Dr. Chambers. If it was up to me we wouldn't even be having this conversation. But your little presentation seemed to impress the men in the room and my reservations were overruled. Frankly, I don't trust that you won't use PTER to satisfy your own priorities."

"Please, Lydia, I need to know who Mason is."

"You don't. And from your tone I'm going to assume he's not fixed."

"I can't possibly know until he's awake and I get a chance to speak with him."

"Then I'll wait."

"I will need to speak with him in *my* office," I said.

"And I will be present for every minute of your interview." Lydia pursed her lips and shook her head. I balled my hands into fists and marched out of the room. Mason was still sedated, so I took the opportunity to quickly change my clothes and come back to his compartment.

"He's waking up," said Rhodes. Mason looked vacantly around the room. Not a good sign.

"Can I help?"

My body tensed with fright. Nurse Suzy had sneaked up behind me.

"Yes, please get him changed," I told her. She took Mason by the elbow and slowly walked him to the change area. The skin on his face was gray and loose. The beard and hair gave him the quality of a sick, wet dog. Each step was slow and laboured. Rhodes whispered in my ear.

"We've never worked on anyone so frail before," he said.

"His mind is stronger than his body," I said, "and it didn't work."

"You weren't able to find his trauma?"

"No, I found something," I said. My hands shook as visions of the little girl's body flitted through my head. I thrust them in my pockets where I found the cool, hardened shell of an extirpation tablet. I rolled it back and forth between my fingers. But it would have to wait until after I spoke with Mason. I looked at Rhodes. "But for some reason I know there's no way it will be that easy," I said. "His lattice, Rhodes; I've never seen anything like it. I don't think it would let me find what's really haunting him without a long fight."

Mason stepped back out of the change-room.

I walked over to him. "Can you please follow me? I'd like to talk about our experience." I led him down the hall to my office and offered him a seat on the couch. When Lydia saw us she lifted her pen. She sat behind the desk watching our every move and immediately started scribbling on her clipboard.

"Mason, can you tell me what you remember from our session. From the memory I shared with you?"

He didn't make eye contact. His vapid stare floated past my right shoulder.

"You were a surgeon. A good one, I presume, who wasn't willing to admit to a problem. We're all guilty of that in our own way. Sometimes the costs are higher than others, but a mistake is still a mistake." When I finished speaking the room was so quiet I could hear every scratch of Lydia's pen. With each passing second the image of the dead child crystallized further in my mind.

"Mason," I said.

He finally turned to face me.

"Are you able to say anything."

More silence. Not even a nod.

"What if I asked you to write it down?" I yanked a pen and sheet of paper off my desk, straight out from under Lydia's clipboard. I placed the pen in Mason's right hand. He twisted his fingers around it and winced. He threw the pen on the floor, crumpled the paper, stood up and left the room. Lydia jumped up and came around the table. She looked out into the waiting area and found the nurse speaking to Mason. When she looked back inside, her brow was furrowed but a small smile curled her lip. "Give me one good reason why I shouldn't cancel this project right now," Lydia said, arms crossed. She tapped her foot against the floor, causing her shoulders to shift back and forth.

All of her stupid little gyrations made me furious, but exploding on her wouldn't further my cause. I sucked in a deep breath. "Lydia," I pleaded. "In my presentation I never promised every patient could be cured in one session. The mind of a drug addict is broken. The space where you expect certain things to be are often empty. A few hours isn't enough time to properly search."

She uncrossed her arms and then crossed them again.

"There's more. This particular patient. He has, ummm, well, he has defenses I've never encountered before. It's like his mind is guarded against intrusion. Like he's had someone meddle with his mind before."

Lydia's shoulders tensed. "Fine, we'll do another day," she said. "But now we need to leave." Lydia collected her things and hurried out of my office.

By the time I got to the door the nurse was already walking Mason out. Each step was no more than a small shuffle. He looked worse than when he had entered. But somewhere in his frailty were hints of the stronger man who resided in his lattice.

"We'll see you the same time tomorrow," said Lydia. A second later she was gone.

Debbie gave me a queer look. "Well that was rushed," she said. Rhodes joined us.

"There's something about our patient she's not telling me," I said.

"You forgot this," Rhodes said. He placed a chrome extirpation capsule in the palm of my hand.

"Oh, right, thank you," I said. "Excuse me." I left them and entered the washroom. I threw the extirpation capsule into the toilet and flushed it down. If I was going to fix Mason, I couldn't afford to forget what I had seen. Extirpation could only stretch back a maximum of six hours. It meant Mason's memory would be my cross to bear for the rest of my life.

CHAPTER NINETEEN

The afternoon was a blur of administrative tasks to properly cover our asses with Lydia. My body was threaded with nervous energy from thinking about my next session with Mason. I needed answers.

Rhodes inspected the sensors and tested the connections. He couldn't find anything wrong with them, but a full system diagnostic was the only way to be sure.

"It'll take hours to finish," he said. "No point hanging around here waiting. We've been working non-stop for days, and I'd love to eat a big meal, watch a movie and come back to this later. I can check in remotely tonight."

"Fair enough," I said. Maybe I could go out for a nice meal with Eric. I needed the distraction.

"I'll see you tomorrow," said Rhodes on his way out the door.

I let Debbie go then called Eric.

"Let me guess, you're working late," he said.

For a split second I almost lied and said yes. But I didn't want to stew all night. "I was thinking we could meet in Gastown for supper tonight."

"Oh, well, okay. Did you have somewhere in mind?"

"I'll meet you at L'Abattoir in thirty minutes."

"See you soon," he said.

The sun poked through the clouds as the final hours of the afternoon waned. I sucked in a deep breath of fresh air. It was then that the magnitude of my day struck me. My hands ran across my neck and dabbed at my chest to check that my bones were still stitched together. The world started to spin. I leaned against the side of my building to steady myself. My stomach growled. I hadn't eaten anything since breakfast and I was fading fast. I popped into the take-out joint next to my building and bought a can of Coke. It was like medicine.

I took a momentary jaunt across the tail-end of East Hastings street along my route. I waited at the street corner and stared down its length. How many more of you will be like Mason? Could I climb that wall of worry every week? I suspected Lydia orchestrated a particularly troublesome patient as my first. She wanted this to fail. I crumpled my finished pop can in my fist.

When I reached L'Abattoir, Eric was waiting outside. He was dressed in a navy sweater, beige khakis and brown leather boat shoes. His hair was curled back in a wave. I felt particularly frumpy after my long day and had to bottle up my self-consciousness. He smiled when he saw me, the skin around his eyes wrinkling. After so many years, his smile wrinkles still made me happy.

"You look great," I said.

"Thanks, you look… like you've had a long day."

He was doing his best, but I was notorious for wearing a bad day on my face. "It was manageable, but let's not talk about that now. First, I want to eat all the food, and drink all the wine. Then I want to talk about you."

Eric gave me an even bigger smile. He took me by the hand and walked me into L'Abattoir.

The restaurant was rustic old Gastown with a French twist. For the area it was a big space, and we had no trouble getting a seat. Eric would have gotten us one regardless. He seemed to know everyone, including the owner, who he helped buy a condo once upon a time. People had a tendency to bend over backwards for that smile.

We sat down and opened our menus. I ordered the scallops roasted in black pepper caramel. Eric decided on the eight ounce steak Diane with bone marrow butter. A $125 bottle of Pinot Noir Bouzy Rouge from Coteaux Champenois France found its way to our table.

"It's on the house," said our waiter.

Eric grinned at me. I took a sip. It was magical.

We spent the evening chatting about old times, eating fabulous food, and pushing our cares away. After two healthy glasses of wine on a nearly empty stomach I was enjoying a wicked buzz.

"We should go on vacation," said Eric. "I've been looking all over and we can afford to rent a villa in southern Italy or France. Really get away from it all. If Point Grey goes through, hell, we could do a whole year if we wanted."

"Eric, I can't go anywhere while my project is in full swing." I didn't like where the conversation was headed, but I was never good at tact when I was drunk.

"Okay, maybe a year is a bit much," he admitted, "but at least a couple weeks would be good, to get our money's worth."

"Eric, you know I'm locked down for the next year. Don't throw all these nice ideas around when you know there's no way I could do it."

Eric's enthusiasm vanished. A shadow crossed his face. "You mean to tell me we can't go anywhere for an entire year. I've gotta sit on my ass in the condo until your little project wraps up." Eric raised his voice and other patrons started to stare.

"Nothing's stopping you from getting out of here. Go to Vegas with the guys or something."

"Vegas? Please. If anyone needs a vacation, it's you, not me."

"It's the first day of my project goddammit. Can we not do this? Seriously." I let out a sigh.

Eric pressed his lips together. Lines ran across his tightened forehead.

"I need to use the washroom," he said. He walked past me. I poked at the last bits of food on my plate. People at nearby tables cast me sideways glances. I reached into my purse and pulled out my phone.

There was a text message from Rhodes: *Diagnostics are finished. You need to see this. Come back to office a.s.a.p. I'll be here.*

CHAPTER TWENTY

When Eric got back to his seat I stood up from the table and told him I had to leave.

"Whatever," he said.

I gave him a peck on the cheek and ran off. Back at my clinic, the lights were off save a softly glowing one that came from the examination room. I knocked on the door as I entered. PTER was closed and engaged in its cleaning cycle. It hissed like a black python in the dark.

"Hey," Rhodes said, illuminated by nothing but his monitors. His eyes never left the screen.

"What was so important that I needed to come back?" I said, secretly thankful to get away from Eric.

"I checked and double checked the sensor connections and there's nothing wrong with them. So I pulled the vital statistics of our patient and yours through the session to see if maybe it was something on his end. What I found was not what I expected." Rhodes turned his monitor to face me. On his monitor were four different charts, each with two lines that ran virtually parallel to one another.

"How high are the correlations?" *Did I want to know the answer?*

"Ninety three percent. It'd be damn near one hundred if it wasn't for those two blips. You can see where you drop way down and he spikes way up. Almost like he surged out the sensors for a second," said Rhodes.

"What does this mean?"

"I was hoping you could tell me."

"His mind isn't like anything we've seen before. Our old models are unlikely to be of much use here."

PTER let out a loud hiss behind us. I jumped out of my skin and grabbed Rhodes' shoulder. "Sorry," I said. "We need to think of something before tomorrow if we're going to make more progress. You don't have to stay here all night doing that. Go home and get a night's sleep. Something will come to us."

"And if it doesn't?"

We exchanged a worried look in the soft glow of his monitors and said nothing more.

*   *   *

By the time I got home, Eric was asleep. Largo waited for me on the rug by the front door. His little tail wagged furiously when I entered. He jumped on to his back legs and pressed against my shin. I knelt down to his level, and he promptly knocked me onto my back and crawled onto my chest and slobbered all over my neck.

"Largo, gross!" I exclaimed. I pushed him off of me. After a solid two minutes of ear and bum scratches he seemed satisfied and sauntered off into the bedroom. I crawled into bed beside Eric. He didn't stir.

Lying on my back staring at the ceiling, I dreaded what dreams the night would bring. I dreaded squaring off with Lydia the next day. And I dreaded wading through Mason's nightmare. As sleep took hold, I relinquished any hope of happiness.

*   *   *

I was inside a dimly-lit living room. Along the far wall was a worn, flower-patterned sofa cornered by end tables. Opposite the couch was a large television encased in decorative wood paneling.

The young girl from the operating table sat on her knees merrily drawing up and down in purple crayon on one of the open stretches of white wall. Long blond hair hung around her shoulders. The drawing was of two scales of a piano keyboard, complete with sharps and flats. When she finished she stretched her tiny hands across the keys and danced her fingers in a pattern. She hummed a tune in her soft, cherub voice.

I backed up and nearly ploughed into the chest of a man looming over me. It was Charles, my father. His face was unshaven, his oxford button-down shirt open to a coffee stained white undershirt. He was tall and imposing, with big hands balled into fists. When he spoke he spit venom.

"Look what you did!" he said as he pointed at the wall. "What a mess. How could you be so stupid?" His feet stomped on the floor as he barged over to the girl, grabbing her by the wrist and yanking her to her feet. The girl's eyes stretched wide. She recoiled from Dad. Each time he gave her a shake her face morphed back and forth from the cherubic girl to my own.

"Who is going to pay to clean this mess up... you?" Spit flew from his mouth.

"I'm sorry, it was for yo-" she squeaked as her eyes darted from Dad to her drawing.

"Sorry... Sorry?" He bellowed. "What is this crap anyway... a piano? There's a real one right there."

Her feet hung in the air. Without warning Dad wound up and slapped her face, then threw her into the piano bench. His fist lashed out again, this time at the crayon covered wall. His fist and arm buried into the drywall. When he pulled his fist out, a black inky trail of ooze followed his hand and wrapped itself around his wrist.

"What the hell," he choked. Dad's fury evaporated. His eyes went wide as the black tendril crept inch by inch up his arm. Terror at what seeped out of that wall turned him into a weak, bubbling shell. As he struggled to pull his hand away, the black tarry substance stretched away with him.

Suddenly, the dark slime consumed his arm. It spat out blood and bone. He let out a blood curdling scream, like a man being slowly fed through a wood chipper.

The girl cowered in the corner of the room. What was left of my father turned towards me. The whites of his eyes had turned black, the face a mask of black veins etching across his skin. One arm had become a tentacle, dripping ooze. The bones in his legs had turned to mush. His torso rested on the pile of flesh left behind.

A demonic laugh pursed his blue lips. With each guffaw, the bones of his jaw extended an extra three inches from his face. Once the jaw was a foot and a half in length it curled back over his head. With each guttural laugh it chewed, crunching through the bones of his skull.

His own mouth was devouring his head. The shambling mass of gore that was left grew with each bite and blotted out the overhead light. *Get out, Get out, Get out!* I hoped beyond hope that someone would save me. My muscles were frozen and useless. The mass enveloped everything around me. Wake up! *Please, God, Please. Wake up!*

CHAPTER TWENTY-ONE

I scanned the contours of my dark bedroom that was illuminated by nothing but the streetlights that pierced the window blinds. The digital clock on the bedside table read five AM. I heaved myself out of bed. The cool air touched the sweat that seeped through my nightie.

The rest of the morning I floated half present, through my routine. More than once Eric tried to talk to me, but I could barely form a full sentence. My mind was preoccupied with the images from my nightmare. Not one piece from that twisted dream was how I wanted to remember my father.

Only once I had skulked back to my office building did my mind fully register the day ahead. *Pull it together Catarina.* I hoped getting to the office a little early would help me focus. To my dismay, Lydia was there first. *Were we racing now?* She was dressed in a white blouse, blue skirt, black heels and sharply drawn red lipstick.

"Pretty early start for a government employee," I quipped as I exited the stairwell.

She pounced. "We aren't the lazy drain on tax payers the papers like to make us out to be. We care more than anyone about what happens in this city."

"Pump the brakes, Lydia. I meant nothing by it," I said.

She narrowed her eyes. "I trust we can leave the matter of our patient's identity behind us today. I don't want to argue with you at every turn. His information is confidential until I've compiled my preliminary report, shared it with our board, and satisfied them you can be trusted."

I unlocked the clinic door. "What can I do to win your trust?"

"Leave that to me." She went straight for my office and made herself at home.

"I expect to have your logs of yesterday's activity on my desk by eight thirty."

Your desk?! "Fine," I said.

"The patient will be here by nine."

I looked at the clock. It was seven thirty. I heard noises as I meandered towards the examination room. Rhodes was still at his computer, much as I'd left him. PTER's compartments were open. The respirator hoses and sensors protruded from the console like the appendages of some great insect slithering out of its nest.

"What the hell is going on?" I said.

Rhodes swivelled his chair. He had deep, dark rings under his eyes.

"Did you even leave last night?"

"No. I found a problem with the patient respirator hose. There was a pin-prick hole that was leaking water. So I swapped the patient hose for your own."

I scanned the hose. "Is this duct tape?!"

"Shhh," he said. "Yes, but I patched it first with one of those kits you use on an inflatable air mattress. Then I secured it with the duct tape."

"Don't give me something else to worry about…"

"Do you want to order replacements? They'll take weeks to get here. They're not exactly standard issue fittings."

"I guess I'll just have to risk it."

"I guess you will," said Rhodes. He was edgier than usual this morning.

"Can I get you a coffee?" I asked in an attempt to shift gears.

"No, thanks." He slid the garbage can towards me. It contained two coffee cups and three cans of Red Bull.

"Any ideas on how we can pinpoint his trauma today. I thought I found it yesterday but…"

"Every time you go in I'll be able to map coordinates. It's like building his lattice from the inside out, but we'll eventually get there. If there's some way for you to pass through as many memories as possible, we'll be able to plot out a lattice more quickly. If I can find some kind of recurring pattern, then I can estimate the rest."

"I'll see what I can do," I said. "Can I get a print log of yesterday?" Rhodes thrust a stack of papers at me without looking away from his computer. They were covered in fancy looking charts, tables and other advanced diagnostic numbers designed to obfuscate the uninformed.

"This should keep Lydia out of our hair for a while."

"That was the plan," said Rhodes. There wasn't enough time to prepare her the executive summary. Convenient. I left the examination room and walked along our darkened hallway. Each day the clinic lost a bit of the warmth it had when I opened the practice and hadn't taken my patients' worries home with me yet. Guilt washed over me at the thought that this project would turn my practice into a turnstile for drug addicts. But it was either that or let my clinic go under and spend the rest of my life wondering if I'd done enough to help those suffering like Dad. I wondered how many other young girls were out there in Vancouver alone. Girls who'd lost their father to addiction and mental illness.

Where do you win in all this Cat? It's only a year. Yeah and then what? You'll be almost forty years old, adrift without an anchor. Maybe I need to be adrift for a while. But what about Dad. He'll haunt you every day until you find an answer. There must be another way. There isn-

The sound of Debbie shutting the clinic door ripped me out of my spiral.

"Morning Debbie," I said.

"Good morning," she said.

I turned into my office and closed the door. Lydia looked up. I dropped the papers onto my desk with a resounding thud. "Here are yesterday's logs you requested." I hoped to see distress cross Lydia's face, but she was unfazed.

"Do you mind telling me what this is?" she said. In her hand were my notes from speaking with Maggie.

I nearly threw up. "Just some of my theories on what's wrong with the patient."

"That's not what it looks like to me. I'll be making a note of a potential confidentiality breach. You were warned, Dr. Chambers."

My stomach gurgled and I was about to speak when the office door opened again. *Surely it wasn't time to start yet.* It was just Rhodes with a greasy bagel wrapped in wax paper.

"Get your own," he smiled.

Time was getting on, so I went into the back and put on my

acusensory suit. I would have to hope Lydia didn't connect too many dots and pry into my recent patient files. I pulled a white lab coat around my suit to hide how skinny I was becoming. Had Rhodes given me his sandwich, I'm not sure I would have been able to swallow a bite. The constant anxiety wreaked havoc on my appetite. Mornings before a session were the absolute worst.

Watching Rhodes eat his bagel sowed doubt into my mind about his ability to stay focused. His shirt was half tucked in and he was leaning back as far as his swivel chair would take him. Grease dribbled down his chin; sweat dotted his forehead. His body odour hung in a three foot radius around him.

"Can I count on you today?" I said.

He shot me a dirty look. "Have I ever let you down before?"

"Well no but-"

"Then you should stop worrying. I'm fine."

What happened to his good spiritedness? Was this a sign of what was to come? No. Once we get Lydia out of here, get a little money to repair PTER properly, and fall into a groove it'll be fine.

"Dr. Chambers," said Debbie from the doorway. "They're here."

CHAPTER TWENTY-TWO

Suzy led Mason to the examination room and got him changed into his suit. He looked no better than the day before.

"Hello Mason," I said. His pale blue eyes looked straight through me. Suzy and I helped him on to the platform and Rhodes got to work setting up his sensors.

"Thanks, we've got it from here," I told her.

"Kay," she said.

"He's all set," said Rhodes. I stepped on to my platform and hooked up the sensors over my head. Rhodes clipped the last cable into the neck of my acusensory suit, injected an extirpation landmark in my neck and then went back to his computer station. I plugged in my headphones and grabbed the respirator and placed it over my face. My hand passed over the taped-up hole looking for a break in the seal. Before I had a chance to fully inspect the hose one last time, the door of my compartment closed, and I was plunged into darkness.

"Test, test," said Rhodes.

"I hear you."

"Good, at least something still works. Now remember, Cat, I need you to pass through as many memories as you can so we can build a lattice. You don't need to spend any significant amount of time in each one. Call to me when you're done and I'll reset you."

"When I called to you last time in there I got nothing."

"I could hear you."

"Okay, well, when I say 'clear' take that as the sign to eject me from the memory."

"Sounds good. All right, here we go."

"Rhodes! Wait!"

"What?"

"Remember to up the SLUMB-Rx again."

"I didn't forget," he said.

"Thank you."

Moments later the walls of PTER changed from black to blue, pink to orange. My compartment grew hot and the smell of smoke wafted into my nose. I landed back on the platform with the tunnels. It was the one point inside of Mason's head we could target, and Rhodes, despite his exhaustion, had landed me right next to it.

The sky was celestial, streaked with pink and blue, bright stars and nearby planets. The odd bird flew overhead. If I kept my gaze upward, and ignored the grinding sounds of battle, it was almost blissful.

At the far side of the valley, the drawbridge in the castle wall opened. Out poured a formation of knights on horseback. Hundreds thundered across the field. A rumble emanated from deep in the belly of the earth.

The sides of the great crack in the ground that ran under the platform burst apart as massive monstrosities smashed their way to the surface. They were nothing like the hell hounds that were running in all directions. The torsos of these monstrosities undulated out of the depths on serpentine hind quarters. Their hands were long wormy outgrowths. Their bodies were coated in a red substance that glistened under the fiery sky. And. No heads. Christ, no heads! Only a hole at the apex of their torsos that gleamed with multiple, circular rows of teeth. Each row gnashed on a different axis. Whatever got caught inside would be shredded to pieces.

The creatures were no less numerous than the knights and slithered at a sickening speed towards the men on horseback. A flash of spears launched from the shoulders of the knights towards the gruesome horde. The first layer of creatures fell. As they did, the group behind them lifted their fallen brethren up in their tentacles. Their bodies splayed out several feet, causing the mouths to yawn wide. The tentacles pushed the dead down into their gullets, which churned through the carcasses. Their torsos ballooned, skin nearly bursting. As it stretched, the red slimy film covering their bodies spilled into the cracks and formed a new layer of carapace. These eaters of the dead were now twice the size of the fallen.

When the two groups were about to clash, the horsemen unsheathed their swords and broke rank down the middle. The creatures' momentum pulled them through the empty space. The knights slashed with their broadswords as they passed. Appendages flew into the air. Toxic gurgles echoed from the injured creatures. Once the knights had fully rounded, they bore down on the backsides of the monsters and trampled them.

The knights' momentum was short lived. The tentacles of the fallen lashed out and wrapped themselves around the passing knights, ripping them off their steeds. The men fell into the maws of the beasts. Bits of bone and armour flew through the air. Horses whinnied and cried out as they, too, were consumed. Other knights leapt from their mounts and hacked frantically at the melee.

From the center of the maelstrom a knight looked straight at me. I stood stock still on the platform. His armour was covered in the crimson gore. He breathed heavily. Until that point I had thought I was safe from the chaos. Would he come for me next?

An arm shaped like the slithering body of a monstrous millipede slipped over the lip of the platform. Then another! Multiple tiny mouths, each with its own set of ventricular teeth, ran along the tentacle. The creature's maw crested over the platform. The space beyond its mouth seemed to stretch to infinity. The gnashing of its teeth rotated hypnotically, and I couldn't help but lean towards this blood-red serpent as its tail swung over the edge.

Suddenly, from between its teeth, protruded the bladed prongs of the end of a spear. I reeled backward before it could touch my face. As the creature writhed on the platform, I stumbled into a tunnel and watched a new memory swirl around the wall of PTER and blot out the unending violence.

CHAPTER TWENTY-THREE

Mason sat on a doctor's table in a small room with sea-foam green walls. White butcher paper crinkled underneath him as he shifted nervously. He clasped his hands in his lap. A woman sat in the corner. Her features were taut; her eyes darted between Mason and the door. The anxious actions did little to steal from her beauty. Her blond hair was straight and silky, her skin bronzed from the sun. Her makeup was light and elegant, her eyes big and dreamy. She wore a white blazer over a low-cut blouse that did a poor job of hiding breasts that were surely fake. She wore tight jeans and gold high heels.

She sat next to Mason's table in a steel chair with fraying black upholstery. Her hand rested on his knee. On the ring finger of her left hand was a huge diamond.

"It's going to be fine. You'll see, the doctor will write you up a prescription and we'll be on our way. In a week you'll be good as new, babe," she said.

"Hmmm," mumbled Mason.

"I know you're scared, I'm scared too, but you gotta have faith."

"Faith?" said Mason, "Wish it were that simple. Faith isn't going to fix me. It's over, Cora… you'll see." Tears welled up in her eyes.

She dropped her head. A moment later a short balding doctor in a white coat entered the room.

"Mr. and Mrs. Dietrich," he said curtly. At the mention of Mason's last name heavy ball bearings seemed to drop in my stomach.

"Pretend she isn't here," Mason said, indicating Cora.

A pained expression crossed Cora's face.

"Oh, I-" stuttered the doctor.

"—Can we just get on with it. What's wrong with me?"

A fissure appeared around the doctor's face.

"I'm afraid it's a combination of repetitive strain injury and degenerative arthritis. The tendons in your right hand and wrist are frayed."

Mason's mouth fell open. "Wha...what do we do about it?"

Fissures formed around Mason's field of vision and crackled like an ancient reel of film.

"I've written you a prescription for Percocet, but otherwise nothing can be done," said the doctor.

"What do you mean nothing?" blurted Cora, her face haloed in fissures.

"Shut up, Cora!" yelled Mason.

The doctor composed himself before speaking. "There's not much that can heal this except time. A lot of time, a lot of nothing. I'm afraid I can't clear you to perform surgery again."

Fissures burst across the memory. Their conversation continued, but it was hopelessly muffled, like listening to a wall of white noise. I sat there for a few more minutes until I heard the sound of a door click shut.

"Clear," I said.

The memory fell away, and I was back on the platform looking over the carcasses of the fallen creature. I broke into a run along the platform. After a couple hundred meters, I launched myself into the closest tunnel.

The walls of PTER took on a new shape. I looked across a great oaken desk at a man in a three-piece suit. He had small dark eyes and a thick moustache. Tiny fissures ran along the seams of his suit. Mason sat across from him.

He folded his hands on the table. "Mason, Dr. Reza told us about what happened in the operating room. I've seen your doctor's report and it disappointed me greatly." He continued, his voice low and authoritative. "How long were you aware you were having problems with your hand?"

"I-uhhh," stammered Mason.

"Longer than you'd like to admit I'm sure. Listen, Mason, we're letting you go effective immediately."

"WHAT!" said Mason. The acusensory suit became a sauna. The chest wrapped tight around my lungs and thudded on my breast as Mason's accelerating heart beat mingled with my own.

The man drummed his fingers on the desk. "I've spoken about the incident with members of the board of directors of other hospitals in the area."

Mason leapt to his feet. "You've bankrupted me and destroyed my reputation! I'll lose everything."

"And what about the family of that girl. Have they not lost everything?"

"Clear," I said into the microphone. A tiny drop of water hit my upper lip. The memory disintegrated; the platform materialized into view. Out in the battlefield the fight between the horsemen and monstrosities was over. A lone knight stood in the center of the gore four hundred meters away. His hand wrenched a spear out of the ground. He wound it over his shoulder and ran in my direction. After ten meters he launched his javelin. It traveled at a blistering speed. I spun my head at the last second, certain he'd shorn off a clump of hair. More spears followed the first. Panicked, I leaped into the closest tunnel. It wouldn't do Rhodes much good in mapping the lattice, but I had no choice.

The memory shimmered into view. I was in a grandiose house with vaulted ceilings that were lined in ornate crown moulding. The furniture was a mix of well-kept antique pieces. Large paintings dotted the various walls. The next room was the foyer, from there a broad staircase curled up to a second floor. A massive skylight was cut into the ceiling.

Standing in the center of the foyer was Cora. She wore a tight-fitting leather jacket, slim blue pants and knee-high brown boots. Next to her was a suitcase.

"I'm leaving you, Mason," she said.

"Everything is already unraveling, please don't do this. I need you," Mason pleaded.

"All of a sudden you need me? For years you treat me like garbage. But I put up with it because we had something." She motioned at the house around her. "If that's gone, I have no reason to stay. I'm filing for divorce and I'll be getting my half before the hospital can get its hands on it."

"You gold-digging bitch," said Mason.

"Rot in hell, Mason!" Cora grabbed her suitcase and walked out the door.

"Clear," I said. How far Mason Dietrich had fallen… That name, why did I know it? With all of Mason's thoughts bombarding my own brain it was impossible to remember anything concrete.

The platform came back into view. A wall of spears jutted out of the brick wall and stretched up twenty feet. They had formed some kind of makeshift ladder to the second level of tunnels. I climbed up the spears to a small ledge that ran along the bottom edge of each tunnel. The knight stood fast in the battlefield. *This wasn't a coincidence.*

My mind and body were exhausted. I only had one more memory left in me. I plunged into the first tunnel at the top of the ladder, hoping for more insight into what happened in the years between Mason's downfall and today. What I found would change everything.

CHAPTER TWENTY-FOUR

Nirali Reza slid into the booth opposite Mason. Gone was the sheen of resident doctor. Her hair was cut short and tidy. Her elegant gold necklace and pearl earrings went perfectly with her red, tailored business suit.

Between her and Mason on the table was a glass half full of bourbon and a notebook with a weathered black cover.

"What do you want, Mason," said Nirali. Her eyes locked on his. Her face looked huge and hateful over the walls of my PTER compartment. "The trial is long over. The hospital would kill me if they knew I was talking to you."

"You look like you've done well since I left," remarked Mason.

A haggard waitress came by the table. "Can I get you somethin'" she asked.

"No, thank you," said Nirali.

"'Nother Bourbon?" she said to Mason.

He nodded as he took a sip from his glass.

"Mason, your departure left a gaping hole in the surgical department I was happy to fill."

"I'm happy for you."

"Somehow I doubt it."

Mason took another swig and set the finished glass on the table. "I'm done feeling sorry for myself. I've moved on to something different. But I haven't forgotten that day. It haunts me, Nirali."

"Think about her family."

"I do. Every damn day. And my self-loathing has twisted and warped that memory into some grotesque caricature of the stupid mistake I made." Mason opened the notebook. "That's why I've asked you here. I need something from you. A few things actually." He turned the notebook towards Nirali. On it was a crude drawing... of PTER. My heart crashed against my chest; my guts twisted in knots. Every inch of skin under my acusensory suit tingled with sweat.

There were two compartments on either side of a central console. A body lay inside each compartment. Wires exited from the console to a nearby bank of computers. Below the drawing were the letters P.T.E.R.

"What's PTER?" Nirali asked.

Mason shifted in his seat. "It means Post Traumatic Exploratory Restitution. It means that deep inside, what someone *remembers* lies the truth. I've developed a way to enter someone's memories and scrub away the degradation of time. To help reconnect with the reality of the past and find closure," he said.

"This is just a drawing..." Mason reached into a bag and pulled out a heavy stack of documents and dropped them on the table with a thud. He took another sip of bourbon. "Here is all the research, models, theories, everything," he said.

Nirali lowered her gaze on him. "Cute Mason. What do you need me for?"

"No one understands exactly what happened that day better than you. I want you to go into my mind and help scrub away all the pain time has created. And I want you to finance the construction of the machine."

"I have nothing to gain from this, Mason. Helping you can only put my reputation at risk."

"Do you think I deliberately killed that girl?"

"Well no," she said.

"Everyone deserves a second chance. But if it's only dollars and cents that matter to you, I can tell you that PTER will make you wealthier than you could ever be from grinding out long hours in the operating room."

There was a faint glimmer in Nirali's eye. "How much do you need?"

"Fifty thousand," said Mason. "I've managed to collect the rest elsewhere."

"I don't have that kind of money lying around!"

"You've taken over my job, so I know you've been able to save plenty," said Mason.

The waitress came back and set down another glass of bourbon and left without a word.

"What if I give it to you and it doesn't work?" Nirali said.

Mason slid the papers to her. "Take these and read them. I don't need the money now, but if you're in, let me know in a week. Otherwise, I'm taking the offer to someone else." Mason pulled back the notebook. He threw back the double shot of bourbon, dropped a wad of wrinkled bills on the table and left Nirali sitting there.

The memory crackled and faded as he walked out the door into the bright sunlight.

"Rhodes, get me out of here," I said. The respirator was filling with more than a mere trickle of water.

"Rhodes?" The water filled my mouth.

"RHODES!"

*   *   *

The door of my capsule folded open. I ripped off my respirator and spit out the salt water. I was consumed with anger. I disentangled myself from the sensors attached to my head and marched out of the room. Rhodes swivelled around on his chair and called to me. I ignored him.

I thrust open the door to my office. Lydia looked up from the log of yesterday's activity. She'd made it about halfway through. The papers were splattered in her red ink.

"Mason Dietrich?" I said. "Dr. Mason Dietrich? You've got to be kidding me, Lydia."

Her eyes flashed wide before she composed herself. She put down her pen and folded her arms. "Well, now, I know your machine works," she said.

"Of course it works. Do you think I'm an idiot? I know what you're trying to do here."

"And what's that?"

"You're intent on making this project fail. Then you can go back to your little committee and say I folded. It saves you the trouble of actually trying to justify shutting the project down, which you know you'll never be able to do under normal circumstances."

"Are you saying you're giving up?"

My body grew hot and sticky inside my acusensory suit. I was desperate to be rid of it. "Of course not," I said.

"Dr. Chambers," Lydia said as she leaned forward in her chair. "The city is bleeding red ink. Any chance to sop some of that up I'll take if it means more funding for well-established programs I know will get results. But you have the backing of a number of important people downtown so I'm here. But don't make me out to be some kind of villain. If the city is going to back this little program you need to prove yourself. And that means throwing the kitchen sink at you."

"How did you even find him," I said. My zeal was fading.

"When I do my research I am exhaustive," she said. "I dug into the creator of PTER's past to find out as much as I could about the machine. When I learned he was based in Vancouver, I followed that thread as far as it would take me. It went cold twenty years ago. I cross-referenced the city's own records. Turns out Dr. Dietrich was in and out of prison for drug possession and assault. He visited the city's clinics and injection sites more than once. It wasn't difficult to track him down."

The room fell silent as we stared at one another.

"You should be happy I gave you such an interesting case to get you started," she said.

I let out an angry groan and turned to leave.

"Dr. Chambers," Lydia called.

"What is it?"

"I see you increased Mason's sedative above the recommended range. I'm making a note of it in my report. If you want to continue your little project you'll stop that immediately."

I grabbed the doorknob and slammed the door shut. I went back to the change room and peeled off the suit as quickly as I could, put on my clothes and marched over to Mason. He was already dressed. Suzy stood next to him. I stuck a finger in Mason's chest. He didn't flinch. His eyes watched me absently.

"I'm not letting everything you've seen Dr. Dietrich scare me from bringing you back to us. I certainly hope you're not taking part in some little game with Mrs. Qiao to undermine everything I've built on the foundation you started."

"There's no need to be so aggressive, Dr. Chambers," said Suzy.

Rhodes hung back and watched the situation unfold.

"Suzy," I said. "You've no idea what I'm being subjected to. This isn't your run of the mill drug addict. Do you see that machine right there," I said, pointing at PTER. "The technology was his design. The only person who has witnessed traumatic memories like I have is this man."

Rhodes gasped as the revelation hit him.

"Well it's time for him to leave," said Suzy, taking Mason by the arm. As he passed he leaned down and whispered in my ear:

"Where I am is where you'll be."

CHAPTER TWENTY-FIVE

My head whipped around once they were out the door. "Did you hear that," I said to Rhodes.

"Hear what?"

"He said 'Where I am is where you'll be'. What is that supposed to mean?"

"You're the psychiatrist, Catarina."

"Rhodes, this is bad. How the hell do we treat the inventor of PTER?"

Rhodes slumped in his chair. His skin was pale; sweat ringed the collar of his shirt.

"It explains so much," he said. "The missing lattice... his mind's defenses."

"That man has seen more trauma than anyone except for me. And he did it all without extirpation. It's no wonder every horror imaginable is spilling out of his past. He has erected a fortress in his mind to keep it at bay, but how long can that be done?"

Rhodes' face drooped, and he shut his eyes.

"Rhodes, I've been given an impossible task. How can we possibly fix him?"

"We'll think of something. We always do."

"Lydia set us up. This whole exercise was designed to fail."

"It's awfully convenient," agreed Rhodes. "How do you figure she convinced him to take part?"

"I'm not sure she did. He's barely coherent. If it wasn't for him whispering in my ear I'd still think he was mute. I can only fathom what we'll need to revisit to bring him back. After so many years of navigating other people's traumas, I can only imagine what finally broke him."

"Everyone has a weak spot. Press hard enough and every one of us folds," he said.

For several hours Rhodes and I hashed out how we'd tackle tomorrow's session. The map of Mason's lattice was far from complete. Each memory formed part of a semi-circle around a central unidentified point. Was this point the gargantuan tower in his lattice?

"How long do we keep at this before we get more experimental?" asked Rhodes.

"What did you have in mind?" I said.

He shifted uncomfortably in his seat. "A targeted extirpation," he said sheepishly.

"No way, too risky," I said.

"If we don't try it on him, who would we ever try it on?"

"There's too much to lose."

"If we don't fix him by the end of the week, there won't be anything left to save."

"I'm not prepared to go that route yet."

"And I'm not asking you to. Just think about it, Cat."

"What time is it anyway?"

"Nine," said Rhodes.

"NINE!" Eric and I were on thin ice and leaving him waiting around when he expected me home would only make him angrier. I went back to my office to grab my cell phone. Three missed calls from Eric. Probably another couple on the office phone. I hit his number.

"Oh my god, are you all right, where have you been?" Eric's voice was loud and angry over the phone. "I've been trying to reach you for hours. I was just about to come to your office building."

"My patient was particularly tough today, and we've been troubleshooting. I lost track of time," I said.

"I guess," he trailed off. "I wish you'd come home. You need sleep. Plus, it's dangerous to walk around too late at night. Let me come pick you up."

"Don't worry, Eric. I have a couple more things to tidy up. I'll find my way home."

"You promise you won't walk?"

"I'll call a cab. Love you," I replied. I hung up the phone and stretched out on the couch. I closed my eyes and ran a kaleidoscope of faces through my mind: Eric, Mason, Lydia, Rhodes, Dad… each one glowered at me. A splitting headache ripped through my head.

Then, the sound of crunching and breaking of bones rattled through my ears. The sound of skin stretching and tearing joined it. My lower jaw jutted out from my face, growing inch by inch. My hands wrapped around my extending jaw and tried to push it back in place; it relentlessly angled outward and turned over itself as a hundred rows of new teeth threatened-

"—Let's leave," said Rhodes.

I shot straight up from the couch and ran my hands over my face.

"You hanging in there, Catarina?"

Rhodes frowned. He rubbed the stubble shadow on his face and neck.

"Sorry, yeah I think so. Just so tired," I said.

"Remember, they're not yours," he said. "These memories you've seen. Don't let them become a part of you."

I stared at him, unsure what to say. "You go ahead, I'll close up," I told him.

When I was done shutting down, I closed the office's outer door behind me and stared at my name pasted to the frosted glass window. *Catarina, what have you gotten yourself into?*

*   *   *

My eyes scanned the pools of darkness at each end of the hallway. I pushed open the door to the stairs. The only light came from the exit signs on each landing. My smart phone had a flashlight. I pulled it out—dead battery. I was nearly convinced that one of the creatures in Mason's head was waiting for me in the shadows.

I had no other choice. Gripping the railing, I raced down the stairs as fast as I could, stumbling around each landing till I finally reached the bottom and burst into the building's tiny lobby. I tripped over my own feet and fell onto the floor. The streetlights bathed the lobby tiles in a soft white glow. I sat with my back against the wall to catch my breath.

I was a couple blocks from the worst part of East Hastings Street and at least ten blocks from home. In my rush to get away from the clinic, I had forgotten to call a cab. But there was no way I could bring myself to go back.

Another deep breath and I was off. *A walk through the scariest part of the city should help get my mind off Mason.* I was getting closer to the heart of East Hastings. Newspaper, Styrofoam cups, old blankets, broken glass, cigarette butts, and used syringes littered the sidewalks. The lights of ancient hotels-turned-housing-projects lit up the street. The denizens fluttered like moths to the failing bulbs of the old marquees.

I was stuck at the streetlights waiting to cross and choking on a thick cloud of marijuana smoke coming from a pair of men beside me. An open case of beer sat at their feet. There were twenty seconds left on the opposing crossing signal.

"Hey," said a man's voice. *Oh God, he is talking to me.* Eighteen seconds. I pretended not to hear him and stared straight ahead.

"Miss, hey, come have a beer wit' us." He held out a bottle of Coors like an olive branch.

"No thank you," I replied, doing my best to keep my voice steady. Twelve seconds left to go. The traffic was thick. My mind envisioned my body rolling over the hood of a passing car as I attempted to escape.

"D'ya smoke?" the other man asked. His voice was hoarser than the first.

"No. Honestly I'm tired and going home."

"O, ya, where's home? We could move this party there." *What have I done?* I was standing at the slowest crosswalk known to man. Five seconds left.

"N..nowhere" I stammered and turned to dash across the street, one foot to the pavement.

"Whoa, where ya goin!" A beer bottle smashed against the ground as a leathery hand wrapped around my arm and yanked me backwards. As I was about to turn and smack the man, a taxi flew by, horn blaring. With my hand still raised, I gazed in embarrassment at him. I was close enough to feel his hot beer breath on my neck.

"Better be more careful, Doc," he said.

"H-How do you know I'm a doctor?" I asked.

"We all know round here. Been reading the papers, ya know. We seen the good yer doing. Yer safe in these parts, don't worry so much. It's the passersby that'll kill ya. Don't give a damn bout us folks livin' and dyin' round here."

I must have stared at him like an idiot for at least a few seconds before my brain registered a reply.

"Thank you," I said and crossed the street before I lost my chance.

The rest of the walk home was graciously uneventful. I pushed open the door of our condo to the sound of gunshots. Eric had a movie blaring. He looked at me with concern.

"You should have let me pick you up," he said.

"I know, but I didn't want to bother you so I called a cab."

"You're all sweaty."

"I was rushing."

He got up off the couch and looked at me with his dark brown eyes. He pulled me into a hug. I stiffened at first, but then melted into his arms.

"Oh Eric, it's all messed up," I admitted. "Part of me wants this to work so bad. The other…"

"… wants to run away," he finished.

CHAPTER TWENTY-SIX

Curiosity will kill the Cat. I've hopelessly entangled myself in Mason's web. The second I left my office I knew my time in his memories was just beginning. If anyone had the keys to rid me of my guilt over my father's death, it was Mason Dietrich. We could help each other if we didn't kill each other first.

Laying in bed was futile. Largo huffed as I got out of bed. He followed me begrudgingly into the living room. Eric had forgotten to turn off the TV before bed, and it played along in mute. I had entered the limbo hour of infomercials for insomniacs: a pill to get skinny, a pill to build muscle, a pill for natural male enhancement, or a tray for cooking grease-free bacon. I like my bacon fully greased, please and thank you. Eventually sleep took me again.

When I opened my eyes, Eric was standing over me, dressed for the workday. "Good morning," he said with a slight smile.

"Morning. What time is it?" I asked. It was light out, but I still felt groggy.

"It's eight o'clock," said Eric.

"Eight! Oh, god, I need to get back to the clinic." I jumped off the couch and accidentally kicked Largo. I leaned in to give Eric a quick kiss. He wrinkled his nose as I got close.

"What?" I pulled back.

"You stink," he said and gave me a peck on the cheek.

"Jerk," I punched him in the arm.

"Largo, let's go do your business," he gave the dog a quick whistle.

Largo hopped off the couch, tags jingling as he went.

I went to the bathroom to clean the stink off. The hot shower peeled the oils off my skin. A good shower felt like it could fix anything. But there was no time for a good shower. Lydia would be waiting and judging every second I delayed. I soaped up the important parts and turned off the faucet.

I knew it was going to be a long day, so I put on one of my more comfortable pairs of underwear and bra and a looser fitting pant suit. By the time I was ready and at the front door Eric had returned to let Largo back in for the day.

Eric gave me a sniff. "Better," he said with a stupid grin. I gave him a look that said *not the time*. The grin faded.

"Let me drive you to the office," he said.

"Sure, that'd be great." The thought of getting in the car filled me with anxiety, but I had no choice. Largo whimpered at us as we were about to walk out the door.

"I didn't forget about you." I grabbed a dog treat from the tin. Largo's ritual: *If you're going to leave me here by myself all day, you give me a treat or say goodbye to the couch.* Largo wagged his bum. His joy melted into my own and, for the briefest moment, I forgot about life. I threw him the treat and Eric and I slipped out the door.

We leased a BMW SUV. Eric always leased. It still had the new car smell. I lifted myself into the passenger seat. It was a big vehicle.

Large enough to throw a house-hunting family inside. Eric pulled out of the parking lot. It was only a five minute drive. But five minutes was more than enough time for Eric to pry into last night.

I tried to head him off. "So who is this potential buyer for Point Grey?" I asked.

"An executive from Hong Kong. Apparently made a killing on company stock options."

"Would be lucky for us if it went through."

"Hardly. I worked my ass off for that listing."

"Sorry, just meant that I'm glad a buyer came along. I know those properties can take ages to move. So what does that mean for your career?"

"Early retirement if I want it."

"I'm sorry I can't be part of that right now."

"I know," said Eric, trailing off. We arrived at my clinic.

"Love you," I said. Eric gave me a sad, half smile.

"Love you, too," he said.

I closed the car door and Eric sped off. Across the street my four-story building seemed to loom a million miles into the sky.

*   *   *

Debbie was already at her desk; Rhodes was plugging away in the examination room; and Lydia was in my office. She came out to meet me. The shoulder pads of her navy blazer gave her frame a boxy look. Her black hair was tied back into a ponytail and reading glasses rimmed her nose. Comparably, my shirt was half-tucked and poked out of my blazer. Creases rippled across my pants, my hair was a mess, and there wasn't an ounce of makeup on my face.

Debbie looked wide-eyed from Lydia to me and back again.

"I was beginning to think you took the day off," Lydia said.

"Then there'd be no one here to keep an eye on you," I said walking past Lydia towards the examination room.

Debbie stifled a laugh. Rhodes spun around in his chair as I entered.

"Talk to me while I change," I said, shutting the door and squeezing myself into my acusensory suit.

Rhodes voice carried through the door. "The respirator hose is fixed. I found a better epoxy, so you won't have any more leaking problems. I saw Lydia's note about the SLUMB-Rx dose. Thankfully with the bit of work we've done there's a better shot I can keep you out of the worst parts of Mason's defenses. The only notable problem is that the cleaning cycle failed last night. The compartment is going to be dirtier than you're used to, could be some residue obscuring your vision."

"Do you have a plan to fix it?" I asked.

"Always, but there's not enough time to get all the work done this morning, so it's going to have to wait until after you're finished." He paused. "It's not going to be cheap, though, Cat. Maybe a thousand dollars."

"Brutal," I said. "Talk to Debbie." I'd lost track of how much money we had left. It was as if the funds I'd withdrawn from our account were being thrown into a dumpster fire. *Only two more days Cat; you can survive two more days.*

Rhodes looked me up and down when I stepped out of the change room. "Looking a little thinner than usual," he said.

Rhodes' own belly was edging over his belt, and the buttons of his plaid dress shirt were straining to hold together. His face was puffier than it had been a few days earlier.

"For every pound I lose, you gain two, so at least I know they're going to a good cause," I said.

Rhodes laughed. "I deserved that."

"The stress is getting the better of us. We just need to get through this week and then we'll regain control of this mess."

"What mess?" said Lydia from the doorway.

We jerked our heads in her direction, neither offering an answer.

"Your patient is here. Perhaps we can wrap this up today," she said.

I was not so optimistic. "Send them in," I said. Adrenaline rippled through my limbs. The gravity of what I was walking into hit me. I hopped up and down to settle myself. A few seconds later Suzy led Mason through the door. His hollow face looked more decrepit than ever. I tracked back in my mind as to how old he might be. I had never thought to look up his birth date but figured he had to be in his sixties. Today he wore the expression of a tired and frightened ninety-year-old man. It wasn't lost on Suzy.

"He's particularly frail today," she said. "I'm not sure we should do this."

"The sensory deprivation might actually be good for him. It will take all the weight off his physical body." My comment was self-serving and made me sick to my stomach. Suzy was right, but I just wanted the whole experience over with and delaying even a day could sink the clinic. One day soon the hydro company would shut down the power and, with my luck, our untested backup generator would fail and I'd drown and die alone inside my PTER compartment. They wouldn't retrieve my body for hours. The last image Eric would see of me was a bloated, purple corpse.

"Dr. Chambers," said Suzy. "You assure me he'll be okay?"

"Our monitors will ensure we keep a very close eye on his health. He's at no more risk inside than he would be laying in bed." Suzy nodded and led Mason to the change room to put on his suit.

Rhodes whispered in my ear. "You're putting a lot of pressure on me. You know as well as I do that SLUMB-Rx will impact his already weakened vitals."

"It'll be fine. If he were going to die he'd have already ended his life long ago. All that fighting in his head is for a reason. It's having a psychosomatic effect on his body. You'll see." My words felt callous; Rhodes said nothing further.

I stepped on to my PTER platform and began connecting my sensors. Rhodes finished the hook-up. I spied a layer of salty residue covering the platform that the cleaning cycle missed. The inside of PTER's doors were likely the same.

Mason gingerly stepped over to his platform and out of sight. Rhodes murmured a few words to him. A couple minutes later I heard his chamber door fold shut.

Rhodes came back to my side. "You all set? Remember, I can't put any extra SLUMB-Rx in his system so you're going to have to be on your toes in there."

I nodded.

He clicked a button on the console to close my compartment. Three quarters of the way across it jammed. The hydraulics groaned.

"Shit!" he said. "The residue must have caked in and jammed the door." Rhodes appeared in the remaining gap. He pushed on the door to make it release. After ten seconds of tugging it pulled free. As he pushed the door the last of the way shut I saw one of his tired eyes observing me. And then I plunged into darkness.

CHAPTER TWENTY-SEVEN

The extra salt in the water clouded the images projecting up the walls of PTER. It would be a distraction. Rhodes didn't live up to his promise. Instead of the platform of memories, he plunged me down next to the castle wall.

I looked up. Soldiers on the parapets were pouring hot tar towards me. I dove out of the way and watched as the salt mixture passed by my eyes. The soldiers continued to rain tar and arrows down on me. I was forced to run around the outer edge of the castle. Their attack was relentless until I reached the base of the mountain. Then suddenly they stopped. Their shouts and yells were replaced by the thunderous sound of giant boulders crashing together.

The men at the back of the castle ignored me as they tried desperately to shore up the wall that scaled hundreds of feet into the sky. No time to marvel at its construction. There was a loud smash beside me. To my right, a five-foot wide rock hurtled in my direction. I dove for the wall but, because of the salt, I mistimed my leap to safety. The rock connected with my right leg; I felt all the bones below the knee shatter. The force of the impact spun me in the air. Everything in my field of vision swirled.

I stopped spinning, but the pain persisted. My mind couldn't let go of the sensory deprivation chamber's hallucinations. My leg looked normal, yet I couldn't will myself to put weight on it.

I looked towards the wall for some kind of escape. There! A large vibrating crack in the brick where it met the mountain. I tried to swish the salt away to get a better look. Crawling on my hands and knees I inched over. I nearly passed out from the pain in my leg. The crack in the castle wall was large enough for me to squeeze inside. From deep in its recesses something shimmered. With the last bits of energy I had, I squirmed into the cavity.

*   *   *

The pain in my leg was gone. My eyes opened to stone arches ensconcing fifty-foot walls supporting the tapestry that blanketed the vaulted ceiling. Large windows let streams of light through three of the four walls. The fourth wall led into the belly of a vast train station. The room I was in was lined with ticket booths and vendors. At its center two stairwells led down to an underground pedestrian concourse. Seventy feet of open floor divided the stairwells that were full of people walking in various directions. And a piano.

It was an old baby grand, painted in a kaleidoscope of colors. Sitting at its bench was a man with wild hair. He was dressed in a plain black t-shirt, blue jeans and army boots. Periodically, he looked around at the people passing by. His face was hopeful when he viewed his potential audience, a mask of anger when he looked down. I steadied myself on something. Then fell through the water inside my capsule. That man was my father.

Once I was within earshot, the sound of soft hammers caressing the strings of the piano drifted into my ears. His masterpiece was soft, haunting, and sullen. One dissonant chord followed another, linked together by a twinkling melody. Each melodic phrase inspired a hopeful resolution that was stolen back with another dissonant chord. The composition modulated ever so slightly to a major key as he raised his head. Once he confirmed he still lacked an audience, he threw his head down in disgust. He began to play a crescendo, smashing through a progression of minor chords, luring the listener into his dissonance. Yet as quickly as it came on, the piece fell into a dolce diminuendo.

The composition was pure ecstasy. I felt every emotional tug each time as he repeated the four measure sequence of its central theme. Each repetition grew more complex and intense. His hands blazed across the keys and created the impression of symphonic accompaniment. The fluidity of his hands, the character of every chord, the erratic movements of his body, all brought me back to my childhood.

The piano had always been an outlet for my over-active imagination, channelling catastrophe into courage as the notes flowed effortlessly out of my fingertips. I was a more technically proficient player than my father but didn't bare my soul in every piece like he did. Only after his death could I see the torture that punctuated each note as he struggled to find an audience in the train station. Nevertheless, watching him play reignited a fire that had burned to the embers.

No one gave my father a second glance. Crowds of people swarmed like ants out of the station. He arbitrarily smashed middle C extra hard every time someone passed close to the piano. This was particularly jarring for the one person paying attention to the piece: Mason. He pushed himself past the people in his path until he was less than ten feet from the piano. He was enthralled by my father's performance. A weight grew in the pit of my stomach. It wasn't a mistake that this was the memory I found.

With each stroke of the piano, a new fissure tore open. The harder Dad banged on the keys, the darker it got, building into a black crescendo. The area around the piano cracked and warped like melting reels of film. Dad lifted his head and stared into the crowd. His eyes were crazed, his grin manic. He whipped his long hair back and forth as he scanned the room. As the piece grew in intensity he rose to his feet, sweeping his hands across the keys in a glissando. He slammed his fingers down into one final massive chord, and then slammed down the lid of the piano. The bang was followed by a silence that hung over the room. The memory fragments floating around my chamber were so numerous that I could feel them vibrate against me.

He searched the room, his chest rising and falling. When his eyes met mine, they lingered and froze. Butterflies fluttered in my stomach. The man who left my life too soon looked very much alive. Several long seconds passed before I noticed that all movement in the memory had stopped.

"Rhodes, the memory, it's... frozen," I said. There was no reply. I moved face-to-face with my father. He was just as I remembered him. Wild and handsome with sharp angular features, thick dark eyebrows and a hooked nose. And those rich blue eyes! They now bore into mine as I stood there and admired him.

"Is it really you?" I said. I rested my hand on his cheek. Fragments of memory followed my touch and sewed themselves to his image. The world unfroze. I was back at the edge of a circle of people who surrounded his piano, head and shoulders over the other spectators. Dad sat at his piano bench. I looked around the room and found myself back at the beginning of the memory. My hands ran through the air like a conductor, massaging out fissures to the beat of the composition. My father's deep baritone voice sang.

> *Shine bright moon tonight*
> *In the sky you held your light*
> *Turn it off your match is out*
> *Stamped smoke into the ground*

It was a beautiful mess, held together by a brilliance I could barely follow.

> *Help, can't help myself*
> *Without, without my breath*
> *Frozen air inside my chest*
> *Exhale but there's nothing left*

As the fissures poured back, the movements of the crowd slowed. People gathered close around the piano and blocked my view. The large crowd attracted even more onlookers, like magnets to a lodestone. His voice rang out above them.

> *Awake but make no sound*
> *A patient of the lost and found*

Come find me where I roam

The sound of change tossed into a bucket next to the piano punctuated the performance.

Buried deep one autumn day
Covered under earth and clay
Hide this man, hide his past
Hide someone who died at last

With the same flourish as before he ended the piece and slammed down the lid of the piano. The crowd burst into applause. There were whistles and hollers. An avalanche of change fell into his bucket. The weight of his words dragged my body into the bowels of PTER. A lump caught in the back of my throat.

Dad scanned the crowd with that same crazed look on his face. His chest heaved. When his eyes met mine I swore a smile crested his lips. It was gone an instant later. After several minutes, the crowd dissipated and Dad collected his things from beside the piano.

Mason walked up to him. He stopped no more than three feet away. Dad recoiled when he noticed him.

"Remarkable performance," said Mason.

"Oh, umm thanks," Dad said.

"I've been listening to your work for years. Where do you find the inspiration for your compositions?" Mason's tone was clinical and disarming.

Dad crinkled his nose as he searched for an answer. "I can't really say. There's a lot running through my head to work with I guess," he answered.

"Have you ever wanted help with the things running through your head?"

Dad took a step backwards. "I don't follow."

"Sure you do. People don't write music like that unless they're tortured by something. Shall I list off the names of famous musicians who couldn't tame the demons in their heads."

Dad worked his jaw back and forth. "Who do you think you are buddy?" He stretched to his full height. He was a tall man, but Mason still had a couple inches on him.

Mason stood his ground. "I'm a psychiatrist," he replied. He handed a business card to my father. Was he *the* psychiatrist? Based on Dad's age and appearance the time lines matched. Rhodes voice crackled into my ears.

"Time's up, Cat."

CHAPTER TWENTY-EIGHT

Before I had a chance to protest, the water inside my capsule gushed down the floor drain. My body sank until my feet landed on the platform. The images that felt so real only a moment earlier became nothing more than projections along the compartment walls. Then they faded to black. The light from the room hit my eyes, and I was welcomed by a blinding migraine. Rhodes was speaking to me, but I couldn't process his words. He sounded like his cheeks were stuffed with cotton balls. The migraine blurred my vision. I stumbled into the bathroom and shut the door.

My stomach clenched when I saw my reflection. The left side of my face hung lifeless. *Did I have a stroke?* I mashed my fingers into the fleshiest part of my cheek. There was almost no feeling at all.

"Oh, god," I spluttered. The sobbing came in an uncontrollable wave. I heard myself choking out deep gasping breaths as I began to hyperventilate. I sat down on the toilet to balance myself.

"Catarina?" said Rhodes from outside the door. "Can I come in?"

Come in? No I can't let him see me like this. But I couldn't bring myself to say no. Rhodes clicked open the door.

"What's wrong?" he asked.

"Look at my cheek… I think I may have had a stroke."

"A stroke. Ha, you're kidding, right?"

"LOOK AT ME!" I looked into the mirror again. My cheek was exactly where it should be. The thought that I was delusional was not comforting. Mentally ill or physically ill. I knew too much on the subject. The former was far worse.

"Catarina, you need to go home. You're delirious. It's been a long day."

"But, I…" I just kept staring at my frazzled and tired, but otherwise normal face. "I don't have it in me to speak to Lydia."

"Leave it to me," he said. "Anything you want me to tell her? Mason is no better than before, if that makes a difference."

"Umm, just tell her the memory was particularly troubling and I need some time to process the experience."

"I'll get them out of here." He shut the bathroom door.

What would I do without him? For the following thirty minutes I hid in the bathroom as the pain slicing through my head receded. Once I heard everyone leave I stumbled back to my office and picked up the phone. I dialled Eric.

"Hey, what's up?" he said.

"Do you have clients? I was hoping you could pick me up?" My voice was unsteady.

"Of course. Everything all right?" he asked.

"Been a real long day. I miss you."

"I'll be there in fifteen. Keep an eye out for me."

I put my head in my hands. Eric coming to whisk me away from it all was the warm blanket I needed.

* * *

I bolted upright. My father was in Mason's memory! I had to tell Rhodes. I leapt up from my seat and smashed my knee on the underside of the desk.

"Jesus Christ!" I cursed. When the pain dulled, I hobbled back to the examination room.

Something wasn't right. All of the vital monitors screamed. Rhodes was hanging limp in one of the compartments, tied up with the respirator hose. Mason was in the other. They were both dressed in acusensor suits. A clear IV bag of saline was turning crimson as blood ran from the SLUMB-Rx injection site in Rhodes' neck. Foam seeped from his mouth as he went into a seizure.

"Oh, my god," I heard myself say. I found a spoon from a finished cup of yogurt by his computer. I jammed it between his teeth to keep him from biting off his tongue. As gingerly as I could, I pulled the catheter from his neck. Blood gushed out of the wound in pounding bursts that sprayed my clothes. His heart rate slowed precipitously; each spurt was weaker than the last. He was turning white. I needed to stop the bleeding. I grabbed the closest thing I could find—my coat. With every ounce of strength I had I tore off the sleeve.

As I wrapped the sleeve around his wound, I felt fingers dig deep under my collarbone. Mason towered next to me. He clamped down with all his strength. The pain was excruciating. I nearly blacked out. He tossed me across the room. I slammed into Rhodes' desk, causing the monitor to crash to the floor. As I writhed in pain, Mason picked up the monitor. It was an ancient, heavy beast of a thing. Then, he whipped round and smashed the monitor into Rhodes' face. It exploded into hundreds of pieces. Rhodes' convulsions stopped.

"NOOOO," I screamed. I pushed myself to my feet and ran for the door. Mason grabbed my shoulder before I could get away. *This is it Catarina, you're going home. Maybe Dad will meet me.* Mason spun me around.

"Cat, CAT," he said. His face was oddly comforting, his voice not at all threatening. "Cat," he said again with a gentle shake. And then I was looking at Eric's face. The tension melted from his shoulders.

"The car is on the street out front. Come on, we have to go or we'll get a ticket. You know how bad the traffic cops are around here," he said.

I was still at my desk. Just a quick, terrible dream… I shook my head to clear the cobwebs.

"Just let me say bye to Rhodes, make sure he's okay to lock up. Wait here."

"All right," he said.

When I got back to the exam room I let out a heavy sigh of relief. Rhodes raised an eyebrow.

"I almost forgot to tell you-," I trailed off. It didn't feel like the right time to discuss my father. I wanted to go home.

"You know, now I forget what I was going to say. Anyway, don't stay too late."

Rhodes nodded.

Eric was by the front door, shifting his weight impatiently.

"Let's get out of here," I said. I needed my husband, my dog, my couch, and a very large glass of wine.

CHAPTER TWENTY-NINE

We jumped into the car, happy to be parking ticket free, and made our way home. It was an uneventful drive through the evening streets of Vancouver. Eric made small talk that I barely registered. A few well-placed nods kept the conversation going. When we reached our condo I peeled myself out of the seat and felt the full weight of my day on my limbs. But before I knew it, Eric had lifted me off my feet and was carrying me up the stairs of our building.

"Eric, what are you doing?"

"You look tired."

"But your back?"

"What about it? I'm fine. Have you been eating? You weigh nothing?"

Eric had always been fit, but dead-lifting a body up three flights of stairs was hard for anyone. When we reached our door he put me down. I could see from the look in his eyes his question was serious.

"Oh, you meant that as a real question… Uhh, I've probably missed a couple meals with all the stress getting the pilot project ready. I'm famished now." Another lie. The idea of food made me sick despite the grumbling in my stomach. Maybe a glass of wine …

or two, would help my appetite.

Thankfully, a bottle was ready to go on the dining room table. I poured a glass right to the brim.

"I'm going to take a shower, hon," I said "I feel gross. It's been a long day."

"Okay, I'll warm up some supper," said Eric.

The shower felt amazing. They always did at the end of a long day. As I finished up, I heard Largo barking incessantly. I towelled off as quickly as I could, threw on my softest bathrobe and went back into the living room.

Eric stood by the front door, an opened envelope in his hand and a broken glass at his feet. The red wine spread across the hardwood floor.

He looked at me. His jaw was clenched, his eyes red.

"Why Cat?" A long pause. "Why?"

My body froze as Eric held my dirty little secret. *Why hadn't I been more careful?*

"You stole twenty grand from our savings. How did the bank even authorize this?"

I shrank into the corner. I wasn't prepared for this fight, physically or mentally.

"Did you forge my signature!? Goddammit, Cat, I can't watch you do this to yourself anymore." Eric waved the letter over his head. "We have a way to leave this all behind, but you keep digging in deeper. Why do you keep hurting yourself? Why do you keep hurting us? Do my feelings not matter? These people aren't worth it."

"You don't understand," I said.

"Then explain it to me!"

"I... this is what I've been working my whole life towards. Finding answers inside the minds of those who can't find those answers themselves. And I'm so close. But it's hard Eric. I was on the brink of something huge, and I needed the money to float the business through the probationary period."

"That doesn't mean you can steal from *OUR* future," Eric waved the letter around again. "Lying, stealing, what's next, Cat? You're en route to join all your *patients* on East Hastings Street. Is that what you want?" I stared at him. I had no idea what to tell him that would make it better.

"IS IT?" he yelled.

"NO!"

Largo peered at us from over the back of the couch. He whimpered quietly. I should have gone to him; instead, I opened my stupid mouth. "My work has meaning Eric. I'm not out there every day trying to find a greater fool to sell the next McMansion to. I help people. I make the world a better place. And when you're not there to support me, when no one has got my back... what the hell am I supposed to do?" I yanked the letter out of his hand. I immediately regretted every word that spilled from my mouth. But everything had gotten so hard and I didn't need Eric making it worse.

He looked hurt and indignant. "I don't help people? The world is worse off because of what I do? That's what you're saying?" He balled his hands into fists and hiked his shoulders. "I'm so sick of this high horse you're on. I've been supporting you for way too long, only to watch you fall apart under this clinic of yours. Always putting everyone else's needs ahead of mine. Now you get a little bite of the good life and all of a sudden my career is under you." A vein throbbed in his forehead. "I've been hanging on, biting my tongue, because I knew you were working hard for something. But now I learn it's all propped up on deceit and contempt. You know what, Cat, I'm done."

Life moved in slow motion as he pulled his wedding band off his finger; the white outline of untanned skin underneath a painful symbol of what I had pushed away. I pleaded with him for the next twenty minutes, but he wouldn't listen. The baggage of my father's death continued to wreak a path of destruction on my life. Now with the strongest mind I could possibly try to penetrate as my patient, the chances I'd find redemption for his death through the pilot project dimmed.

I was now nothing but a puddle of emotions on the floor of our bedroom. I heard a jingle of dog tags. Eric attached Largo's leash to his collar.

"What, no," I said, "not Largo." My hand stretched out for Largo. Eric yanked him away. Largo yelped.

"You're in no shape to take care of yourself," Eric said, "let alone a dog. He's coming with me. We're going to my parents."

My face burned red through streams of tears. "Eric, please. I might have found a man who can give me the answers I'm looking for. But I, I, I can't figure him out. Please, I'm so close."

"You'll lose your mind in his memories. This can never work between us until you decide to stop taking responsibility for all the world's problems just because you feel you let your family down." He looked down at me for an answer, but I could only stare blankly at the deep grooves cutting across his cheeks and forehead.

"Everything you want is walking out this door, and you can't even promise to stop. You didn't even try." He slammed the bedroom door shut behind him.

CHAPTER THIRTY

I sat at the end of my bed with my knees tucked into my chest and arms wrapped around my legs. I scanned the room as I wallowed in my dysphoria. *I wish I could look at something and feel love. Feel happy. To feel any way but the way my heart feels, full of worry and despair. To let go of the idea that tragedy will reach out and steal everything I care about. That everything wonderful will someday become a burden to endure infinitely.*

When I finally stopped crying my entire body felt numb. *How could I get back everything I had lost?* My world was shattered to pieces. My mind was incapable of putting it back together, like trying to mend a smashed window with nothing but white school glue.

A switch went off in my head. I got out of bed and found my glass of wine in the bathroom. It was still brimming. I chugged it back in one long, disgusting swallow. A pathetic sight stared back at me from the mirror. My head swam when I finally put the glass back down. I staggered out into the living room. My purse lay on the floor, sopping up the puddle of red wine.

Trying to avoid the broken glass in my bare feet, I wound my way to the couch. My mind and body were so defeated that, had I cut myself, I'm sure I'd have felt no pain. My head was spinning. I collapsed on the couch and passed out.

*   *   *

The remains of an upright piano were scattered on the floor. A chipped and dented Louisville slugger sat beside it. Sheets of music were strewn everywhere; most of the music was in scribbled pencil; a few of the sheets were covered in drops of blood. A single bulb, hanging onto life in an old chandelier, barely lit the room.

In the middle of the mess sat my father. No shirt. No socks. He wore only a pair of old, loose jeans. He was panting and covered in sweat. His long hair hung down around his face. His voice broke the silence. "I know you're there," he said. "You come and you go. Watching everything, doing nothing. Hide in the shadows and say nothing you coward. I don't need you. I don't need your help."

"How do you know I'm here?" I replied. I had never had a memory interact with me.

"I know what you're thinking. How could he say these things? After everything we've seen and done together, surely he understands me, surely I understand him. But you don't. You haven't taken away the fear. It eats me up, and ruins everything, everyone who comes across my path. I worry I'll do it again."

"Please, let me try to help you." The words fell out of my mouth before I could stop them.

"A devil's empty temptation."

"Why do you want to push me away? No one else can help you understand the way I can."

"Save your sympathy. You should have known it'd never work.

All you cared about was what fame I could have brought you. Now that I'm more broken than ever, you're scared I'll jeopardize this new life you built, and it will disappear like the one before it." Dad's voice was laced with anger. "And you know what, you're right. But I was never going to be your saviour. Hate me a little now, but I'm saving you a lifetime of pain."

I was lost and heartbroken. I tried to convince myself these weren't Dad's words, that it meant nothing to me.

"How do I go on..." I began to say before I was cut off by a girl's voice.

"... without you. I've been where the light ends and I still came back, Dad." It was my teenage self standing in the doorway, tears streaming down my face. My cheeks were flushed and my posture slumped. *How long had I been standing there?*

Dad lifted his head from the floor and looked at my younger self. "How would you go on with me?" he said. "I've lost whatever shreds of resolve were keeping it at bay. It will come and find me and pull you under with me. Don't pretend the little peeks you've had are close to what I've fought for thirty years."

My younger self looked at him imploringly. His jaw was clenched and veins throbbed in his forehead. His beard had grown out.

"This is our home," she said, "I can't leave."

"Then it'll be me who leaves you behind. There's nothing left for me here." He motioned to the debris in the room.

"Don't give up!" she cried.

Dad got to his feet and made for the door. My teenage self didn't move out of his way. Instead, she pressed herself against him, her head rested against his chest, her hands on his wrists.

"Please," she sobbed "Don't."

Dad stood there awkwardly. She put her arms around his back. Dad's face softened. He lifted his arms, unsure what to do. Then he wrapped his long arms around me and kissed me on top of my young head.

Fissures coursed around the embrace. I massaged them away. With each push my teenage self faded from the memory. When the fissures cleared, Dad stood alone in the cold, dark room that was lit only by sunlight seeping through a window in the hall. He choked back tears as he looked at a picture on the wall.

It was a photo of him and me as a little girl. I was standing on a bench in front of a grand piano so that I stood a couple inches taller than he did. My head was tilted over his. He had a big arm wrapped around my hips. We both had silly smiles on our faces. Behind us was an empty concert hall.

Dad slid down to the floor and leaned against the wall, clutching the picture close to his chest. Out of the darkness of the room Mason's voice echoed. It was cool and deep and it wrapped around the room. Shadows cast their dark fingers across my father's body.

"Please, try," said Mason.

Dad lifted his chin from his chest, and stared at Mason with puffy eyes. "I'm not ready to do what you're asking of me."

"Charles, I'm dedicated to making things right and helping you get better."

"Then why do I feel like some pawn in your quest to make up for whatever mistakes you made in the past."

"I mean to lead you out," Mason replied. "There's a world of people out there who need you."

My dad let out a heavy sigh. "Fine," he said. He stood up and moved to a stereo on a nearby shelf and hit the play button. Soft piano music filled the room. He opened the curtains and the shadows fell away. Out of the stereo his voice sang over the music.

> *One time we are here, one time to get it right*
> *A chance to rule the world or lie in rags*
> *To explore its depths or run away, terrified*
> *Heartache, heartbreak, all alone*
> *Love, laughter, build a home*
> *One time to get it right*
> *all the time to get it wrong*
> *Remember, Remember, Remember*
> *Where I am is where you'll be*
> *Be me, be you, be alive*
> *Or lose yourself in the darkness and die*

CHAPTER THIRTY-ONE

I awoke hours later. My head was pounding and my stomach growled. I couldn't remember the last time I had eaten. I spent the next hour eating dry toast, cleaning up the puddle of wine, and taking care of myself.

What waited for me at the office? What was real and what was a dream, a hallucination, a splintering of my brain? I wanted to fill my mind with an absence. A cold empty place to retreat and to forget. It was my profession to tell others that the road to peace was a long, daily slog. There was no instant gratification. Not a sustainable one at least.

And here I was with the sands of time passing through my fingers searching for a quick release. Witnessing Mason's memory of my father opened up a sick curiosity, and it was the only thing motivating me to finish.

But that curiosity was mingled with a sickening dread about the answer that might follow. As these thoughts swirled through my head I finished the walk to my building and ascended the stairs to the clinic. For the first time all week I was the first to arrive. I flicked on all of the lights and walked back to the examination room. Under the track lights PTER loomed like a sleeping giant. It hissed at me as the cleaning cycle finished. Its great folding doors yawned open. A lightning flash of pain split through the top of my nose and between my eyebrows.

Inside my compartment was a black pit without a bottom. When I leaned out over its edge, my feet slipped and my body plunged into the dark. My hands grabbed futilely at the edges of the platform but they, too, slipped on the freshly cleaned surface. The lights of the exam room faded away to nothing.

* * *

"What's wrong with it now?" It was Rhodes' voice. He knelt next to me and gave me a half smile. I turned back towards the void where my eyes had been glued a moment earlier and saw nothing but the drain pipe.

"It's fine," I finally said.

"You look like you've seen a ghost," he said.

"Promise me you won't go into Mason's head. I can't lose you, too," I said.

"Lose me, too?"

"There was a dream…" I trailed off. "Just-"

"Just what?"

"Eric left me last night," I blurted out.

"Oh, Cat." While we were both kneeling he wrapped his arms around me and squeezed. I leaned my head on his shoulder.

"We don't have to keep doing this, you know. Losing your husband isn't worth the money."

"It's not about the money anymore. Rhodes, I saw my father in Mason's memories. I think Mason is the doctor who looked after him just before he died. There are so many unanswered questions inches away. I can't squander this opportunity. There's a real chance to give both Mason and me peace if I can solve this."

Rhodes' body stiffened and stopped hugging me. He looked me in the eyes. His expression was difficult to decipher. After a couple seconds, he stood up. "Let's end this today," he said. "Whatever it takes. I want it done as much as you. I hate seeing you like this."

I got to my own feet. "Deal," I said, unsure how we'd actually solve our mystery.

The rest of the morning was a mindless shuffling of papers and emails as we waited for Suzy to arrive with Mason. When they did, we wasted no time getting started. The room-temperature water enveloped my body and drowned out my thoughts as the walls lit up with images projected from Mason's brain.

Rhodes landed me inside the castle walls. The soldiers marched to their posts, oblivious to my presence. I skulked in the shadows close to the outer wall to avoid being seen. The inner courtyard floor was caked in mud and debris. Men dragged the bodies of the dead to an immense funeral pyre at the center of the courtyard. It was a macabre pile of burning flesh, bone and steel. I averted my gaze, but the toxic smell of sulphur, ash and smoke couldn't be ignored.

The great tower at the back of the courtyard spiralled up into the clouds, the peak impossible to see from my vantage point at its base. There appeared to be a single entry point: a large gate that would open every thirty seconds, letting out a new battalion of armoured knights. Otherwise, the walls of the tower were nothing but large polished stone stacked on top of one another and sealed with cement.

I angled deep into the back of the courtyard where fewer soldiers milled around. There was at least a hundred meter gap between the shadows where I hid by the wall and the side of the tower. I'd be completely exposed if I ran across. There were no hiding spots along the route to the gate. God knows what waited for me in the tower.

"Rhodes, it's impossible for me to get to his memories," I said, not expecting to get a response.

"I landed you practically on top of it. What's wrong?"

"Uhhh, hard to explain. I really need to inject him with more SLUMB-Rx to make this work."

"You know we can't do that."

"They'll tear me to shreds."

"It isn't real Cat. I keep trying to tell you that."

"Perception is reality. You try navigating through here." A soldier halfway across the courtyard cocked his head in my direction. He marched his immense eight-foot tall frame towards the wall.

"My, god, Rhodes, he heard me. He's coming this way."

The soldier gained speed. He was only twenty five meters out.

"What should I do!" Rhodes yelled.

The soldier's movements were lightning fast. He unsheathed a six-foot long sword.

"YOU!" bellowed the soldier.

"Who was that?" Rhodes asked.

The soldier heaved the sword over his head and leapt into the air. The blade slashed down.

"RHODES!" I screamed. I shut my eyes tight. After a couple seconds of nothing, I opened my eyes. The tip of the soldier's sword was inches from my forehead. Instinctively, I rolled to the right and came up on to my knees. His blade plunged deep into the earth, sinking an inch per second. Time almost stood still.

"Cat, whatever you have to do, do it now!" shouted Rhodes in my ears. I leapt to my feet and ran for the gate to the tower. Every few feet I ran, more soldiers noticed me, their heads wheeling slowly in my direction. Their movements were delayed but quickly gathered speed. Whatever temporary injection of SLUMB-Rx Rhodes had given Mason was dissipating. I pushed my limbs as hard as they could, swishing through every ounce of water in my PTER compartment. Tiny air pockets formed in the top of the deprivation chamber from the current. With each push, I plunged deeper into the lattice as dream merged with reality.

The gate was beginning to close. The gap had shrunk to five feet. When I was no more than a couple of yards away I dove the remaining distance. My torso plunged into darkness. An armoured hand wrapped around my ankle. My bones splintered under its crushing grip. I let out an agonizing moan. My free foot lashed out and connected with the face hiding behind the helmet. He released his grip. I pulled my legs inside the gate as it slid down and shut.

Large lights flickered on overhead. They were ancient and monstrous fixtures with broad metal covers and wire cages covering the bulbs. Two rows of three lights each dotted the ceiling. Small blue tiles covered the walls and extended down to a different, larger tile design on the floor.

I pushed up to a standing position. The pain in my ankle was gone. At the center of the room was a large console covered in chrome buttons. From the console a series of thick wires ran to a computer system that spanned the rear wall. On either side of the console were two glass chambers. The drawing that Mason showed Nirali floated through my memory. I was looking at the original incarnation of PTER.

The sound of a fist thudding against a heavy slab of iron rang out behind me. The field of vision turned. The vast wooden gate was gone. In its stead was an iron industrial door, a small, plexi-glass window at its top. The point of view through the glass showed a man dressed in white. He had black skin and short cropped hair.

A hand reached out and pushed down on the lever, which controlled the door from the inside.

"Dr. Dietrich," said the man. "I have your patient here." The man stepped aside and revealed Dad.

CHAPTER THIRTY-TWO

Dad's hair was long and wavy. His face and neck were covered in stubble. He took Mason's extended hand willingly, but his eyes darted around the room.

"I'm not sure-" He tried to pull his hand from Mason's grip. Mason's fingers firmed around the handshake.

"Charles, I know it looks intimidating. I completely understand your hesitation. But you've come this far. At least let me show you what I've built and explain how it works."

The man with the cropped hair made his way to the computer station and sat down. He rattled away on the keys until the monitors came to life. The wall glowed with output images of EKG's, MRI's, and a host of other vital statistics. They sat idle, waiting to be fed.

"You've already met Bruce," said Mason. "He will be providing technical support and keeping an eye on us." Mason led Dad to PTER and outlined all of its specifications. Dad tried to keep up with his explanation but from his blank stare it was clearly going over his head. *Was this how my patients felt? Intimidated by technical speak into undressing their memories?*

My PTER construct was significantly more advanced than the original model. The major difference was the orientation of the patient compartments. These lay flat like large glass bathtubs. Instead of acusensory suits there were dozens of small electrode patches. Beside the machine were two huge oxygen tanks that connected into the respirator system. The computers were large and cumbersome but otherwise comparable.

As I stared at the device, I couldn't shake the familiarity of this room, with its institutional color scheme, sterile smell, and aged lighting.

"Dr. Dietrich, do you promise this will work? I want to believe everything you've told me but-"

"I promise Charles," Mason interrupted. "I've spent years working to this point. You're not my first patient."

"I-I don't want to die," said Dad. The man I remember being a tall, strong and confident performer looked shrunken, pale and weak. From Mason's perspective, Dad was just another blubbering patient.

"The machine is harmless and well-monitored. Like I said Bruce here-"

"That's not what I meant," Dad said. "My memories, they eat away at me. I'm afraid of what I might do to myself to make them stop."

Mason squeezed Dad's shoulder. "You can hear it in your music, Charles, see it in your performances. You yearn for a normal life. For peace. I wanted the same thing and built this machine to give it to me. It helped me find peace with my own trauma. I can do the same for you."

Dad's eyes were bright and hopeful as all the right words poured from Mason's mouth. "Okay," he said, "let's do this."

Mason directed Dad to undress; Bruce placed the electrodes over his naked body. Dad covered himself up with his hands in embarrassment. Bruce helped Dad up a couple steps and into the sensory deprivation chamber. He placed what looked like a scuba respirator in Dad's mouth and turned on the oxygen tank.

"Breathe deep," said Mason. "It'll give you a slight high that will help keep you calm."

Dad nodded and Mason turned from him, undressed himself and applied his own electrodes to his body. Bruce helped him with a few on his back, and then Mason laid himself in his capsule. He wedged a respirator into his own mouth, then Bruce turned on the flow of oxygen.

Mason raised his hand and gave a thumbs-up to Bruce. A few seconds later the sound of metal scraping on metal filled the room. Slats extended from inside the console, and above Mason's head. They slowly traveled alongside the compartment until it was completely shrouded in darkness. Cold water trickled in from a spout near his feet and rose an inch every ten seconds. After a minute, Mason's breathing became more rapid as the claustrophobic effect of PTER took hold. After three minutes the water had completely filled the tank, and I felt his body become weightless. Would I finally see the memory that had stolen my father from me?

*   *   *

I was enveloped in an obsidian blanket where neither light nor dark could breathe. Yet I stood illuminated in a spotlight— an actress in a black box theater. My body floated effortlessly through the vacuum. I was in the starless dark of a broken lattice. A mind gone blank. The silence, perfectly absolute, was my prison cell.

"HELP!" I screamed. My voice fell flat against the hollows. Needle-like pains ran through my chest. My skin was drenched in sweat.

How do I escape? I thrust myself straight ahead, drifting instead of walking, hoping if I pressed on in one direction I'd eventually reach an exit. But the black curtain, like the line of the horizon, was endless. Maybe I would be lucky enough to fall off the edge of my world.

"LET ME OUT!" I screamed. The words died an inch from my mouth. THRUMP! The sound of a heartbeat thundered through the space. The walls shuddered. THRUMP, THRUMP. Each wave was stronger than the last. The walls of PTER were compressing. The blackness beat against my body like a drum as my heart raced in my chest. I tried to expand my diaphragm, but it was impossible under the weight of the intensifying vibrations. With each beat of the walls my feet and knees were pressed deeper into my chest. Against my will, I curled up into the foetal position.

"Help…" I tried to scream. My bones pressed against my stretching skin. They were about to snap. *It waits for you in the holes of the earth, Cat.* My own voice echoed through the room. *Don't go down there.* But it was the only way. I let my body sink into the abyss. Instantly, hundreds of arms the color of coal reached out of the darkness and ensnared my wrists and ankles. They pulled me down and away from the crushing walls. More hands inched their way up my body. They crawled in and out of my clothes and left a cold emptiness behind.

Their strength was omnipotent. I couldn't keep them away from my face. A set of fingers latched onto my bottom teeth; another grabbed my top teeth to pry open my clenched jaw. Out of the gloom, floated my father's lifeless body. It hovered inches over my own. He opened his eyes to reveal milky, dead irises. His mouth yawned wide and then inhaled. As he sucked the last breath from my body, his eyes came to life.

*   *   *

Mason's hands trembled as they wrapped around the edge of his tank. Once he was upright he pulled the respirator from his mouth. It fell from his hand and clanged heavily against the tile floor. The sound echoed off the walls. He yanked carelessly, desperately at the mass of cords. His skin stretched away from his body before the electrodes came free. A couple snapped from their cords and remained attached.

He crawled out of the capsule and picked up a towel that was hanging on a stainless steel rack beside PTER.

Bruce clomped over to Mason and surveyed the broken sensors. "You need to be more careful Dr-"

"Shut up!" groaned Mason. He stumbled to his clothes on a nearby bench and put them on. His fingers fumbled with each button. He stopped twice to steady himself. When he was finally dressed he sat on the bench and put his face in his hands.

Eventually, he lifted his head and looked with glassy eyes as Bruce guided Dad out of his compartment, helped him towel off, and then got him into his clothes. Dad was silent the whole time.

Finally, Mason got up from his seat. "Charles-" he started.

"Get away from me!" Dad cried as he retreated to the opposite wall. His skin was pale and clammy. He looked like he had seen a ghost. *How did I not witness the memory? What happened while I was in there?* Mason stopped in his tracks.

"Why did you have to resurrect what I'd been burying so deep?"

"I-" said Mason before stopping. He bent over and put his hands on his knees.

"What were you expecting to see?" yelled Dad.

"Not that. Anything but that. You don't understand…" Mason trailed off.

Dad's entire body was quaking in fear. A gate in his head had been opened. That was the day the demons spilled out. "Now you see my guilt," Dad said through quivering lips.

Mason staggered over to Bruce's desk and opened a drawer. Lying there was a prescription pad. He pulled it out and scribbled clomipramine 3X and then his signature underneath.

"NOOOO!" I screamed, "Mason don't!"

"Charles, take this," he muttered.

"All this, and it ends in you giving me pills. You're a goddamn fraud!" Dad grabbed Mason's shirt and shook him. His words were laced with anger, but the whites of his eyes gave away his terror. Dad ripped the prescription from Mason's hand and then pushed him away. Mason staggered into PTER. Dad turned and walked to the door, jammed down the lever, and stepped outside.

Mason fell to his knees and wept.

CHAPTER THIRTY-THREE

Instead of emerging into the all-consuming blackness of my PTER compartment, I stepped back out of a memory tunnel and onto the platform that looked out over the battlefield that substituted for Mason's lattice.

The very thing I staked my life's work on, the machine I had built from nothing more than the sketches of an obscure medical journal, was responsible for destroying the last good parts of my father's mind. I felt wretched for perpetuating a practice that mentally crippled my own father.

How in good conscience could I ever continue with my clinic? The weight of wasting more than a decade of my life burning other people's trauma into my mind was an anvil around my waist. I fell to my knees and looked out onto the battlefield. The war raged on. Opposite me, the mountain continued to pour down on Mason's fortress. The black sky above the scarlet clouds was dotted in stars.

Blood boiled in my veins and surged through my body. My fists lifted above my head. A scream bellowed out of my lungs as every ounce of frustration erupted from my body. I punched the platform until my fists were bloody.

A thunderclap deafened me. I raised my eyes to the fortress. Pitch-black lightning bolts split the sky and struck the tower's peak.

Massive cracks formed across the castle walls and up the tower. The spire buckled and its huge stones splintered as it crumbled under its own weight. A cry of despair erupted from the soldiers. The tower swayed over the battlefield and rained huge stones onto the valley floor. Man, horse and hound tried to escape the devastation as others were crushed. Running was futile. Everything was swept up in the devastation. Its full weight collided with the ground.

The earth trembled and shook.

Without the wall to hold back the avalanche, the boulders from the mountain rolled free. The rock grew upon itself and became an avalanche. The avalanche picked up speed until it was a wall of stone and dust traveling at hundreds of miles an hour. I stood up from the platform and let it strike me with all its might.

*   *   *

PTER's door opened before all the water had drained out. The vital monitors in the room screamed. My lungs sucked in air from the respirator greedily as hyperventilation took over. Rhodes rushed over to my platform and unhooked me as quickly as he could. My body collapsed into his arms; my limbs paralyzed with shock. He fell down to his knees trying to support my weight.

Lydia's heels clacked quickly down the hallway tiles. Water had spilled out onto the floor. She ran into the room, slipped and landed hard on her ass. "This is a safety hazard. I could have killed myself," she whined.

"Mrs. Qiao, shut it!" yelled Rhodes. He glared at her, then turned back towards me. All I could do was follow their movements around the room. My own body wasn't functional. Slowly, Lydia got back to her feet and came over. She rubbed her elbow.

Hovering over me, she said: "What happened?"

"I have no idea," said Rhodes. His eyes suggested otherwise.

"Isn't it your job to know?"

Rhodes gave her a dirty look. She pursed her lips petulantly.

"It's my job to keep her and the patient safe," Rhodes said.

"Looks like you're not doing a very good job of that either." Lydia crossed her arms.

I couldn't move or speak and had to passively absorb their conversation.

"Listen you ice queen, can't you see something is wrong." That shut her up. Rhodes looked into my eyes. "Can you hear me Cat?" he asked.

I blinked to confirm.

"And can you feel your limbs?" he asked.

I blinked again.

"You're likely in shock," Rhodes turned to Lydia. "Whatever memory she saw in there today, it must have been bad. Real bad."

"I thought she was conditioned for this kind of thing," said Lydia.

"She is, but our *friend* over there is in a league of his own."

Despair washed over Lydia's face as she awoke to the danger she had exposed me to. It was at that moment that Mason entered my view. He towered over me as I huddled on the floor. Without a word he passed his eyes through each one of us. His irises were the color of a dead body floating to the surface of a lake after the winter ice melt. But a cold lucidity had returned. They told me that our time together was far from over.

CHAPTER THIRTY-FOUR

Mason emerged from the change room dressed in his own clothes. Skin that was loose and pale had regained its color. His movements were swift, as if his mind and body had reconnected with one another. He flexed his hands open and closed. He lifted me up off my feet by the front of my suit. His eyes blazed with madness and fury.

"Hey!" yelled Rhodes. He grabbed at Mason. Mason smashed his fist into Rhodes face. There was a sickening snap as the bones in his nose shattered. Blood splattered across his mouth and cheeks as he tumbled on to the floor.

Lydia crawled to the corner of the room and pressed herself against the cupboards.

"I WANT IT BACK, CATARINA!" he bellowed.

I couldn't speak. What did he want? He shook me violently.

"I built my walls to keep people like you and the rest of the world out." Spit flew out of his mouth and hit me in the face with each word. "You're going to put them back, and then you're going to stop looking for answers to your own problems in my head."

"I-I-I," was all I could manage.

"Spit it out," he yelled with another shake.

"I don't know how?"

He tossed me on to the ground. Pain shot through my wrists as I caught myself awkwardly on the wet floor.

"You have until tomorrow morning to figure it out," he said.

"What if I can't?"

"I'm going to give you an incentive." He left and a moment later the clinic door slammed. It was followed by the sound of shattering glass. Debbie shrieked. Lydia and I stared at each other in stunned silence. Rhodes groaned on the floor next to me.

Lydia finally spoke. "I'm calling the police."

"And tell them what?" I said.

"He assaulted your technician."

"I'm fine," blubbered Rhodes. "Ugh, what did you do, Cat?" he said.

"What did I do? What did you do?!" I replied.

"I did what you couldn't."

"What do you mean, what I couldn't?"

Rhodes sat up and touched his nose gingerly. "That bastard destroyed my nose."

"What did you do?" I pressed.

"A targeted extirpation."

"No... No, please no." I looked at my research notebook lying open on Rhodes desk. He had put our little theory to the test and excised a memory from the distant past. It was like tearing a great red cedar, roots and all from the earth and watching the rest of Mason's world fall into the giant hole left in his being.

"I had to. We had to be rid of him. Can't you see how bad everything has gotten this week? It's not worth it. I'll take a broken nose for that man to be out of our lives."

"You heard what he said. This isn't over, Rhodes." What did he mean by an incentive?

"We must call the police," Lydia said.

"Let's think about this for a few minutes before we do anything," I said. "If we get the police involved this is no good for any of us. It would be terrible for the city's reputation. The newspapers would crucify us."

"Fine," said Lydia.

I quickly changed out of my suit and went back to help Rhodes. "You need to get to a hospital," I told him.

"And tell them what?"

"Just say you got mugged and didn't get a good look at the guy."

The bleeding had slowed and was starting to dry and cake to his chin. I found a cloth and ran it under some hot water to clean him up.

"I'll take care of it," said Rhodes. He trudged to the bathroom.

Lydia continued to sit there uselessly. I held out my hand to help her to her feet. She stood on her own. Her legs were shaking. "I'm going home," she said.

"That'd be good," I replied. I walked her to the front door. Debbie was trying to sweep up a pile of broken glass. She looked at me with eyes full of fear.

"Did he hurt you?" I asked.

"No, he just walked right past me and slammed our door so hard the glass blew out. Suzy ran after him. What does this mean, Dr. Chambers?" Debbie glanced at Lydia.

"It means we're getting close. We start back same as always tomorrow." While we spoke Lydia threw on her coat, put her bag over her shoulder and walked out the front door. A minute later Rhodes walked through the waiting room. He had a wad of toilet paper under his nose. He was down the elevator before I could think of anything to say.

"What happened to him?" said Debbie.

"Same thing as the door."

We spent the next thirty minutes cleaning up the waiting area and rigging up a sheet of plastic over the window. Debbie made some calls, but no one was available to fix it until next week. When we were all done, I let her go.

Once I was satisfied we had done our best cleaning up, I slid on my coat and locked the clinic door, not that it mattered. I decided to take my usual route down the stairs. Inside the stairwell was more broken glass. A few larger chunks were rimmed with blood. The stairwell door closed behind me. It occurred to me that Mason could be in here with me. I turned to go back to the elevator when I noticed writing carved into the paint of the stairwell door.

> *I know what you love*
> *It is not safe*
> *Fix me*

CHAPTER THIRTY-FIVE

I ripped through my purse for my phone. My hands shook. I punched in Eric's cell number, making several mistakes before I finally got it right.

The call wouldn't go through. I pulled the phone from my ear and looked at its screen. No signal. My legs coursed with adrenaline as I sprinted down the stairs two at a time. I burst into the lobby and out into the street and redialled Eric's number.

"What the hell do you want, Cat?" he answered.

"Where are you?"

"I'm at home getting some of my things. Why?"

"You need to leave right now."

"This is as much my house as yours, so just back off."

"No, you don't understand."

"I understand just fi-"

There was a knock at the front door, heavy enough for me to hear through the phone. Eric grunted, "just a sec."

"Eric NO! Don't answer it." But he was gone.

I heard the front door creak open.

"Can I help you?"

A second later there was a loud thud as something hit the floor. Largo exploded into a fit of barking, then yelped and went quiet.

Oh, my god! Oh, my god.

"Almost, Catarina," said Mason's deep voice into the phone. "I'll hold onto them for now. Time for you to get to work."

"You bastard! Let them go. They've got nothing to do with this!"

"THEY HAVE EVERYTHING TO DO WITH IT!"

"I'm calling the police, Mason," I said. Any fallout to the project ceased to matter.

"And I have a steel blade pressed against your husband's jugular. Whatever happens to them is on you. You have until nine AM tomorrow morning. No police or I won't even give you that." He hung up.

My knees buckled and I slumped next to the wall of my building. People shuffled by but said nothing. After several minutes I regained my composure. *What in god's name are you doing sitting here on your ass, Cat? Do something!*

I jumped to my feet, wiped my nose and ran for home. I was nearly clipped by more than one car as I sprinted through traffic. I was home in less than twenty minutes. It was too late. The apartment was empty, and there was no sign of anyone nearby. The only evidence anything had happened were a few drops of blood by the front door. Where could they have gone? I ran back down to the street.

I stopped a woman who was walking by with her dog. "Have you seen two men and a dog come by here recently? One of them may have been hurt. Maybe they got into a car?"

"I only just came by here." She stared at my face. "Is everything okay? Can I call someone for you?"

"No I-" What was I? "I'm just late for something important." A thought crossed my mind: Eric's car. I circled around the building to the parking lot. The BMW was gone. They could be anywhere by now.

I staggered back up to our condo, locked the front door and leaned against kitchen island to think. My mind replayed the mountain crashing through the fortress in Mason's lattice he had worked so hard to defend. I could barely explain what the targeted extirpation Rhodes executed had done to Mason's brain and even less on how to reverse the damage. Frying an ancient memory with such influential links to every part of your personality left you with god-knows-what for a human shell afterward. Every thread connecting him together may have unraveled. Did we create a monster?

My head was spinning. Searching for Mason and trying to rescue my family was futile. I couldn't call the police. I had to figure out how to fix him. My only hope was that there was a hole in the extirpation theory. Could we be sure that something deleted from the brain is actually gone? It's not clear if the traumatic memory can truly disappear. It could simply spread its poison around to other places. But like the bricks of a torn-down house, the materials remain. Could his memory be rebuilt? If so, how?

All I knew was that evil was gushing out of Mason's mind and infecting whatever good parts were left. I had to stop it before he hurt Eric or my little Largo.

I thumbed through papers I'd left out on my writing desk. In the middle of the stack was a mock-up of how I expected the next year to play out with the project, this project that Mason had thrown in to a tailspin. A wave of nausea washed over me. My jaw clamped down to help the episode pass.

Staring back at me from one of the shelves of my desk was my PhD thesis. I yanked it out and sat down. The document was nothing short of epic. Three hundred plus pages of academic surveys, theoretical models, data analysis and results. At the back was an index. I flipped through it for some kind of clue. It yielded nothing promising.

Just ahead of the index was the bibliography. A nervous energy swept over me. I quickly went to the D's. One third of the way down the page was his name: Dietrich. I had cited three different papers. It was the third that sounded the most promising: Ignite - A study of the medial temporal lobe and memory reconstruction.

One perk from my university I hadn't lost was full-time access to the library archives. They included all of the major academic journals and plenty of the more obscure publications. I typed in Mason Dietrich and the paper's title into my laptop and clicked 'search.'

It was the first item on the list. I printed the document. The paper was one of the most complicated forty pages of text I had ever read. These papers were hard enough to pierce on my best day. I settled into my seat and took the printed pages into my hands. *The medial temporal lobe houses the bulk of the brain's memory functions* the paper started. *A study of cancer patient survivors with tumours on the medial lobe demonstrate impaired memory function post surgical removal. A model of electromagnetic brain activity shows that memories can be reignited via non-invasive exploratory restitution techniques to restore full recall.*

The rest of the paper was a sea of equations and jargon I used to be able to understand with ease. My mind kept drifting to images of Mason tying-up Eric and jamming him and Largo into the back of the BMW. Sticky sweat clung to my body. I wandered into the bedroom with Mason's paper and put on a fresh pair of yoga pants and a gray sweatshirt.

Finally I hit a point in the paper with some promise. *Igniting a suppressed memory in the medial lobe requires mapping out the location the memory ought to be via interpolation between adjacent memories. Adjacency is not defined by the passage of time. Neural connectivity is secured via shared linkages between like items. The memory of a car accident is not recalled by going to the memories that immediately preceded or followed the event. The traumatic memory is remembered by getting back in a vehicle. Groups of neurons ignite when they follow patterns that mimic the original experience. To rebuild forgotten memories for brain cancer survivors, the therapist must work with the patient to retrieve these patterns.*

The passage was littered in shades of PTER. Obviously the technology must have been Mason putting his paper into practice. I glanced at the Yogi Berra quote pasted inside my desk.

But dad never suffered from brain cancer. Something else was troubling him. And from my last session with Mason, I guessed that same something now haunted Mason. How then can you ignite a memory when it was never your own to begin with? What patterns are there to follow?

It was six in the evening, my head was pounding, and I wasn't getting anywhere. All I could do was worry. How do I figure this out? Who in the world could help?

I wandered around my condo, each step and creak of the floorboards a reminder of how quiet it was. The fireplace mantle was littered in cruel little photographic reminders of everything that was and all that was not to be. My eyes were drawn to the important men in my life: my dad, my husband... all of them had left me. Had I driven them away? Had they driven me away? I reached back into my own memories of my childhood and pulled up blanks. Anytime I looked at Dad's face, I felt an emptiness longing to be filled. But I couldn't recall anything but pain. I was like a jack-o-lantern, all cruel image on the outside but no substance at the center.

There was one other familiar face on the mantle, and the best hope I had. I picked up the phone and dialled a number etched in my memory.

CHAPTER THIRTY-SIX

After three rings she picked up. Her voice sounded tired and wary. "Hello," she said.

"Mom, it's Catarina."

"Who?"... and we picked up right where we left off. For Mom, Dad's death had turned her mental health into a car with no brakes, skidding towards a cliff. Time was severing the brake cable. With each passing year, she accelerated to madness. But Mom was still in there if you dug hard enough.

"Your daughter," I said.

"Oh Catty, you never call."

"I'm calling now. Can I come see you?"

"Oh, I don't know. I have nothing prepared, nothing to put out. I wish you had given me more notice. It's not right, Catty, barging in on someone like that."

"Mom, don't worry, I already have something." It was a lie, but she'd forget by the time I got there. We had done this dance enough times in the past to know that putting something out didn't matter. It was hard to speak constructively with Mom, but she still had her moments of brilliance. *I was hoping one of those would happen tonight.*

"Oh Cat…" she fretted.

"I'll be there in an hour, Mom." She lived across town in a crappy part of Richmond. Her apartment building was a dive, but the rent was cheap for Vancouver. There was no time to waste. A cab drive filled me with anxiety, but every other method would be too slow.

I rang a taxi and waited for it on the street outside my building. The sun was setting over Vancouver harbour, drenching the water and mountains in an orange glow. For everything this city put me through, it was still beautiful. Mountains on one side, the ocean on the other, comfortable climate year-round. Aside from the rain, it was the closest thing to tropical one could find in Canada.

Early in his career Dad used to drive all over the country, spending long hours on the prairie highways. I wondered what he thought about in those solitary moments. He found Mom in Winnipeg at a show during one of the city's negative forty degree winter nights. She was only nineteen and all too eager to follow Dad, a fact she reminded me of whenever she had the chance. After Nan and Gramp passed away she never returned to Winnipeg.

My cab finally pulled up to the street corner and shook me out of my daydream. I got in. It had the big soft seats of an old Lincoln and the nostalgic odour of leather and stale cigarettes. It was my kind of cab.

"1180 Granville Avenue in Richmond, please," I said. The cabbie nodded, punched the address into his GPS and started driving. My palms were sweating and butterflies flew through my stomach. I stared out the window at the passing buildings as we wound our way out of Gastown and emerged into sunlight blazing off the glass condo jungle that had become the Vancouver skyline. When the light hit my eyes, it flared up a sharp pain across my forehead.

I kept my head down as we wound our way onto the bridge over Granville Island and hit the Ninety-Nine south to Richmond. The drive to Mom's was thirty minutes door-to-door on a good day. Because I was catching the tail end of rush hour, it would take closer to forty-five.

The traffic started to let up once we passed Forty-first avenue. The cab picked up speed and I sank lower into my seat. The driver hadn't said a word since I got in. It wasn't unusual to get a cabbie who wasn't chatty, but this guy was mute. His head skirted close to the roof of the car. He was thin and had long, dark greasy hair that passed his shoulders.

My intestines knotted. *It couldn't be him.* I dug frantically through my purse for my phone to see what number I had dialled. My hands were so sweaty that when I did finally pull it out, it flew out of my hand and under the driver seat.

I swore under my breath. I didn't dare lean over and try to fish out my phone. That's all it would take for me to have a knife stabbed in my back. Instead, I poked around the floor with my foot till I found it and slid it back to my seat. As I reached down to grab it, I bumped my head against his seat. Not a word.

I scrolled through my call list. The last number I dialled was my mother. *The last number... but how did...*

"You can let me out here," I squeaked. The car didn't slow or veer off course.

"Excuse me. I'd like to get out. Now."

Still nothing. His hand went up to the GPS and clicked it off, followed by the fare meter.

"Where I am is where you'll be," he said. The locks snapped down into the doors. The car accelerated. Mason kept his eyes fixed on the road. I gripped the seat and the handle above the window. He wove between each car, and sped down the busy four-lane street at over a hundred kilometers an hour. We blew through a red light. I watched in horror as the headlights of a delivery truck skirted feet from my window. At 140 kilometers an hour, we still hadn't crashed.

The car moved into oncoming traffic. As cars swerved, accidents piled up in our wake.

He took his hands from the wheel and turned to face me. "You stole everything from me!" Before I could reply, bright headlights filled my view, and then... impact. The world moved in slow motion. The frame of the car buckled and crumpled as my body lifted from my seat. The tractor trailer we hit rolled over the car. Mason's body and the dashboard hit me like a tidal wave of blood and steel.

After the initial impact, the blow-back sent me, but not my legs, hurling through the rear window. I was momentarily airborne before I landed like a butchered pig on the grass next to the crash. Warm blood trickled down my face as I lay dying.

CHAPTER THIRTY-SEVEN

"Miss." A man's voice.

"Miss." It was unfamiliar.

"Miss!" He had a foreign accent.

"HEY!" My eyes filled with the glow of street lights. My face was pressed up against a pane of glass. I pulled away and turned to the sound.

"Sweet dreams, yes?" the man with the Chinese accent said. "We're 'ere, $32.50."

"I…" I didn't know what to say. My hands ran up and down my legs. Rifling through my purse, I found my wallet and pulled out a pair of twenty dollar bills. Without checking where I was I handed them to him and jumped out of the cab.

The graffiti on the side of my mother's building was unmistakable. The ten-by-ten foot mural was remarkable because the artist's talent was wasted on an unremarkable building. It was the face of an old man and woman staring into each other's eyes. Set back from each were four younger versions of themselves, all the way back to childhood. But instead of pupils each person's eyes contained an hourglass. The man's eyes had the sand running out of the top, while the woman's eyes showed sand collecting in the bottom.

Outside the front door was an older woman taking a drag off a cigarette. She gave me a nod as I approached. Mom. She blew out a plume of smoke and spoke in a hoarse voice. "Took you long enough. Smoke?" She held up a fresh cigarette. "You look like you could use it."

"Mom, what are you doing out here? You know I don't smoke," I replied.

"Don't play dumb with me. Sure you do. Well at least you did. Here." She dangled the cigarette in my face. This wasn't a negotiation. *What could it hurt?* I took the cigarette in my fingers while she produced a lighter. With a flick, she lit the end of my cigarette. Truth was, I'd smoked plenty before I met Eric.

"You didn't bring anything," said Mom.

"I was hoping you wouldn't notice. Listen, I need your help."

She stared off into the night sky. Her red hair had lost its fullness. Her skin was worn out from years of smoking. She looked older than she was. Her voice had taken the brunt of the damage. On her sweatshirt a white wolf walked across a patch of snow. She was always on the hunt for *fashionable* thrift store bargains.

But her eyes sparkled. Even at dusk, their emerald green couldn't be missed, like staring into a gemstone. But the smile I had cherished as a child was lost the day Dad died.

"I guess you want to tell me what's wrong," she said.

I let out a sigh, "I'm a mentally ill psychiatrist trying to help people put their lives back in order and its cost me everything."

"So you admit it then. I knew this day would come. Your profession is nothing but a bunch of pill-pushing, gaslighting frauds. I wish you'd never gone down that road."

"Maybe you're right, but it doesn't matter anymore. One of my patients kidnapped Eric and Largo."

Mom's harshness evaporated. "Oh, god, Catarina, I'm so sorry. Have you called the police?"

I proceeded to recount my week in as much detail as I could. She snapped her focus on me when I mentioned Mason's memories of Dad and his treatment.

"You found that son of a bitch," she said when I finished. She flicked her finished cigarette on the ground. Mine had blown itself out.

"Mom, I need to know what he saw in Dad's head. What was Dad fighting all those years?"

"Let's go inside," she said. "I'll tell you everything I know."

* * *

The stairs to the front door were a patchwork of cement repairs. The buzzer board was an old-fashioned collage of label maker names. Most of them were yellowed with age. No new tenants here. That was co-op housing for you. The button on my mom's was particularly worn down. She'd been living at the apartment for almost twenty years, ever since the bank foreclosed on our house. That was the beginning of a long and drawn-out bankruptcy for mom.

I was at university when most of this was happening, but I had gotten at least one panicked phone call a week. I got involved when the creditors tried to take the rights to the royalties from Dad's music, not to mention the audacity to suggest they auction off all his unrecorded work. Bunch of vultures. We spent a year in and out of courtrooms fighting while my student loans piled up. The deterioration in my mother's mental health and her eventual inability to continue working ultimately won us the case. It was a hollow victory.

Mom finally found her keys buried in her purse and unlocked the door. We wound our way up the three flights of stairs to her apartment. The hallway was hot and thick with the aroma of ethnic cooking. A heavy layer of dust on the lights made the old building extra gloomy.

Mom opened the door to her modest apartment. To my left just inside the door was the bathroom and straight ahead, a single small bedroom. To my right was her little kitchen, sizable enough to boil a pot of noodles or make toast, about all she ate these days. The tiny living room was nothing but a TV, couch and an uncomfortable arm chair reserved for guests. The apartment was covered in knitting. Most of Mom's hours passed watching daytime cable while she knit blankets, sweaters, mittens, and hats for the homeless on East Hastings.

Mom took my coat and hung it up in the small closet. It was jammed with junk that threatened to crash down when she opened the door. She took the opportunity to sift through the mess. Various items spilled out as she dug up to her armpits into the back of the closet. She eventually yanked out a long metal box.

"Your father never spoke about his past. I asked and asked but it was this great big mystery. He'd always say he didn't want to talk about it and that he wanted to just let it go. As he got sicker I tried to find more creative ways to learn about him."

She opened the box. It was full of a few pictures, song lyrics, and scraps of paper covered in music staffs and notes. A photograph was stapled to one of the pages of music and lyrics. It was of a young girl, likely no more than eight, with blond hair and a warm smile. Her cheeks were chubby and scrunched up around her green eyes. She was wearing a pink dress.

I folded back the photo and looked at the sheet music. Usually I could recognize one of my Dad's songs from a mile away. This one wasn't familiar.

"Who's the girl?" I asked.

"Your father never said anything about his family. Maybe a sister?"

"You mean I might have an aunt out there somewhere."

"Maybe."

"Why did dad never release this work?"

"There's a part of every artist's soul they're not prepared to show to the world. This was probably his."

I longed for a piano so I could play the music and hear first-hand what secrets his composition held. I read through the lyrics.

> *In hiding I found the secret to the end*
> *Your light came in when I wished it gone*
> *Out of shadows I came to bring you oblivion*
> *And forever wrapped an anchor to my neck*
>
> *You opened your heart and I took your soul*
> *Wove a wound into a gaping hole*
> *Down I plunge into a crimson tide*
> *On the sea in which I live my life*

I had to stop reading to compose myself. Dad's work was always melancholy, but this piece was tragic. Mom moved into the living room and sat on the sofa. I followed and sat beside her.

"Have you read all this?" I asked. She put her hands over her face. She pressed her fingers against her forehead, then smoothed back her hair.

"Every word a hundred times."

"What do you think?"

"I can't say specifically, but your father felt weighed down by a tremendous burden of guilt. He must have done something terrible."

"Dr. Dietrich must have gotten in Dad's head and laid it bare."

She glared at me. "Isn't that what you do everyday?"

"That's not how it's supposed to work, Mom. The point is to wipe away the effect of time and how it mutates a memory into some perverted version of the truth. Then the doctor can speak candidly with the patient about their experience and work through those feelings. It's supposed to be a way to get people off the drugs."

Her face didn't soften.

I continued. "Dr. Dietrich wasn't prepared for what he found in Dad's memories. All he could do was write Dad that goddamn prescription. He never gave Dad the opportunity to sort through all the emotions that episode brought roaring back."

Mom shifted uncomfortably on the couch.

"The man was a neurosurgeon," I said, "not a therapist, not a psychiatrist. It's like getting a dentist to fix your car engine."

"He's dead, Catarina!" Mom's eyes were full of tears. "What does any of this matter?"

"My husband isn't dead, Mom! If I don't figure this out, who knows what could happen to him?"

A shadow passed across Mom's face. She crossed her arms and sunk into the corner of the couch. "Then you better figure it out."

I closed the lid of the metal box and stood up. My knuckles were white from squeezing it so hard. Even though I knew Mom was battling mental illness, her callousness still infuriated me.

"I'm leaving and I'm taking this with me," I said. I put my shoes back on and retrieved my coat.

"Fine," she said. She stared absently into the glow of the television. I shut the door and walked back downstairs with the box in my hands, hoping that somewhere in the scraps of paper was an answer.

CHAPTER THIRTY-EIGHT

Back outside I pulled out my phone. It was on silent and I had missed a parade of calls, all from Eric's number. There were ten messages. It felt like a thousand rubber bands were wrapped around my chest as I tried to suck in breath. I hit the voicemail icon and pressed the phone to my ear.

"You have ten new messages," said the automated female voice. "To listen to unheard messages, press one." At first there was only silence on the line. Then I heard heavy breathing. After ten seconds a man's voice growled, *'I'll call back'* and then hung up.

My hands were trembling as I pressed seven on my keypad to delete the message. The next message fired up. The same silence, the same heavy breathing and then *'I'll call back'*. I cycled through each message, my guts churning over themselves with each one and seven. Every message was the same. When I finished I pulled the phone from my ear and looked at the call log. Every call was exactly five minutes apart. The last call had come in four minutes and fifty-five-

The screen lit up in my hand. Incoming call. One ring, two rings, three. I hit the answer button.

"H-hello," I stuttered.

That same heavy breathing hung on the other end of the line. He smacked his lips.

"Mason?" I said.

"I wouldn't advise ignoring my calls again." It was the articulate voice of a man awakened from a dark past.

I drummed up as much courage as I could hoping to swap fear for anger. "What do you want?" I asked.

"I want what you took from me."

"I'm working on it."

"Work harder," he barked. "I'm going to give you some more incentive. You hear that?" There was a jingle of something in the background.

I was speechless.

"DO YOU!" he shouted.

Largo's barking erupted across the line.

"Yes, I heard it" I stammered. *Oh, God no.*

"Me and Largo are best buds now. I'd hate for anything serious to happen to him," said Mason.

A moment later Largo yelped and whimpered.

"Stop! You piece of shit!" It was Eric's voice.

"No, please no," I said, "leave my poor dog out of this."

"You brought him into this. I never asked to be part of your project. You've seen too much, taken too much, and put nothing back, Dr. Chambers. I looked as deep into your mind as you looked into mine. I know what you love, what you want, and what you're running from. Don't use me."

I could practically feel his hot breath through the phone as he said those last few words.

"But… but"

"I'll be generous, my love. You have twelve hours. After that I can't make any promises."

The line went dead.

*   *   *

My body turned into jello, and I fell hard on the concrete steps. Poor Largo. Poor Eric. None of it made any sense. Mason was one step ahead of me, walking through my life, dipping into every corner as if he knew it like the back of his hand.

My hands squeezed the cold steel box. Then I was beating the metal over and over with my fist. Rhodes and his stupid extirpation had threatened everything. I had it under control, and now I had nothing. But I couldn't run anymore. Running had gotten me here… rock bottom.

Galvanized to action I called a cab. My despair transformed into a fury so strong and desperate for change that I was willing to do whatever I could to rid myself of Mason and the panic he had sowed in my life.

A long, black taxi appeared after five minutes. The interior smelled like freshly cleaned leather. The driver turned to me as I sat down. He was an Indian man with a neatly trimmed moustache. He wore a leather coat and driving gloves. His starched white shirt collar practically glowed in the dark.

"Evening, Ma'am. Where to?"

"East Pender Street please. 151." I had to get back to the office. There was no time to figure this all out myself. I called Rhodes.

After a couple rings, he answered.

"Catarina?" he said incredulously.

"Rhodes, I need you at the office. I'm on my way there now. Mason called me. It's not good. Not good at all. We have to undo what you did."

"What I did? All I did was what was best to solve the situation you put us in in the first place," he replied.

"There's no time for this. Get to the office now."

"I'm still in the waiting room at the hospital."

"Your nose can wait. Get to the office now. It's urgent."

"What could be more urgent..." he trailed off and sighed. "Fine, I'll be there in forty-five minutes."

"Make it thirty." I hung up.

"Rough day at the office eh?" asked the driver.

"You don't know the half of it," I replied. The rest of the way was spent rebuffing the driver's attempt to make small talk as his nattering invaded my attempt to sort out how to get Eric and Largo home safely. When we finally arrived, I paid the driver and stepped onto the sidewalk.

A note was taped to the door. It flapped in the wind.

The note, scrawled in pencil, simply read *11 hours*. I pulled it off and crumpled it into my hand.

"What's that?"

I spun to face Rhodes.

"Whoa, easy now," he said, "you're so jumpy."

"Oh, thank god it's just you. Look. Mason kidnapped Eric and Largo and is threatening to do something terrible to them." I shoved the crumpled note in Rhodes' face. His nose had swelled, his eyes dark-ringed. "We have eleven hours to undo the extirpation," I said.

"He did what? But how did he even know where to find them?"

I pushed into the lobby and entered the stairwell before replying. "I don't know what traces of my own memories got lost in his head, but he has them, and who knows what he'll do, who he'll hurt next if we don't figure this out."

"But he's not even here. How can we work on him-"

"He knows we have no idea what we're doing," I interrupted. "We have eleven hours to figure it out."

"It only took seven years to theorize it was even possible. We aren't miracle workers, Catarina." He jammed his hands in his pockets.

"Answers crop up in the darkest moments if you know where to look." I took the stairs to the clinic two at a time. "I'm willing to believe anything if it will get me out of this mess."

"Where do you want to start?"

"Start by telling me how you determined which memories to wipe in the first place," I said. We sat on the couch in my office.

"I had this revelation when staring at the data on his lattice," Rhodes said. "Save the memories you revisited, there was nothing connecting his memories to his present self. The entire neural recall network you or I rely on to call up past experience was severed by some kind of wall around his consciousness."

"You still haven't explained how you extirpated the memories."

"That's because I didn't. All I did was calibrate a landmark at that central point and injected it into his SLUMB-Rx drip feed. The extirpation cocktail was fed through after and burned a hole straight through the landmark. My thinking was that if I cleared that blockage his remaining memories would re-pattern themselves like a regular lattice. I thought I was being so clever." Rhodes looked pained telling me his story. He fidgeted incessantly on the couch.

"You didn't hit the wall, you hit his trauma, *the trauma*. He locked it away in a fortress. The extirpation rolled an avalanche over everything he'd bottled up. Who knows how far the trauma's disease has spread now."

"I only did what I thought was best. I mean look at you, Catarina. You've been falling apart. When I started working for you, you had so much energy. But after each patient I swear a little life got sucked out. And then he came into our lives. He's nothing but an aggressive cancer that took over the last good bits of your mind. I got arrogant because I thought you couldn't handle it. So I did what anyone would do for a person they love. I got rid of the problem. At least I thought I did."

Rhodes' words cut through me. I put my hand on his for support to steady a dizziness that washed over me. My anger evaporated. I wanted to be everything for everyone, but it only made me fall apart like a house of cards. "I'm sorry. I wanted it to work so bad. I wanted all of this to happen. To help people in a way they've never been helped before. And when there was a hint Mason had answers to my father's death. I clung to it. But I can't keep it up anymore, Rhodes. There's too much disappointment. Am I broken?"

"All the king's horses and all the king's men," said a deep voice.

Rhodes stiffened. "Who the hell was that?" Rhodes said.

I reeled back on the couch and looked around the room.

"Ten hours," said a voice. It came from my purse, "and now I know what you did… Rhodes. I may have to hurt you, too."

CHAPTER THIRTY-NINE

I must have bumped my phone and accidentally dialed Eric's stolen cell.

Rhodes bolted out of the chair. "What the hell was that? Oh, Cat. Oh, god, no, he wasn't listening. No, he couldn't have been. Oh, god, he can't hurt me. Why? What have I done!"

I watched in awe as Rhodes melted into a pathetic pile of anxiety, the same way I always did. My skin crawled and my hands sweat. The room shrank with each word of panic spilling out of Rhodes' mouth. The idea of Mason, anywhere and everywhere at all times, was overwhelming.

I pushed up from the couch. Face to face with Rhodes, two sets of panicked eyes staring into each other, I saw us drifting out to sea like survivors on the wreckage of the Titanic. So I did the first thing that came to mind: I slapped him across the cheek.

His face flipped from fear to surprise, then confusion, and then anger, the emotion I was hoping to uncover.

"What the hell was that for?" he blurted. He dabbed at a drop of blood seeping from his broken nose.

"It worked didn't it?"

He eyed me seriously. "What do we do next?"

"Show me everything you drew up of Mason's mind during all the times I was in there."

"Okay," he said and led me back to the PTER room. He plunked down hard into his chair and swivelled around to the computer. His hands were shaking and he fumbled with the password a few times. I squeezed his shoulder.

"Don't worry, we'll figure it out. If he seems to know everything about us, that means I must know everything about him somewhere up here," I said, tapping myself on the forehead.

Rhodes gave me a wan smile and punched in the password. His double monitors came to life. "This is a two dimensional scatter plot I put together of the coordinates of all of Mason's memories we've encountered and where we'd expect to find the rest through interpolation."

The graph on the right monitor looked like a mess of a thousand dots.

Rhodes looked at me. "Doesn't make any sense, right. But watch this," he clicked a different diagram. "This is the same data, but in three dimensions." The dots had taken on an orb like shape with a thick dark spot at its center. "Now compare it to a sample of our other patients." Rhodes pulled up a series of other graphs. Each one looked like a cone, starting at a singular point and emanating outward. Unlike Mason's scatter plot the dots were connected to one another by millions of tiny lines.

"I kept trying to make his data fit the conical structure but it just wouldn't map properly. Then I remembered another person with a scatter plot like Mason's," said Rhodes as he called up another patient.

"This is her graph when she started with us years ago." It maintained the conical shape. "And here it is from last week."

Another orb like diagram appeared on the screen except it had lines that ran through the memories to its dark center.

"Who is this Rhodes?" I said.

"It's you Catarina," he said.

*   *   *

"I have to go to the bathroom," I said. I barely made it, retching violently into the toilet. My mind raced as I knelt there, struggling to believe what Rhodes had just showed me. *What had I become?* I stood and stared at my hollow appearance in the mirror.

Where I am is where you'll be.

Could it be true? My tenable grip on reality was already lost. Was I a burnt-out shell of a human like Mason? An emotional garbage dump? *Impossible*. I'm here, aware of all that's happening. Here, making a difference. Mason was almost catatonic when he came to us. I went back into the PTER room to find Rhodes working away at his graphs.

"Are you all right?" he said without looking away from the computer.

"What do you think?" I shot back.

"Ummm, well, I wasn't done showing you the data when you ran out of the room. Prolonged PTER use does something to the composition of the brain," Rhodes said.

"I've seen enough. I think your data is wrong. There's nothing similar about our behaviour."

"You could be right. The process isn't perfect, but I've done my best. Either way, it's what we have to work with to figure out how to fix this guy. Frankly it would be easier if we bought a gun and shot him."

Mason would see through any facile plan that involved an ill-conceived rescue mission by two people completely incapable of the task. "We do this right," I said.

"Fine, then look at this." Rhodes clicked another button and the space between each dot on Mason's graph filled in with more dots. The sphere looked almost opaque. "I overlaid your data on his and discovered that your lattice links up nearly perfectly with his, but never crosses. It's truly remarkable. But I don't know what to do with this information."

Rhodes was on the doorstep of a breakthrough. I would get him the rest of the way there. I thought back on all of the research Mason had written and what Maggie had said about him being disconnected from everything. The footnote in his paper about mindfulness stood out.

"I know what we need to do," I said.

*   *   *

I went into the closet and took my acusensory suit off the hanger.

"What are you doing?" Rhodes asked.

"That orb is like an onion. We have to peel back each layer until we reach its center. You're going to sift through my past and build a path, a blue print we can use to stitch Mason back together. Him and I are connected through my father, by PTER, and who knows what else. My memories are our best chance at helping Mason heal the way all my patients do; by coming to terms with whatever that black ball is at the center of our being. That weight that has followed us for decades."

Rhodes looked scared. "Why are you putting me in this position?"

"Eric and Largo are in danger. I can't do this without you. I promise we're almost on the other side." I paused to gather my thoughts, realizing Rhodes might not be ready for what's in my head. "If I'm as much like Mason as it appears, my mind is going to defend itself against intrusion. I can't promise it's safe for you."

"I'll do my best," he said.

"Let's set PTER up to eject us after four hours. It will be three thirty AM by that point." I was only guessing it would be enough. Four hours was pushing it for Rhodes. I struggled with sessions that long and it was Rhodes, not me this time, going into the mind of a trained PTER practitioner. "We can do this Rhodes."

"All right," he muttered. He went to the closet and donned his own suit.

He waddled back over to me and pointed towards the patient platform. "Well, let's hook you up."

I stepped on to the platform and lowered the headset over my forehead. It pinched. "Has this headset always been so uncomfortable?"

"How should I know? Anyway, I've got to connect you to the SLUMB-Rx drip. It's going to pinch." Rhodes pushed my hair aside and then pressed the back of the headset along my neck. There was a brief flash of pain as the SLUMB-Rx injection needle pierced my skin. He attached the bottom of the device to the spine of my suit.

"When was the last time you used SLUMB-Rx, Cat?"

"Years ago."

"It's going to feel strange."

"Good luck in there," I said.

Rhodes walked around to the console and out of my field of vision. Without a word he clicked a button. I felt the world drift away; the bright lights of the room replaced by pure oblivion.

CHAPTER FORTY

Everyone in the room counted down. *Three, two, one, snip.* The scissors I was holding sliced through the red ribbon. Cheers and applause exploded through the examination room. The ribbon fell away from PTER. Its hull was pristine. My hand grazed the cold dark metal. With a tear in my eye I turned to my audience.

The room was full of bright, shining faces from my past. Rhodes was there, skinny as a rake in a blue dress shirt, red tie and dark-rimmed glasses. Short dark curls covered his head. He had a goofy crooked smile while he clapped. He gave me a thumbs up.

Beside him was Debbie in a tight dress and high heels, catching stares from some of the men in the room. The wrinkles that characterized her worried face were gone. She walked over and gave me a hug.

"Can I steal her for a second, Debbie?" said Eric. He put his hand on the small of my back, spun me around and planted a kiss on my lips. The memory revealed how much he had aged the past ten years. The man I thought was timeless wore more worry on his face than I had realized. His decade-past self was almost childlike in his exuberance.

"I'm so proud of you," he said. "You've worked so hard to get here."

"I couldn't have done it without you," I replied. My voice sounded light and youthful.

"You would have found a way. You always do. But thank you." He let me go. My PhD supervisor Dr. Arthur Young angled around Eric and thrust a bottle of champagne in my hands.

"Congratulations, Catarina! I can say this is one of my proudest moments as a professor and mentor. You're about to make history with the pioneering work you'll be doing. I can't wait to see the difference it makes." His words were a punch in the gut after how far from that idealized moment my life had traveled. He whispered in my ear *"Please be careful Cat. Great power rests in this machine. You're not always going to like the truth buried in the past. The darkest hours will take courage you didn't know you had."* He put a hand on my shoulder and announced to the room "TOAST, TOAST!" After a few cheers the room fell silent.

I cleared my throat. "I want to thank all of you for being here to celebrate this special day. Opening my own clinic has been a dream for years, and I couldn't have done it without your support. I'd like to thank my husband, Eric, for his unfailing encouragement and understanding, Dr. Young for his guidance and mentorship. Rhodes and Debbie for embarking on this journey with me. My mother for her love..." I scanned the room for Mom. I spied her red hair at the back of the room. Her face was a black hollow mask of fissures. Each break in her visage snaked away like serpents into their hovels until her frowning face emerged.

"... and I'd especially like to mention my father, Charles Chambers. He couldn't be here because mental illness stole him from us. He was a remarkable but tortured man. Post traumatic exploratory restitution is my epitaph to Dad, a way to create a world where mental illness doesn't end in tragedy. I hope he'll be proud of me." I hoped it would allow him to forgive me, was what I didn't add.

I gripped the champagne bottle. "Why don't we do this the fun way," I said. I shook the bottle until the cork popped out and dented the ceiling. Champagne sprayed everywhere. Dr. Young frantically tried to collect the spill-over with plastic wine glasses. When it stopped foaming, he took the bottle from me and served everyone.

I walked over to my mom. Beside her at the back of the room was a heavy-set man I didn't recognize. He did his best to obscure his face, but I noticed bruising around his ear and neck.

My mother took me by the hands. "I wish you could remember the beautiful soul trapped inside your father, Catarina. The therapists promised things like you did, but they couldn't help. I certainly hope you're different."

"I miss him as much as you do, Mom. No one feels worse about Dad's death than I do. I am different, and I can do better." With those words the memory disappeared.

CHAPTER FORTY-ONE

Eric pulled his Acura into the parking lot of the university's psychology building. He turned off the engine. He wore a white dress shirt and black tie. His wedding band still had a fresh shine. "You tell that asshole you deserve a better grade!" Eric said.

"He's not that bad, hon," I said.

"Okay, well then, you tell him I said 'hi' instead." Eric flashed me a big smile. He ran his fingers through my hair and rested his hand on my cheek. "Have I told you how much I love you yet today," he said.

"I literally think the first words out of your mouth this morning were just that. I love you, too."

He pulled me into a deep kiss. His hand ran up my leg. I swatted it away.

"Eric!"

He laughed and leaned back in his seat. "Good luck in there."

I marched up to the building's third floor and knocked on my psychiatry professor's door. Dr. Arthur Young opened it. He had handsome age lines running along his face I liked to think came from smiling too much. His hair was thick and dark. His shirts were always the starched, crisp white of regular dry cleaning. He smelled of discrete, expensive cologne. I hated him in that moment. All my resolve melted away in the face of his charisma. I needed more strength to confront him about the grade on my essay.

"Do you have a minute?" I managed.

"Sit down," he gestured, "and close the door." He sat there, one leg over the other, a hand on either arm of his chair.

"I don't understand why you gave me such a low grade on my essay," I said.

"Were my comments not clear?" he asked.

My mind raced over the specifics.

"I'll take your silence as a no," he said. "I bet you marched over here, full of worry and frustration ready to take a strip off me. You strike me as the type who is full of anxiety Catarina; but you do a better job than most at bottling it up. Listen, I wasn't trying to scare you. I wanted to talk to you because I think you show great promise. But this," he waved a hand at my essay, "is a mess."

Arthur crossed his arms. He studied my face and continued: "Why are you taking your Masters in Psychiatry, Catarina? I swore you were a music major in your undergrad. I heard you are quite the pianist."

My hands shook at the thought of the piano. The instrument made me want to retch. "I've fallen out of love with it. I can't find inspiration when I sit down. Instead my hands shake- I just get angry with myself for ever dreaming that life as a musician was realistic."

"So why the field of mental health?"

"I want to understand why I feel this way and maybe help others figure out why they feel the way they do too. I have an obligation to do more and make a bigger difference for others instead of just thinking about myself and my little dreams."

Arthur rubbed his hand across his chin. "We could spend hours delving into what you just said, and at some point, when we have more time perhaps we should. I have no doubt you'd be great at whatever you set your mind to. You have a dedicated spirit."

He pulled a book off the shelf behind him and tossed it onto the table in front of me. It was a book of psychology journal articles.

"Why are you showing me this?" I asked.

He opened the book to a page marked with a sticky note. The title of the article: *Exploratory Therapy Techniques by Dr. Mason Dietrich*. I held my paper next to it, dismayed. It was like Columbus landing in the new world and finding a well-worn path trampled by Dutch boots. What had I missed? When I looked up at Dr. Young he was smiling.

"Do you know this man?" he asked.

I studied the name. "No," I replied.

"You're full of good ideas, Catarina, but ideas take work for them to become great. And I hate to give you a sixty when you took a leap of faith from the safe work you've submitted in the past. Maybe some day you could stand on the shoulders of greats like Dr. Dietrich. Build on what he wrote. I gave you a sixty on the essay because you just weren't rigorous enough with your research. Some of your ideas are brand new, others have been tried. Put in that extra effort and you can be great. But I just can't justify giving you any better than a sixty now."

His words, though well intentioned, felt like an icy dagger in my belly. My mind raced. I had never seen this article before and felt like a fool for missing it. "Dr. Young, my grades mean everything to me. If I don't keep my GPA above four there's no way I'll be able to get into a school like Berkley. Please, is there nothing you can do?"

I sounded too desperate.

Dr. Young gave me a long hard look and folded his hands behind his head. "For one, a mind like yours doesn't need the mark of a Berkley to be successful. There's so much more to it than a game of credentials." He paused to chew on his next words. "Catarina, have you considered getting your PhD here?"

"It crossed my mind."

Arthur gripped my essay in his hands. "I'd love to help cultivate your ideas."

"Are you proposing to be my supervisor?"

"I guess I am," he said.

Instantly I forgot about the grade. "That's fantastic news!"

As Arthur tried to speak again, fissures crept across his cheeks. His mouth fell away from his face and muttered at me from the top of his desk. The curtains rustled and tore my attention from him. A dark red stain ran up the gray drape.

"How did you come up with neural imaging on your own?" Arthur's face was back in one piece.

"I could never get the image of this machine in the basement of a sanatorium where I interned one summer out of my head. Do you think it may have been Dr. Dietrich's?"

CHAPTER FORTY-TWO

"I'm sorry, I'm going to be late, honey. Someone went home sick."

"But I bought a really nice bottle of wine. Who else am I going to share it with?" said Eric on the other end of the phone.

"Stay up late for me. I'll make it worth your while," I said.

"Does that mean what I think it does?" he said.

"Bye, Eric."

"Just checking what kind of underwear to put on…" I laughed and put the phone back on the receiver. A nurse stared at me impatiently. Her name was Jill, a crotchety fifty-something woman with jet black hair and sharp cheekbones.

"The mess isn't going to clean itself," she said. "Go down to the basement and bring up some extra cleaning supplies. Dan the custodian took home his key, and I can't get into his closet up here."

The mental hospital was built after World War I to deal with all the soldiers coming home with post-traumatic stress. It wore its age poorly and was slated for demolition once a new facility was finished.

Most of the light bulbs in the basement had burnt out. The few that remained flickered intermittently. Other than the janitor, no one came down here anymore. Dan went home early that day due to back pain. So when a patient crapped himself and made a mess it was the responsibility of me, the intern, to take over his responsibilities. Not exactly the glamorous start to my career I had imagined.

The paint on the cement walls was peeling badly. The concrete floors were littered in puddles. The drainage had backed-up long ago. The lone elevator behind me sat at the junction of three long corridors. The supplies were at the end of the one in the center. The problem was that Carlyle Mental Asylum was huge. It was one of the biggest institutions in the country for these traumatized soldiers. The basement was where they kept the most dangerous and violent patients. *So, no need to be scared, right?*

The sound of an enormous furnace turning on made me jump out of my skin. *Stop being irrational, you twit.* I took one step, then another. Once I had momentum I did my best to keep my eyes focused straight ahead. For a split second the lights flickered off.

When they came back on, I heard the sound of metal scraping on metal behind the door next to me. Each door had a plexi-glass window, but it was too dark to see inside without getting close. *Not a chance.*

My pace quickened. As I passed by one of the windows, a man's bruised and bloodied face stared back at me. The curve of his lips and curl of his hair were strangely familiar. A scream escaped my lips and echoed down the hall. Then the face was gone. My feet picked up speed. Towards the end of the hall the lights were barely functional. Half of the doors to confinement cells lining the walls were ajar. The puddles of water in the hall sank into each room's black belly.

Out of the darkness of one of the rooms came a low moan. The scraping of metal grew louder. From within the doorway to my left a hand emerged. It was wrapped around a long steel bar. Adrenaline surged through my legs and pulled me down the hall as fast as I could go.

The moaning turned to grunting. *He's chasing me!* The metal rod scraped along the floor like a task master's whip prodding me onward. I looked back to see his free hand outstretched towards me. His fingers opened and closed. My mind twisted in panic. The walls around me crackled with dark lines at the edges of my field of vision. They became haloed in bright white light as tunnel vision took over.

Blind terror prevented me from being able to see where I was going. My body smashed full force into the concrete wall at the end of the corridor. When my vision cleared, I was staring up at a blue door with white letters that read *Cleaning Supplies*. The rest of the hall around me was well-lit, save one flickering bulb over the door. I rubbed the back of my head and found a sizable bump forming.

Groggily I got back to my feet. *What the hell were you doing on the floor, Cat? Seeing things again...* My head throbbed. Still in a daze, I watched myself turn the knob of the supply closet door like I was a spectator to my own life.

It was dark inside. I flicked the light switch and was relieved to find the bulbs still worked. Calling it a closet was conservative. The room was cavernous and absolutely loaded to the ceiling with shelves of toilet paper, cleaning solution, rubber gloves and a host of industrial products you had to wear a mask to use. The entire set-up was impeccable. *If we met the zombie apocalypse, at least we'd be sterile.* There was a spare cleaning cart in the room which I loaded full of anything I thought we could use. Anything to get me out of this basement. Even with all the lights blazing, it gave me the creeps.

Too many memories down here.

I wheeled the cart around and back out the door, turning off the lights and shutting the door behind me. The elevator stared me down at the other end of the long hall. The floor along the hall was uneven and caused the plastic wheels of the cart to bounce noisily. The echo wrapped around the corridors. The door to the room on my right was open. Lights flickered inside.

"Hello," I called from the hallway. *Hello, Hello, Hello* repeated my echo. No answer. I shrugged and took a step towards the elevator. Just then a shimmer caught my eye. I yanked the mop out of the janitor cart and used it to push the door the rest of the way open. I waved it through the darkness but connected with nothing but air.

In the center of the room under the few remaining working lights were two rectangular glass tanks of water edged in rusted metal sheathing. Nevertheless, the device was much newer than the building itself. The tanks were approximately seven feet long and four feet deep. Between the two of them was a console. Wires ran out of the console into each tank. It included what looked like a pair of scuba divers' respirators. The water in the tanks was murky and fetid.

I pressed a button on the console. With a loud hydraulic thunk, metal plates sprang out of the console and enclosed the tanks of water. No light would be able to get inside. *What kind of experiments were they doing on the patients here?* I had read about electric shock treatments that were borderline medieval, as well as hydrotherapy and sensory deprivation techniques, but this machine looked like a different beast altogether.

Dust caked the top of the console. I swept it away to reveal four large letters engraved in the metal: PTER. *Wonder what that means...*

I ran my hand across the rest of the metal and found another indentation in the bottom right corner. I leaned over as far as I could to see what it said. The area was hopelessly covered in black cracks. It was a set of initials: M.D.

I pushed away from the console and stood up, as I did I accidentally hit a button. The metal plating outside the tanks scraped back into the console.

What the hell! I fell down into the darkness of the room. There was a man floating in one of the tanks. The putrid water was turning red from the blood weeping out of his body.

'Help' I tried to say, but the words never escaped my lips. The man lifted an arm out of the water and grabbed hold of the side of the tank. Still on my ass I skittered back towards the door. I'd left the mop in the center of the room.

His head emerged from the water. He turned towards me. Water and blood dripped over his eyes. He looked like he had been in a brutal fight. His nose was badly broken. The water in the tank sloshed as he tried to pull himself out.

"Please," he moaned. I retreated on my backside and inadvertently pushed the door closed. I jumped to my feet and heaved on the handle. The man threw one leg over the side of the tank. When he swung his other leg over I saw that, below the knee, it hung at a grotesque angle.

"No, don't come any closer," I screamed.

He was fully out of the tank. He flopped onto the ground under his own weight. His wet skin slapped against the concrete floor. An agonized scream escaped his lips as he reached for his broken leg. He crawled towards the mop I had dropped and used it to stand up.

I frantically worked the door knob; it finally clicked open. I raced back down the hall and slammed the door behind me. I wedged the janitor cart under the door knob, and then ran for the elevator.

My palm smashed repeatedly on the call button. Behind me I heard the man struggling with the door. A couple of seconds later there was a crash as the janitor cart toppled onto the floor. The elevator still hadn't reach the floor. *Where the hell are you? Come on, come on, come on.* I paced back and forth. From the bowels of the hall, I heard the sound of wood scraping against concrete as he slowly made his way towards me on his makeshift crutch.

"Please, don't leave me down here," he moaned.

A loud ding echoed through the halls. The elevator finally arrived. I backed inside then reached around to the large lever outside the elevator that controlled the basement lights. I yanked down the handle and the lights went out.

"No, wait!" he called out of the darkness as the doors shut.

The second floor was all bright and sterile compared to the dank and mouldy basement. Heaven. But it was also unreasonably quiet. And no matter how clean it was kept, it didn't change the fact that the structural integrity of the building was beginning to give way. Large cracks ran along the top of the walls. A few even criss-crossed the floors.

Behind me the elevator descended. It was back at the basement. I swallowed a lump in my throat and backed away from the doors.

"Hello," I said. My mouth was so dry that I was barely audible. There was not a soul on the floor. When I went to the basement I remembered the floor staffed with a handful of nurses and doctors, in addition to several patients. The closer I got to the mess I was originally sent to clean, the worse it smelled. The walls and floors were a welter of black cracks. *Was it so foul that it was destroying the old building before my eyes?*

The elevator rang out. I stopped dead in my tracks. There was a clack of wood across the tile floor. My body was covered in a cold sweat. *Where did everyone go? Why did they abandon me here?* Instead of going back to the mess I went into an empty patient room and unscrewed one of the rods used to hold IV solution from its base. The top was a pair of harmless metal hooks that curled inward. I needed to break the rod to get something sharp. The metal was old and brittle. I might be able to snap it.

I walked back into the hall, wound up and swung the rod with all my strength against the corner of the closest wall. The rod didn't break. Instead, the entire wall crumbled. A giant web of black cracks spread in all directions. The walls fell back into a black void. Under my feet the ground gave way and I started to fall into darkness. I screamed and reached towards the sky.

"Catarina," said a woman's voice. "Catarina!" She was yelling.

I shook my head and looked into eyes of the nurse Jill who sent me into the basement.

"Welcome back," she said sarcastically. "Where are the cleaning supplies?"

I couldn't form a sentence.

She raised an eyebrow. "It doesn't matter. The mess can wait. I need you to help me with this patient. He keeps hurting himself. We have to restrain him."

The man in the bed was badly beaten. His left leg was turned at an awkward angle. Jill held down the man's left arm. An orderly held the right.

"You need to put the straps around his wrists and ankles," said Jill. I couldn't take my eyes from the man's face. It was the man from the basement. He was Caucasian and couldn't have been past his late thirties. His hair, though matted, looked like it had been styled recently. His arms and legs were covered in coarse black hair. He was overweight, which was unusual for the patients at Carlyle as they were kept on a strict and mundane diet.

"NOW," said Jill.

I emerged from my daze. "Around this leg? It looks broken," I said. My stomach lurched.

"Yes, just do it, and I don't want to hear again about how your little degree puts you above the dirty work," she said.

I began strapping him down. He fought ferociously, but any time his leg moved he wailed in pain. Through it all he never took his eyes from mine. Every time I looked at him, I couldn't escape the thought that he knew me.

"We have to move on," he yelled. "We can't stay. We can't. No time. No time. I can't do it anymore." When he was completely strapped in, Jill grabbed a syringe that was filled with a bright red liquid.

"What's that?" I asked.

"It'll help sedate him," she said. She moved quickly, stabbing the needle into the vein in the man's inner arm. As she withdrew the needle I felt his fingers wrap around my hand. His grip was ferocious. As his eyes glazed over, he looked at me and said, "Time to go."

CHAPTER FORTY-THREE

The sheet music on the piano was torn and wrinkled. The piano transcription was from a song written by my father. His album *Blood and Ivory* was almost legendary in circles of aficionados of contemporary piano. This particular piece was one of his more challenging compositions. It was just me and his music in one of the university's small rehearsal room. My fingers fanned the top of the keys.

One note after another fluttered from my hands. As I deftly plucked out the complex melody and rhythm I sang the words I'd long forgotten.

> There's a day when they'll come bury you
> The doctors and their scribes will write
> She may have lived but died tonight
> And when everyone forgets your name
> It'll be chiselled to the back of my brain
> In the blood and the ivory of forgotten memory
> The broken bones and bleeding envy
> The cracks in my heart will blow wide open
> Will you fall right in as you fly to heaven

Sweat ran across my hands. My fingers slipped off the keys and the melody collapsed. Hyperventilating breaths replaced my singing. Dad's dying face invaded my consciousness. He choked out the lyrics of the song through his death rattle.

"Nooooo!" I screamed and slammed the piano cover over the keys. Teary-eyed, I gathered my things and left the rehearsal space. My feet landed in the sprawling void of a hallway, infested with squirming fissures. The nest of fractured memory exploded outward before imploding like a supernova. I collided with a boy. My things scattered across the floor.

"Hey, watch where-" he stopped himself when he looked into my eyes. He was an Asian guy with thick wavy hair. He wore a fitted t-shirt, shorts and running shoes.

The hallway came back into focus.

"Are you all right?" he asked. He helped me gather my belongings. He and I were worlds apart. I was in a pair of ripped jeans, Converse sneakers, and a thrift store leather jacket over a white tank top.

"I'm fine," I whispered. He put my sheet music back into my hands. His hand lingered on mine for just a second.

"Was that you singing and playing in there?"

"It was."

"You have a remarkable gift," he said. We both stood up to face each other. He had a couple of inches on me.

"No, I can't do it anymore. You heard my last requiem."

"Huh?" he said.

"A song for the dead, my father…" I trailed off, "It's not important."

"That's too bad. I'd love to hear you play again some time." A pen appeared and he scribbled his name and phone number over top of the title of my father's song. *Eric.* "Don't be afraid to call me. I'm a great listener." He backed away down the hall.

"Bye…" he raised his eyebrows.

"Catarina," I replied.

"Catarina," he echoed. "I like that." He turned down the hallway and disappeared through a door that led outside. Further down the hall my eyes caught those of a badly-beaten man before he scurried into the shadows. A trail of blood followed him. I gave my head a shake, then looked at Eric's phone number and the title of my father's composition: "Soul of a Dying Memory."

The route back to my dormitory took me through the student union building. My mind ran over what a life without piano would mean. The instrument, the compositions, they were all I knew. They formed the foundation of my relationship with my father. No matter how cruel he could be, we found love for each other through the music. Without him, all of the notes had gone flat.

There was a job fair happening in the cafeteria. On a whim I stepped inside. The room was lined in booths for everything from heavy equipment corporations, engineering firms, banks and insurance companies, and some of the big pharmaceuticals. Tucked in the corner was a booth for the Provincial Department of Mental Health.

"Hi there," said the woman at the booth as I approached.

"Hello," I said, suddenly feeling under-dressed for the occasion. The room was full of students in suits and dresses. "Umm, I hadn't actually intended on attending but had a last minute change of heart," I said.

"What drew you to us?"

In that moment, I felt unafraid to bear my soul.

"Well, my father recently committed suicide."

The smile vanished from her face, replaced by a sympathetic nod.

"He was struggling with darker mental health issues than either my mother or I ever recognized. I'm wondering if maybe I'm on the wrong path. That maybe I should try to make a difference and honour his memory. Help those who've struggled in silence for too long."

"What's your name, dear," said the woman. Her round rosy cheeks and short blond bob set me at ease.

"Catarina Chambers," I said.

"Chambers," she repeated. "Your name sounds so familiar."

"My father was the musician, Charles Chambers."

"Oh my," she swallowed. "I'm so sorry for your loss. He was a remarkable man."

"He was," I said, "but now he's gone."

"Listen, I'm really at a loss for what to say, but I admire your honesty. We have an internship with Carlyle Mental Hospital this summer that may be of interest to you. The poor souls up there have lost everything and could use a heart like yours." She handed me an application. "Please fill this out and I'll put a good word in for you. My name's Mary." She shook my hand.

"Thank you," I said. "I hope to make him proud."

CHAPTER FORTY-FOUR

My reflection stared back at me from a mirror over a makeup table in a small bedroom with pink walls. The edge of the mirror's glass was etched in heavy dark cracks that ran around the frame and vibrated like fissures splitting the ground during an earthquake.

No more than seventeen in an ugly white sequined dress. The makeup on my teenage face was heavy and stark against my pale skin. As if my past self sensed my judgment, she reached for the cream on the desk and wiped away the foundation, eyeshadow, and lipstick that painted her face.

My younger self's brow furrowed as she analyzed her makeup-free visage. Plain but pretty, like a character in a renaissance painting. She picked up her makeup again but this time went easy on the foundation and blush, ditched the tacky eyeshadow for a bit of mascara, and went with a neutral shade of lipstick. She pushed against her puffy hair that was stiff with hair spray.

"Catarina, what are you doing up there? We needed to leave five minutes ago," said a woman's voice.

"Sorry, Mom. Coming," I replied in my teenage voice. Young me stood up and went into the closet, pulled out a simple black dress, tore off the bedazzled mess I was wearing and put on the replacement. Seventeen-year-old Catarina looked herself up and down in the mirror. No wrinkles. Good.

"CATARINA!" yelled my mother.

My younger self quickly turned for the door and then ran down the stairs at the end of the hall.

The hard lines that ran across mom's forehead eased when she saw me. "Well, look at you."

"Not so bad yourself, Mom." A smile lit-up Mom's heart shaped face. I've never seen it glow the same way again. She wore a form-fitting sleeveless blue velvet dress that fell above the knee, black three-inch heels, and a gauzy white scarf.

But there was something wrong with the foyer. It was haloed in tiny black cracks and fissures that made it appear like Mom was a piece of torn newsprint, and made it seem as if it were about to crack away from reality, and come loose from the rest of the house.

She smirked at me and said, "Come on, we've gotta go."

"Is Dad in the car?"

Mom's face darkened. "Your father is… well, he's being your father. I tried to persuade him, but we don't have time to wait any longer."

As we spoke the foyer stitched itself back together.

"Where is he?"

"Downstairs." My teenage self turned the corner and raced to the basement. Fissures broke off in all directions across the stairs with each footfall.

"Catty, we have absolutely no time for this!"

I ignored her. My hand wrapped around the knob of the basement door. The fissures caused it to break off into my hand. I twisted it back onto the door and turned. The fissures ebbed, but the door still wouldn't budge. The heavy thing always closed on its own, and there was a trick to getting the sticky latch to release. I lifted up, pushed the door in its frame to the left and then twisted the knob. The door swung open.

Dad sat in front of the television watching MTV. Instruments surrounded him. An upright piano stood next to the far wall and an electric guitar sat in his lap, connected to a Fender tube amp by his feet. Tucked away into the corner of the room was a makeshift recording studio. Dad spent most of his time squirreled away down here. On the coffee table in front of him was an empty pill bottle.

"You sure you don't want to come?" I asked him.

He never did. For a man who tried to teach me everything he knew on the piano, he had no patience for school or recitals. All the form and structure, the incessant small talk. He turned to look at me. Instead of a face, the center of his head was a hole, the edges a cliff face eroding into a Stygian sea. It was those same black cracks that invaded the foyer.

"Huh?" the sound reverberated out of the pit in his face.

"My recital, you wouldn't want to miss it would you?" I prodded.

"I'm not feeling well." With each word the edges of his head collapsed around the void. Open, shut, open, shut.

"What are those?" I gestured towards the pill bottle.

"A prescription," he said turning the hollow opening of his face away.

"You didn't take all of these did you, Dad?" The area where his face should have been exploded like a punctured pane of glass. The room began to collapse into the black hole left behind, causing massive fissures to ripple up and down the walls. A monster of a man emerged from the darkness as the cracking of the memory ebbed. His body was mauled and shredded. He clutched at his guts as they bled out. In that moment I felt my adult mind dip into my past and register the event for what it was, a memory. *Rhodes* I tried to say. But then the grizzly image of Rhodes was gone. Was that why Mason was so furious with me? Did the countless hours in PTER mean he could see me trespassing in his memories?

"Goodbye," said Dad.

My mother yelled into the basement. "We are so late. You're one of the first people on stage. If you screw this-," she interrupted herself. "Universi- let's just go. It's not worth wasting time on your father. Just give him his space."

I raced out of the basement. "I'm sorry, Mom. I'm ready." Mom's face softened and she squeezed my shoulder. She went out the front door to the car idling in the driveway. I sat down in the passenger seat.

She put the car in reverse, and then I called out: "Mom, wait, my music."

She slammed on the breaks and let out a heavy sigh. "Just go and get it."

The final images of a once simple life passed through my vision as I ran back into the house. My feet carried me down the stairs to the piano where I'd left my sheet music for Claude Debussy's "Clair de Lune." The heavy basement door clicked shut behind me. Once the music was safely in my hands I glanced at Dad. He was laying on his back on the couch. His eyes were half open and foam spilled out of his mouth. His breathing was shallow and rapid. The guitar slipped off his lap and clattered to the floor. Deafening feedback emanated from the amplifier.

"Dad!" I screamed over the noise. "DAD, can you hear me?"

There was no response. I grabbed the pill bottle on the coffee table and peered at it. The bottle said *Clomipramine - 30 doses. Refills 3. Dietrich, Mason M.D.* At the time clomipramine meant nothing to me, but after years of psychiatric training I knew it was a dangerous tricyclic antidepressant.

Dad's pulse was thunderous. At that rate he would go into cardiac arrest. I awkwardly jumped over the coffee table in my long dress and grabbed the phone and dialled 911. My own heart thundered in my ears.

"911, what's your emergency?" said the woman's voice on the line.

"It's my father. He's overdosed on pills. Something called clomipramine. He's foaming at the mouth and his heart rate is going crazy. What do I do?"

"I can't hear you, some noise in the background."

I stretched the phone cord as far as it would go and clicked off the amp. The only remaining sound in the basement was Dad's wet raspy breathing punctuated by choking coughs as the bile caught in the back of his throat.

"What's your address?"

"421 Richmond Street," I said.

"I'll send an ambulance right away. Please stay with him and turn him on his side so that he doesn't choke if he throws up. You will need to administer CPR if he stops breathing. Do you know how to do that?"

"I think my mom knows," I said.

"Get her and go help him. An ambulance is on the way."

I raced up the stairs, through the foyer and to the driveway. I banged frantically on the car's driver side window. The color ran out of my mother's face as she opened the car door.

"What is i-"

"IT'S DAD, he's dying," I yelled and ran back into the house. I heard her heels click on the driveway as she chased after me. We reached the basement door. My hands were slippery with sweat and fumbled over the knob. The sequence wouldn't go. The door was stuck.

"Out of my way," said Mom. She frantically jammed on the door. Several seconds later, it finally gave way. Dad was convulsing on the couch in the throes of a violent seizure.

"Mom! We need to turn him on his side."

Dad's convulsing stopped. He gasped faintly. He rolled off the couch and fell face first on the floor.

"Oh, Charles no," Mom said. She flipped him over and started CPR. With each compression she put on his chest, a black fissure cracked around the scene. The memory decomposed with each attempt to save his life. Mom became desperate and started hyperventilating as she tried to breathe into Dad's mouth. The sound of her breath grew louder and louder until it was deafening. It caused the image of her and him to shake and crack until it broke away from everything around it. Suddenly the last memory I had of my mother and father together sank into a crevasse opening up in the carpeted floor. My limbs trembled as the rest of the room crumbled into the vortex created in the faltering memory. My body became weightless as it fell into the darkness.

But then I was beside Mom, doing my best to help when she faltered. Rhodes body lay next to my father's in a pool of blood. I wiped my eyes, and he disappeared.

Fists pounded on the basement door. The paramedics! I leapt to my feet and ran up the stairs, following the light at the edge of the door frame. The integrity of the memory eroded with each step. My hand pulled the door open and blinding light cut out a silhouette of the other witnesses to the final minutes of my father's life.

CHAPTER FORTY-FIVE

PTER's doors opened on cue. Blinding white light pierced my compartment. My limbs felt weighed down with cinder blocks. I couldn't lift my head from the back wall. SLUMB-Rx left a brutal but mercifully brief hangover.

The ringing in my ears eventually subsided and was replaced by the sound of Rhodes hyperventilating. *Huff, huff, huff, huff.* Short, wet, shallow breaths. *Huff, Huff, Huff, Huff.* He was in trouble. *Huff, Huff, Huff, Huff.* But I still couldn't see past the blinding lights. My tongue was fat and it stuck to the roof of my mouth. My body was completely useless. *Huff, Huff, Huff, Huff.*

When you can't move or speak, minutes feel like hours. I found myself counting each distressed breath. *Huff,* seventy nine, *Huff,* eighty, *Huff.* Then my head raised an inch, my fingers tingled, and my eyelids opened a sliver.

My strength started to come back. I went down on my knees and slowly crawled across the floor to find Rhodes hanging awkwardly from his respirator. *Huff, Huff, Huff, Huff* his chest rose and fell in quick spurts. He was soaked in sweat. The colour had drained out of his face. He looked like a corpse.

"Rhodes," I whispered as I lifted myself onto his platform. I stood up straight and wobbled like a toddler on new legs as I looked down at his pallid face. *Huff, Huff, Huff, Huff.* Spit flew out of his mouth in spurts. We hadn't hooked ourselves up to the vital monitors, so I had no idea how bad it was. But my eyes weren't lying to me.

I was awake. He should be too. I grabbed his shoulders and shook, not sure what else to do. "Rhodes! Rhodes wake up!"

His eyes sprang open and locked on mine. *Huff, Huff, Huff, Huff.* His breathing grew faster. *Huff, Huff, Huff, Huff.* His hands shot up and wrapped around my upper arms. *Huff, Huff, Huff, Huff.*

"Rhodes, it's okay, you're all right. It's all over." *Huff, Huff, Huff, Huff.* No response. His eyes burned into mine. The pupils were enormous and blotted out the rest of his cornea. *Rhodes, you never should have gone inside my head. You weren't ready.*

He was unnaturally strong and his grip hurt. Suddenly he yanked me face-to-face with him. The respirator fell away from his mouth and his hot stale breath hit me with each *huff.* He opened his mouth wide and let out an excruciating scream. He arched his back and threw his head into the wall of PTER as he released his grip of my arms. He collapsed into the chair and went silent. His eyes closed. His breathing slowly went back to normal. He looked like a child with the flu.

I went to the closet for a towel to clean him up. When I returned, he was already sitting upright with his eyes open.

"No, stay there. Don't come any closer. Please don't hurt me again," he croaked. His voice was hoarse. I stopped dead in my tracks.

"Hurt you?" I asked, taking a step forward.

"No games," he said, pressing as far back into the PTER

compartment as he could.

"Rhodes, I'm sorry." I slowly moved forward. He quickly slipped out of his chair but miscalculated his step off the platform and tripped onto the floor. He skittered the last of the way across the tiles until he was pressed against the cupboards on the far wall.

I leaned against the wall kitty corner to him. "Here," I said, tossing him the paper towel.

He cowered away and the roll of paper towels smacked into the cupboard over his head. He looked sceptically at the roll. Finally, he ripped off a few sheets and wiped the sweat off his head and neck. He grabbed more and blew his nose. I went to the sink in the opposite corner and poured a cup of water. I set it on a counter between us.

Rhodes eyed me and the water carefully. *What did I do to you in there?* I looked at the clock on the wall. It was four in the morning. The whole city was asleep.

"Please, drink, Rhodes, I'm not going to hurt you," I said as kindly as I could. The clock reminded me that this day was far from over. He grabbed the cup of water and drank it hungrily. He put it back on the table.

"More," he said, then backed away to his side of the room. I went back to the counter and took the cup. As I refilled it in the sink I caught my hazy reflection in its stainless steel. I looked... better. The cup overflowed onto my hand. I shook my head and turned back to Rhodes. Some of the water sloshed onto the floor as I walked.

"Did you find what you were looking for in there?" I asked Rhodes as I set the water cup down on the counter.

"Too much, I found too much," he said. He looked away from me.

"I'm sorry. I wish I could have made it easier. But I can't control what happens behind my waking mind."

"So much violence. There's so much in there fighting to get out. And even more fighting to get in. I was stuck in the middle of it. There was no way anyone could be ready."

"Did you find what you were looking for? Can we fix him?" I asked.

"Are you not hearing me?! PTER does something to the brain. What you described in Mason's head… this was the same. You and him are more alike than you appreciate. Are you ready to admit how much your mind mirrors his?"

"Rhodes, please answer my question. Eric and Largo's lives are at stake." My eyes were watering. I clasped my hands into fists to keep them from trembling.

He tilted his head back against the cupboard and spoke to the ceiling. "I nearly died trying to reach your trauma, but I found it. I'm sorry about your father. Now I know why you do what you do. But you've put an enormous burden of guilt on yourself for his death. Did you have any idea what Clomipramine was at seventeen?"

"I should have," I said.

"You know that's bullshit. Don't put me through all that and come out the end the same. You were just a girl. You didn't jam those pills down his throat. He made his choice. I'm sorry he abandoned you."

The world spilled out. I crumpled up on the floor and cried for my father. Even if the guilt was a creature of my own design I still longed for the dad every little girl wanted. Rhodes crawled over and wrapped his arms around me.

I reached into a drawer and pulled out a bottle of extirpation tablets and looked into his eyes. "Document what you can of the experience for reference. We've got the data. Then take one of these.

No one should have to remember that experience."

He wrapped his hand around the pills and went to his computer.

I left him in the PTER room. The sound of keys clacking away furiously was encouraging. The more detail the better. I paced around my office, waiting for him to finish. He stepped into my office a moment later in his regular clothes. He handed me the papers. His fingertips held the pill.

"Bombs away," he said. He swallowed the capsule and closed his eyes. He entered a hypnotic state, swaying left and right. After a minute he opened his eyes.

"Welcome back from your first extirpation, Rhodes," I said.

*   *   *

I put down Rhodes' reports and leaned back in my chair. *Who is this person I've become?* Every time I felt like I was getting closer to figuring it all out, a tree would fall across my path. The years of education and training that led up to this moment meant nothing. There was no manual, no reference guide to undo the effects of PTER. Reliving my father's death released some tendrils of guilt, but it didn't undo the shock waves his overdose was still having on my life.

My cell phone stared back at me on the table. The call had to be made. I punched in Eric's number and hit dial. After three rings Mason picked up.

"Do you have something for me, Catarina?" he said.

Eric moaned in pain in the background.

"Cat, help! Ple-"

"SHUT UP," screamed Mason. It was followed by the sound of

something heavy thudding against flesh. Largo growled.

"LEAVE THEM ALONE," I yelled into the phone. My body broke out in sweat. I heard Mason's phone scuffle across the floor and then Largo whimpering.

"That will keep them quiet for a while," said Mason. He smacked his lips.

"You bastard."

"It wasn't me hurting them, Catarina. It was you who swung the gates wide open. I was keeping everything at bay." He took a deep breath. "I didn't want to do these things, but you made me."

"Please stop. I've figured out how to fix you. I need you to come back this morning."

"You haven't told anyone about the evening we've shared have you, Catarina? You remember our agreement don't you?"

"I remember."

"Because if you don't you'll never see these two alive again."

"I remember Mason!"

"Thata' girl."

His patronization infuriated me but I had to hold back. "Be here in the morning and we'll make this right," I said, ending the call before he could say anything more.

CHAPTER FORTY-SIX

"Where should I wait for him?" said a woman's voice I didn't recognize.

"Sessions usually last up to four hours, so you could be waiting a while. Do you have a cell phone number? I can call you when Dr. Chambers is finished," said Debbie.

"The city would like me to stay close in case anything happens. Do you have any reading material?" the woman asked.

"This one is good," said Debbie.

I whipped my head off my desk. Despite everything I had fallen asleep. Slowly I stood up and stepped out of my office to see the two women facing each other on either side of Debbie's high desk. Our guest was young and pretty. She was dressed in light blue scrubs and had curly, shoulder-length brown hair.

"Where is he!? And what happened to Suzy?" I demanded.

Dismay flashed across Debbie's face, then she composed herself. "Dr. Chambers, this is Heather. She brought our patient over today."

"I see that, but where's Suzy? And Lydia, for that matter."

"Uhh, pleasure to meet you, Dr. Chambers," said Heather. "Suzy injured herself yesterday, so I'm filling in."

I squeezed her little hand tight.

"Mrs. Qiao had to catch up on some things at her office this morning. She said she'll be here by noon," she mumbled.

"Great," I cooed. This girl didn't deserve my scorn. But playing nice wouldn't give me the resolve I needed to stand up to Mason. Lydia's absence wasn't a good sign. At best she was too scared to face Mason again. Worst case she was in meetings trying to convince the rest of her committee to shut me down. It didn't matter. I had bigger concerns.

"Do you know when Rhodes will be joining us?" Debbie piped in.

"He's-"

"-right here," finished Rhodes as he walked through the door. He'd found time to shower and shave. His hair was slicked back under a heaping of product. He eyed the waiting room coldly. "I'll be in the back getting everything ready. Should take about fifteen minutes."

I rounded the reception desk and looked down at Mason. He was slumped in his chair, his long legs stretched across the floor. His arms hung limp at his sides; his chin rested on his chest. He was in a pair of clean blue jeans and a plain white t-shirt. Nothing about his appearance suggested he was the man making my life a living hell.

"Listen," I said loudly. "I ought to-" Everyone's eyes were on me. "-show you how we'll be adjusting today's treatment before we start."

Their shoulders softened but Mason didn't react.

"I don't think you'll get much out of him. He hasn't said a word since I met him," Heather said.

"He understands more than he lets on." I heaved Mason up to a standing position.

"I should really help with that," Heather said.

I glared at her. "It's under control."

"Dr. Chambers," said Debbie despondently.

"Debbie, it's fine."

They went quiet and looked at one another. I pushed against Mason's back, down the hall. Once everyone was out of earshot, I yanked him down to my level and whispered into his ear: *"Where's my husband? If you hurt him I will scramble your brain until there's nothing left but pulp. Where I am is where you'll be... bullshit! I'm nothing like you. You're a coward who hid in his shell, too afraid to face the truth."* I spat the last few words. The corners of his mouth turned up, but he didn't break character. His feet shuffled along the floor. His shoes were worn down from constant dragging. Just before we entered, he stopped and centered his cold, dead stare on me. The hairs on the back of my neck prickled.

"If you figured this all out you'll see that truth." He paused. "Then we'll see who's the coward." He shuffled himself into the examination room and continued his act.

I stood in the doorway. An image of Eric's bloodied face flashed through my mind. Rhodes was sitting by his computer waiting for us. The largest acusensory suit swung like a pendulum on a hanger in the open closest.

"Put that on," I barked to Mason.

Mason dressed in the suit with the door open. His leathery skin hung from his bones and reminded me of death. I looked away. Rhodes swung around on his chair.

"Are you ready for this," I whispered to him.

He nodded. We both sat Mason in his PTER compartment. Rhodes continued hooking up the last of the sensors while I changed back into my own acusensory suit.

Rhodes silently administered Mason's sedative. From the changeroom I heard the door of PTER close with a thud. When I finished dressing, I stepped on to my platform and let Rhodes inject an extirpation landmark.

"Let's hope this is the end," I said.

CHAPTER FORTY-SEVEN

My feet sprinted along a loose stone path. With each step the gravel fell away into an abyss that yawned over a pool of growing hellfire. Tongues of flame lashed up the back of my legs, giving me no choice but to press onward. *What the hell happened to his lattice?*

The path ended in a sheer cliff face. The other three directions would surely end my attempt to fix Mason. Who knew how long it would be before he sustained a complete psychotic break? A lack of options must breed courage, because I leapt out from the path and past the point of no return. The sky was dark with archers' arrows; smoke choked the air; and I had just committed myself to a cliff jump with no parachute. The floor of the valley was lined with armoured soldiers clashing against hellhounds, who crawled out of the depths of the massive tear in the earth that had quadrupled in size. The mountains ringing the valley rained boulders from an unending rockslide onto the men below. The remains of the tower were strewn across the battlefield.

I fell through the debris like a novice skydiver, waving my arms in all directions, vainly attempting to slow down. *I'm going to hit the ground and die. My body will break into pieces at the force. Will it end instantly?*

Only a few feet from the ground, a rush of air coursed under me and I floated like a feather the rest of the way. I bolted as soon as my feet touched bottom. Rocks crashed haphazardly around me. I veered left, took four steps, jumped to the right, ran five more and then dove forward under the next rock. I had to roll to my left, push back to my feet and sprint ten more meters. I cleared the worst of the avalanche.

A massive horse ran in front of me and nearly clipped me with its broad chest. Men in gleaming silver armour, wielding giant broad swords, surrounded me. Others sat atop great stallions. Each man held a six-foot long shield in one hand and ten-foot spears in the other. They were the remaining legion of soldiers, the ones who had survived the tower's collapse. There would be no reinforcements. Nevertheless, they advanced steadily on the great crack in the earth.

Unholy monstrosities, big and small, crawled out of the hole. The barbed tails of hellhounds swung menacingly back and forth as they paced around the crevice. One leapt on top of a horse and knocked it over. Its head gnashed through the rider's armour, rending his limbs from his body. His screams pierced my eardrums. Fear seeped into the gaping cracks in my confidence.

Another knight launched his spear at the hound, piercing through its neck and locking it to the ground in a bloody mess. He rode past, ripped his spear out of its body and turned to find another. A winged demonic harpy flew at his head. He dodged it before it could decapitate him. It glanced off his helmet and tore it from his head, exposing the face underneath.

The giant, strapping version of Mason was everything an

egomaniac would aggrandize about himself—strong, dark eyebrows and a closely cropped beard under strands of sweaty long hair. The veins in his neck pulsed as he took deep, heaving breaths and scanned his surroundings. He looked like the hero of a harlequin romance. There was a crest on his tower shield that read: *Sequere Lucem Mori.*

A snarl sounded to my left. A hound approached. We locked eyes, and it pounced. I fell backwards over a rock as I tried to evade it. Out of my peripheral, something streaked by. A giant hand grabbed my arm and heaved me up into the air. There was a sickening thud as the great chest of the stallion I was suddenly riding crushed the skull of the hound.

My arms wrapped around the waist of the bear of a man in front of me. He looked at me… and smiled. Then, without hesitation, he turned the horse towards the tear in the earth. He threw his spear in a hurtling blur towards the opening, catching an emerging hound square in its mouth. It lifted the creature high into the air and carried it across the valley until it plunged into the far hillside.

Mason bore down close to the horse and pushed it into a full gallop at the fissure. *Wait, a fissure!* This was no great crack in the earth, it was the largest memory fissure I had ever seen. Its edges vibrated as we approached. Mason reined up his stallion at the mouth of the fissure, grabbed me by the back and placed me down on the ground. He jumped off the horse and drew a sword that was as tall as he was. He looked at the fissure, then looked back at me and nodded.

"This isn't real," I said.

His voice boomed from vast lungs. "My fiction has become your reality, Catarina. The mind is the only thing that is truly real."

"But that, no, I can't, it's impossible," I said. The violence around me was too chaotic. I couldn't concentrate hard enough to fix a minor fissure, let alone one four hundred feet across.

"Once upon a time, I was where you are now. But now I am what you will become if you don't fix this. The fissure is consuming my remaining memories, my lattice, everything. It will overwhelm us soon. Only you can save me and your family." He took a deep breath. "Only you can save yourself." His voice was now measured and hopeful. A twenty-foot centipede crawled out of the fissure next to me. Mason's sword flashed down and cleaved it in half. It twitched on the ground. He planted a giant boot in the creature's face and kicked it back into the void.

"GO!" he bellowed. I rushed over to the far corner of the fissure and placed my hands on its edge. I folded one side into the other; it started to close like a zipper. Filled with hope, I continued to seal the gap, even as its widest point loomed before me. After covering no more than thirty feet, the sound of the battle grew frantic.

"Faster," Mason yelled. A bloodcurdling shriek cut through my ears. I looked up to see Mason's great sword heave through a winged creature coming my way. Each half of its body fell to either side of me. Splattered in sticky black blood, I put my head back down and continued to squeeze the fissure shut.

"Brothers, to me!" bellowed Mason.

The sound of hooves beating across the valley floor charged me on. With every ounce of concentration I could muster, I pushed harder on the fissure to close its gaping maw. *Fifty feet.*

I had become the eye of the storm. But the helmetless Mason next to me was an implement of death. He swung his eight-foot sword as if it were weightless, butchering anything that came close. Horses crushed the demons into an oozing black paste. But my little honour guard was surrounded on all sides by hell-hounds, harpies, and every other creature buried deep in Mason's imagination. *One hundred feet.*

"Ugh," he grunted. Mason toppled over and lost his sword as a hound tackled him. It snarled on top of him and opened its mouth of razor sharp teeth to rip out Mason's throat. Mason's hands shot up, caught its jaws and pulled, rending the creature's face apart. He rolled it over and straddled the beast. He slammed his fist down through the beast's chest and yanked out its heart.

Mason looked at me, clearly pleased with himself. I managed to smile back. Suddenly his face contorted into an agonized scream as a giant spike impaled him from behind. He was lifted up into the air by a thirty-foot tall behemoth with massive bone slivers for legs. Its body was hollow, skeletal. It looked like an emaciated animal dipped in tar. The life went out of Mason's eyes as he was tossed aside. The creature rushed towards me. I still had two hundred feet to go.

A spike throttled down. I rolled right to avoid being impaled. The earth around the spike exploded. Its talons rained down mercilessly. I bobbed and weaved like a fly on the head of a snare drum until my feet tangled under me and I fell.

As it wound up to thrash at me again, a formation of spears traveling in perfect unison caught it in the chest. They lifted it up into the air momentarily. It reeled back in pain and rolled along the ground in its death throes. Seven equally massive knights stood around me. They still wore their helmets, but their eyes were all Mason's familiar icy blue.

I crawled back to the fissure. The more progress I made, the faster it closed. The soldiers had formed a semi-circle around me, and I felt safe from what surrounded us. But down in the fissure I could see something awful making its way up from the bowels of the abyss.

Its putrid stench caught me first. As its shadowy figure shambled up from the pit, I tried to work faster.

"Look," a voice yelled. For several seconds the fighting stopped. I looked up but couldn't see anything from my crouched position behind my retinue of soldiers. *Two hundred and fifty feet.*

The air grew hot, demons shrieked and men's voices cried in dismay as the sounds of battle resumed. One of the Masons turned and prodded me to move faster. Over his shoulder I saw what had caused the commotion. A great oily black appendage had found its way out of the fissure. Swarms of the demonic creatures formed a defensive ring around it. Those soldiers not protecting me were concentrating their efforts on the black shambling mass creeping out of the far end of the fissure. *Oh, god, what is that thing? It has to die. I can do this. I can do this.*

"You're so close," said Mason. He was right. Only one hundred feet left. With the hole in the earth so much smaller it forced the creatures to emerge from a tighter space and it seemed like the soldiers were having an easier time keeping them subdued. But then the shambling mass emerged from the crevice. Its misshapen bulbous body blotted out the sun. As its appendages lashed out and grabbed at everything in its reach it pulsed, it grew, it devoured. With every foot I progressed on the fissure, the oozing creature opened its belly and sucked everything in its path through its rows of jagged teeth. The iron stench of blood and the wails of the wounded was overwhelming. My peripheral vision darkened as I started to experience extreme tunnel vision. I tried to draw breath but none would come. My skin was soaked in sweat. I collapsed, my knees unable to support my weight.

A big hand grabbed the back of my shirt and lifted me into the air. With the other hand he removed his helmet and held my gaze.

"Do you think breath is needed here? You are nearly a god in this place," he said.

I stared back at him and said nothing. My chest still felt like it was wrapped in metal cables.

"Where I am is where you'll be. Don't you understand? You must finish." He was shaking me.

"I...I don't know what you mean," I replied.

"If you still don't know then all is lost. Don't become me just because I was like you once. Please, it's coming." He pointed his great sword at the ghoulish creature that blotted out the sun. He donned his helmet and charged off towards it. His words ran through my head.

Mason leapt into the air with his sword raised over his head, only to have a black tentacle wrap around him, pull him close and envelope him in its quivering body.

I finally understood.

I worked at the fissure with every last bit of energy I possessed. The wind picked up around me as my body moved faster than seemed humanly possible. The whole world faded as I closed the fissure. *Three hundred and fifty, sixty, seventy.* I was almost there. Whatever I was doing seemed to work because the mass cried out. Its voice wailed, gurgled and choked on familiar words.

The silhouette of a man pressed against the inside of the monster's body, and my father's voice echoed out of a spluttering hole, "Who is going to pay to clean this shit up... you?"

Another shape pressed against the skin nearby and a girl's voice, high and sweet, echoed through the valley: "I'm sorry."

A hand pushed out of its belly and then the fingers turned into a mouth that spoke through two rows of toothless gums. "It's your little chemistry experiments that make me nervous. They were why I objected to this project. What's to keep you from doping up the patients coming through your door who already suffer from drug addiction."

The side of the creature throbbed again and I heard Eric say, "I've been hanging on, biting my tongue because I knew you were working hard for something. But now I learn it's all propped up on deceit and contempt. You know what, Cat, I'm done."

One of the creature's great tentacles slammed the ground next to me. A face pressed against its undulating skin and spoke in Mom's voice. "Your profession is nothing but a bunch of pill pushing, gas lighting frauds. I wish you'd never gone down that road."

I thought it was finished, but the creature began to whimper like a dog. Like my Largo. Every last thing that haunted me poured out of its mouths. I had reached three hundred and eighty feet.

Tears streamed down my face, but I pressed on. The soldiers had faltered. Save my six man honour guard, nothing was left. *Three hundred and ninety.*

"Please- stop- wait- you don't understand." It was speaking to me in Rhodes' voice.

"No," I yelled. *Three hundred and ninety-two.*

The silhouette of Dad's body pressed through its dark, oily skin. He spoke in a youthful voice. "Past, present and future we are bound together. Resolve yourself with me. You need me."

I tried to block out its words.

Three hundred and ninety-five. I was so close.

"QUIET," I screamed.

"I will find you again." The whole oozing mass formed into a grotesque face, each word coming out of its dripping black lips. "I am never far away," it gurgled in a deep monstrous voice.

"I know what you are and you are nothing!" I said.

Three hundred and ninety-nine. The mass retreated back into the hole until it was the size of a small man. I pushed the fissure the final meter. *Four hun…*

It grabbed hold of my wrist and yanked me down into the fissure. I tried to pull free, but its grip was too strong. I looked up to see Mason withdraw his outstretched hand.

"You're in the heart of the wound now," he said.

CHAPTER FORTY-EIGHT

"Charlie, stop it!" said the pretty little girl with long blond hair and freckled cheeks. She giggled relentlessly. It was the same girl from the photograph in the metal box mom gave me. She couldn't be any more than eight years old. A pair of boy's hands was tickling her.

"I can't help it Ivory," he said. "You're way too easy to make laugh."

"Charlie, please. Let's do something different," she pleaded.

"Do you have any ideas?"

"Let's play hide and seek!"

"Not it!" laughed Charlie.

"Oh, fine, you go hide and I'll find you in no time. You're a terrible hider."

"Am not," he said.

"Prove it."

The image of the girl's face disappeared as Charlie whipped to the left and down the hall. I was in Mason's memory of my father's trauma. The fissure was like a rift that pulled me deeper than I had ever gone in someone's mind. A memory of a memory.

It should have been plastered in fissures and hopelessly decayed. The possibility of retaining such a crisp recollection was near impossible. But I might as well have been living out the memory myself. It was retained with such vivid clarity it was obvious neither Mason or my father had ever stopped reliving this moment.

Charles ran into the master bedroom at the end of the hall, lifted the blue-flowered bed skirt and crawled under the bed. The foot of the bed was littered in craft supplies and wrapping paper.

"Ready or not, here I come," said Ivory.

Charles breathed more rapidly. His neck ached, so he turned it to the opposite side. At the other end of bed was a black shoebox. He inched across the carpet and gave it a shake. It felt substantial, but it was too dark under the bed to see its contents. The bed skirt lifted up a second later and Ivory peered under.

"You're not supposed to make any noise, dummy. I told you, you were too easy to find."

Charles squeezed himself out from under the bed and brought the box with him. "Check this out," he said. He placed the box on the bed. On its cover it said *Jefferson's Pawn Shop, 500 East Hastings Street, Vancouver, BC*.

Charles removed its cover, reached his hand inside and pulled out a revolver.

"Whoa," he said. It had an oily black finish and gleamed in the sunlight. The barrel was stubby and the five visible chambers were empty. Charles wrapped his small hand around the handle and pointed the gun around the room.

"Charlie, put that away right now. It's not a toy," Ivory said.

"It's not loaded, Ivy." A nervous energy coursed out of the memory into my acusensory suit. *Put the gun down Dad. Please put it down.* I knew he wouldn't. I wouldn't be here if he did. My stomach churned.

"I don't care. If Daddy found out you were playing with this he'd-"

"Shut up Ivy. He's not gonna find out unless you tell him. You wouldn't betray me would you?" He lowered the gun in Ivory's direction. Her eyes went wide and the color drained from her face.

Charles started laughing. "I'm just messing with you," he said.

Ivory scrunched up her nose. "It's not funny," she said, "I'm leaving."

Charles ran around her and pushed the bedroom door closed. "Promise you won't tell!"

Ivory grabbed the door handle and pulled.

"Promise!" he shouted.

"Charlie let me out!"

Charles lashed out his hand holding the gun to push Ivory away from the door.

"I said prom-"

A muzzle flash. The room erupted with a bang. The gun pitched up and hit Charles hard in the cheek.

Ivory stumbled backwards and then collapsed in front of the door jam. A small red hole dotted the corner of her forehead. The curls on her head sopped up blood as her freckles seemed to fade from her face. Footsteps raced down the hall and boomed in my ears.

Charles sat stunned on the floor watching Ivory's body cling to life.

"WHAT THE HELL WAS THAT?" yelled a woman's voice behind the door. She pushed it open a crack, but it got stuck on Ivory's body.

"Oh, god, Ivy!" she yelled. "Charles help move your sister, I need to get in." Charles sat in stunned silence.

"CHARLES!" He still didn't move.

With all her strength she forced the door, pushing Ivory's limp body across the floor until the opening was wide enough for her to squeeze through. Her eyes passed over the gun on the floor beside Charles right hand. She knelt down and lifted Ivory out of the pool of blood forming underneath her and cradled the little body. All of the color had drained out of Ivory's face.

"My baby. Oh, hold on baby." She stroked a hand through Ivory's hair and looked helplessly at the blood coating her fingers. "Charles call an ambulance," she said as she laid Ivory back down and applied pressure to the exit wound at the back of her head.

Dad might as well have been me helplessly watching the memory play out. He didn't move.

"Charles!"

"I just wanted her to promise," he said softly.

"Charles, call an ambulance."

The memory started to fade to black.

"Charles!"

I was in complete darkness.

"Charles…"

*   *   *

The PTER compartment went dark. The memory was over, and I was left with an imprint in my brain of an aunt I never knew dying a tragic death. My body floated listlessly in the salt water. I tried to call out to Rhodes to get him to eject me from the session, but my voice caught in my throat. Oh, Dad… a stupid mistake robbed you of a happy life.

My brain throbbed from the sound of the gunshot. The walls of PTER closed around my body and pressed the air out of my lungs. I'm trapped in a pinhole, filled with water, and absent of light, sound or air. An instant later my respirator stopped working. I tried to thrash against the walls but the salt water stole all the force from my limbs. *Are the monitors not working? Let me out!* The searing pain running through my head felt like the same bullet that ended Ivory's life was piercing my brain. A hand reached up out of the depths of PTER and ripped the respirator from my face. I gasped and water filled my lungs and choked out the last bits of oxygen in my body. My legs and arms flailed in all directions as my body succumbed.

CACHUNK. The compartment door of PTER folded open and I spilled out along with hundreds of liters of water onto the floor of the examination room. I barely had the strength to cough. Dark tendrils crept into my vision as the room fell away.

Rhodes hovered over me and started compressing my chest. As my eyes closed he plugged my nose and put his mouth over mine and started CPR. For the briefest moment, I felt nothing but the warmth of a blue ball of light. It was serene.

I rolled onto my side and coughed up the water in my lungs. The bright lights of the examination room burned my eyes. Rhodes cradled me in his arms.

"I thought I'd lost you, Cat," he said.

My limbs were heavy and weak. My muscles ached all over, and I could still barely breathe. "It was my dad's trauma," I said.

"Huh? I don't understand," he said.

"It's what destroyed Mason. It was crystal clear. It rhymed too closely with a trauma of his own. He couldn't let go of the experience." I pushed myself out of Rhodes arms and leaned up against a pair of cabinet doors. "He deserved it for turning my dad into his guinea pig."

"What happened?" Rhodes asked.

I described the memory to Rhodes. His face turned grave. We both looked at the other PTER compartment. Anger bubbled up inside me. Regardless of the circumstances, Mason should have known better. He manipulated my father. He preyed on his weakness. Just another patient to pad the bank account. Dad may have been sick but he didn't have to die.

I went over to the console at the center of PTER and pressed a sequence of buttons. My open compartment closed. A moment later I heard the water inside Mason's capsule drain out. I clicked a button to begin the cleaning sequence, which scoured the inside of the capsule with intense heat.

A warning popped up on the screen. *Foreign object inside capsule. Please remove before proceeding.* I started pressing a key sequence to override PTER's failsafe.

"What are you doing?" said Rhodes.

"Ending this," I replied.

CHAPTER FORTY-NINE

Rhodes jumped to his feet and ran over to me and grabbed my hand before I could finish punching in the numbers. "Please don't," he said. "Don't you think he's already done enough damage. He's not worth it. Don't throw your life away."

"What life, Rhodes? PTER is built on a twisted foundation I can't bring myself to inflict on anyone else any longer. I don't have a compass left. It's been nothing but a lie for the last twenty years. I don't care what happens to me, but I do care what happens to Mason. He can't be allowed to come back to the world and restart where he left off."

"But that's what we've done for hundreds of people all these years. Are they worth nothing?"

"Every single one has left an impression on me. I feel... branded."

Rhodes let out a sigh and lifted his hand off mine. He leaned against PTER and rubbed his eyes.

I returned to the keypad and continued reprogramming the cleaning system. I would scour Mason Dietrich, creator of PTER, literally and figuratively from the earth with his own invention.

"Wait!" said Rhodes. "What about Eric? How are you going to

find him?"

I stopped. The hold Mason still had over me made me furious, but Rhodes was right. I punched in a few more keys on the console. Mason's capsule opened. He was leaning against the small bench. A wet old man with long hair matted against his forehead. He was still unconscious, but the look on his face was serene. His sedative was close to wearing off.

"Look," said Rhodes, pointing at the computer screens showing Mason's vitals and neural activity. The MRI showed that the left and right hemispheres of his brain were glowing a soft blue. His heart rate blipped at a steady and even sixty beats per minute. His body temperature was a regular thirty-six degrees. Complete mindfulness.

We stared at the screens in wonder. I had success with clients in the past, but what we were witnessing was nirvana. Mason's mind had gone silent. My skin tingled. The brain scan started to stir.

"Thank you, Dr. Chambers," said a deep voice behind us.

Rhodes and I spun around and gripped each other tight, unsure what Mason might do next. He stood up and removed all of the sensory attachments covering his head.

"Don't come any closer," I said.

"That's fair," he replied. He leaned back down against the bench. His eyes were bright and alert. This wasn't the broken man the city brought to the practice a few days earlier. He shifted his gaze from me to Rhodes.

"Catarina, I'm sorry," Mason said.

"Sorry!"

"I don't know where else to start…"

"Start by telling me what the hell you've done to my husband!" I yanked open one of the drawers beside Rhodes computer and hauled out a heavy wrench. I held it up between Mason and myself.

"I...I don't remember," Mason said.

"You're lying!"

"I'm not," he whispered. He looked PTER up and down. I gripped the wrench and waved it in his face.

"Wherever your husband is was lost in the memories you just helped me release."

"You have to remember!" I shook him by the shoulders.

Mason raised his voice, "Do you know how many years I spent building that fortress in my mind? You laid bare all the trauma I was trying to suppress."

"I don't care about your problems. Where's Eric?"

"You can find your husband and dog at the address that was crystal clear to me once, but is now fading away. I'm happy I can't remember it."

"Happy? How can you say that, you narcissistic piece of shit?"

He lowered his gaze on me and tightened his jaw. "Other people's traumas have stolen our own lives. Maybe we were never meant to gaze so deeply into memories that are not our own." He pushed himself off the bench and stood up straight.

Was he really coming around? No, don't humanize him. He doesn't deserve it. He hasn't earned it yet. He's manipulating you. You saw what he did to Dad. You heard what he did to Eric. It's just more manipulation. But what if it isn't? I saw the screens. His mind, it was at peace. Could this be the start of something new?

"Don't change the subject," I said. There was so much to process and anger was the only tool I had to keep me focused.

Mason stood back up and held his arms out wide. "My apologies still feel empty to you. I understand I haven't earned your forgiveness."

He stepped off the platform. It was like we were having two different conversations. "But look." He reached a long arm past me and touched the screen that showed a snapshot of his brain scan. Each hemisphere glowed a brilliant blue.

"So what, we already saw that you've found peace." I spat the last word.

Rhodes gripped my hand. "Check the name," Rhodes said. Over the brain scan was… my name. That brief moment unlocking the ugly truth had released my mind from all its baggage. I lowered the wrench and looked deep into Mason's eyes. There was no maliciousness there. He looked like nothing more than a tired old man who was happy to have just reached retirement.

My shoulders sagged. "For twenty years my mind- my mind fought against itself. All the pain and frustration, the relentless searching for something bigger trying-" I sucked in a deep breath, "-trying to straighten out the scrambled mess my dad left behind. You ripped his gates wide open and gave him nothing but a bottle of pills to defend himself afterwards."

"The regret I felt for your father's death was the final straw that broke my mind apart. If I could take it all back, I would. But don't you see that, had we never met, someday you might have a patient walk through that door whose trauma looks and feels too much like your own. Then what. You'd crumble apart just like I did when I saw the cruel rhyme of the world in your father's memory."

"Good god, Mason. It was my dad who was supposed to find peace, not you or me!"

"I know," he said. *Does he? Is he still trying to worm his way out of this. Why should I let him off the hook? He doesn't deserve it. NO! Don't be another Chambers who falls for his tricks.*

"YOU DON'T," I yelled. I swung the wrench towards Mason. He recoiled and put his hands in front of his face. I brought the wrench down and started smashing mercilessly.

"Cat, NO!" said Rhodes, but it was too late. Bits and pieces of my nightmare burst across the room as the wrench cleaved through it like butter. I grabbed the wrench with both hands, lifted it over my head and then swung down and crushed PTER's console. I ripped through the respirator hoses, splintered the metal doors over the compartments, tore up the drainage system and then turned my fury on the computers at Rhodes' desk.

Mason stared at me with wide eyes and the faintest smile on his lips as the wrench blew through the monitors. I grabbed the wires running up the walls and ripped them down. I picked the computer off the floor and threw it into what was left of PTER. It split apart and its motherboard skittered across the floor. I hurled the wrench at it; it exploded into pieces.

The sound of high heels clicked quickly down the hall and Lydia barged her mousy face through the door. "What in god's name is going-"

"Shut your mouth Lydia," I said pointing the wrench at her menacingly. Drops of blood trickled off my hand.

"If you think the city will go through with this now—"

"—You can keep your damn money. You can keep your addicts. And you can get the hell out of my life."

"Well I never," she spluttered.

"And take him with you," I gestured with the wrench at Mason.

"Catarina," said Mason, "I-"

"—I don't want to hear what you have to say." I waved the wrench from him to the door. He retreated, hugging the edge of the room.

"Rhodes, give him his clothes. You can keep the suit, Mason. It's a token of my gratitude for revealing to me why I should have ended PTER long ago."

Rhodes shuffled into the closet and pulled out the bundle of Mason's belongings and handed them to him.

"You'll be hearing from our lawyers," said Lydia.

"I dare you," I taunted her.

Mason pushed Lydia towards the door. "Come on, put it to rest," he said. She looked at Mason in wonder. It was the most words he had ever said to her.

"It worked?" she said. Mason ignored her question and pushed her the rest of the way out the door. He turned back one last time and studied me with his cool blue eyes.

"I was where you were, I was where you were going," he said. "I am not where you end." He withdrew through the door.

My breathing was heavy and laboured. My arms ached. But I felt...free. Rhodes stared at me, not sure what to do. The wrench fell to the floor with a clang.

"You're just going to let him leave?" Rhodes asked.

"What's the point?"

"He deserves to be punished for what he did to you."

"He has been punished enough. I'd rather cut him out permanently than press charges. I'm finished letting his mistakes rule my life."

Rhodes stood up and took an extirpation capsule off the counter, poured a glass of water and handed both of them to me.

"Sounds like you'll need this." The pill was extra heavy in my hand. Its chrome shell reflected my wet and tired face. My eyes closed and Ivory's pale listless body being rocked back and forth in her mother's arms replaced my reflection. The young boy's hand that held the gun trembled. I opened my eyes and placed the capsule on my tongue and then brought the glass of water to my lips.

No, I can't. I took the glass away from my mouth and set it on the floor. I spit the capsule out.

"What are you doing?" said Rhodes.

"I can't forget that memory."

"But... why?"

"Closure. The reason my lattice and Mason's fit together so well was because the most important thing we share was a memory that was neither mine nor his. That memory formed the path we followed for decades. I can't forget that memory or I'd never come to terms with my own father's death."

"What's changed?"

"Dad was struggling with a pain that stretched back to something long before I was born. He fought depression ever since. I can't change his choices. I can only choose to make peace with it. I'm done letting Dad's mistake bleed into the rest of my life."

"It's been a long week, Cat."

"It has," I said.

"What about Eric?" he said.

I walked into the change room and took off the acusensory suit and dressed in my regular clothes. There was a smile on my face when I stepped back out. "I know where to find him."

"What?" said Rhodes, his mouth gaping open.

I tapped the side of my head. "Five hundred East Hastings Street. It was an address in my father's traumatic memory. That's where I'll find him. It's the only place that makes sense."

CHAPTER FIFTY

My shoulder burned from carrying the heavy duffel bag. I found a discarded wheelchair and set the bag on the seat. The sound of my sneakers squeaking on the freshly mopped floors mingled with the murmurs of doctors, nurses and their patients in the neighbouring rooms as I pushed the chair down the hall. Finally I reached room 32B.

Eric was asleep, propped up in his bed. The swelling on his face had gone down. His ocular bone was bruised. His right arm was in a cast. I slid my fingers between his.

At my touch his eyes opened. "Catarina?" His voice was hoarse.

"Yes it's me." I put my hand on his cheek.

"Don't let him hurt me again," he groaned.

"It's over, Eric. He'll never be part of our lives again. I destroyed him."

"What! You killed him?" His eyes shot open.

"Not exactly, I killed the part of him that hurt you. It was the only way I'd have found you. He'll never be a problem again. But PTER. The machine. It's gone. My clinic… It's all over. It's over, and it's never coming back," I said.

"Are you serious?" he asked.

"Yes."

"You did that for me?"

"No, I did it for me. I'm done letting my father's past ruin my future. I want to live a life doing what I love, being with who I love."

His eyes filled with tears.

"I missed you, Eric, and I'm so sorry I deceived you."

A whimper came out of the duffel bag.

"Shhh," I said, looking over my shoulder. I reached into the bag and pulled out Largo and set him on Eric's lap. He had his own cast over his right paw.

Tears streamed down Eric's cheeks; Largo lapped them up with his tongue. Eric wrapped his arms around the dog.

"Oh, my sweet boy. I'm so happy you're all right." Eric turned to me as Largo nuzzled his chin. "I love you, Cat."

"I love you, too. Now let's get you out of here. The doctor cleared you hours ago." I helped him out of bed. We stood face to face.

"I thought I'd never see you again," Eric said. "That man almost stole everything from us. How did you manage to turn everything around?"

"I can explain the whole story on the plane," I said. He cocked his head to one side as he registered my comment. A smile spread across his face.

"The Mediterranean sounds nice," he said.

"It does, doesn't it?"

ABOUT THE AUTHOR

Since childhood David has dabbled with writing, composing music, drawing comics, and designing board games. Formally educated in economics, finance and business management, David also has significant experience writing non-fiction. For several years he authored the website the Dismal Scientist. In addition to writing, David has also self-published two board games and continues to lend his creativity to his personal and professional life. Originally from the Canadian East Coast he now lives with his family in Toronto. To find out more about the author and his upcoming books, please visit www.DavidDonaldson.ca, Facebook at the page David Donaldson – Author, or on Twitter @authordonaldson.

Made in the USA
Columbia, SC
10 September 2018